Pictures
at an
Exhibition

Camilla Macpherson studied Classics at Oxford, graduating with a First in 1998. After University, she qualified in law, working in Milan and London. She is a previous winner of the Promis Prize for short stories and has been short-listed for several other writing awards. *Pictures at an Exhibition* is her first novel. Camilla lives in London with her Canadian husband and their young daughter Freya.

How to use the QR codes

To view the beautiful paintings described in *Pictures at an Exhibition*, scan the QR code at the beginning of each chapter with your Smart phone. If you have a BlackBerry or iPhone, you may need to download a free app.

The QR code will take you directly to the relevant National Gallery site with the painting and information about the artist.

Happy viewing!

Pictures
at an
Exhibition

CAMILLA MACPHERSON

To Amy,

With all best wishes
and thanks for your contribution
to my "literary" career!

arrow books

Published by Arrow Books 2012

2 4 6 8 10 9 7 5 3 1

Copyright © Camilla Macpherson, 2012

Camilla Macpherson has asserted her right under the Copyright, Designs
and Patents Act 1988 to be identified as the author of this work.

First published in Great Britain in 2012 by
Arrow Books
Random House, 20 Vauxhall Bridge Road,
London SW1V 2SA

www.randomhouse.co.uk

Addresses for companies within The Random House Group Limited can be found at:
www.randomhouse.co.uk/offices.htm

The Random House Group Limited Reg. No. 954009

A CIP catalogue record for this book
is available from the British Library

ISBN 9780099560449

The Random House Group Limited supports The Forest Stewardship Council (FSC®),
the leading international forest certification organisation. Our books carrying the
FSC label are printed on FSC® certified paper. FSC is the only forest certification
scheme endorsed by the leading environmental organisations, including
Greenpeace. Our paper procurement policy can be found at
www.randomhouse.co.uk/environment

MIX
Paper from
responsible sources
FSC
www.fsc.org
FSC® C016897

Typeset in Bembo by Palimpsest Book Production Limited,
Falkirk, Stirlingshire
Printed and bound by CPI Group (UK) Ltd, Croydon CR0 4YY

To my husband, with love.

Acknowledgements

I would like to thank the following: Luigi for being a wonderful agent, I am very grateful for everything that he has done for me; Gillian Holmes at Random House for her insight, support and encouragement; Kate Elton for her enthusiasm; Gillian Stern for her perceptive comments on an early manuscript; all those who gave me the time I needed to write this book, in particular my husband and family; and, finally, the many museums, galleries and libraries through which I have wandered in the name of research, first and foremost amongst them (naturally enough) the National Gallery.

The quotations in Chapter 14 come from Mary Howitt's poem of 1855, Buttercups and Daisies (page 378), and Robert Bloomfield's poem of 1800, The Farmer's Boy (page 380).

Prologue

Young Woman among Roses

'Come on then, Claire. Are you or aren't you?'

Rob was right outside the bathroom door. She could hear the floorboards creaking as he shifted impatiently from one foot to the other.

She held the test in her hand, gripping it tight.

It's positive.

I'm pregnant.

How would they shape her lips, these unfamiliar phrases? How would they sound in her voice? Now it came down to it, the words were stuck inside, just like the very first *I love you* she had spoken to Rob, hesitant, voice shaking because it meant so much. In the end she just opened the door wide, passed him the test and said, 'Yes.' Straightaway he took her in his arms and swung her around, and set them both to laughing like they would never stop.

'We're having a baby,' he said at last, when they had collapsed, dizzy, on the floor.

It was as if he had released the words inside her,

1

because now they came tumbling out and she couldn't stop them. 'We're having a baby. We're having a baby.'

He got to his feet, put out his hand and pulled her up, and back into his arms. 'Not a moment to waste,' he said. 'Let's celebrate.'

He sat her in state on the sofa in the living room, then left her while he fetched the champagne that was chilling in the fridge. There were roses on the coffee table, a vase of them, the flowers flushed pink. Idly, she reached out and stroked the petals, smiling, thinking how impossibly soft they were, but nowhere near as soft as her baby's skin would be. Then Rob was back, the open bottle in one hand and two of the crystal glasses they saved for special occasions in the other, already full.

'I shouldn't really,' she said. 'Not now.'

'Just a sip,' he said. 'That would be fine.' He drank, and then he kissed her, carefully, deeply, and let the cool liquid run between her lips. Inside she felt the excitement of those earliest of kisses, and found herself responding as she always did, putting her arms around his neck and bringing him close, no space at all between them and the beginnings of their child.

At last Rob pulled away and leant down, his head against her stomach, one hand resting lightly upon it. She shut her eyes, feeling the warmth of the sun upon her as it shone through the window, smelling the summer scent of the roses, the only sound the murmur of whispers.

'What are you saying?' she asked.

'Just how lucky this baby is going to be, to have you as a mother. Just how much I love you.'

'I love you too,' she said. 'More than anything in the world.'

Noli me tangere — Titian

Don't touch me. *Noli me tangere.* That was what it meant. Don't touch me. It was a strange name for a painting.

Claire knew that poison dripped from words like these. It was a poison that she had learnt to use, slowly at first, and then, too soon, without even thinking about it. Rob had become familiar with its bitter taste. Only this morning, as she felt his smooth, sleepy hand creeping underneath the duvet towards her warm breasts, her mouth had opened to say the words. Don't touch me. The ugly tone that had come into her voice still had the power to shock her, and as for Rob, he pulled away at once as if he had burnt himself on the embers of what was, she knew, a dying fire. They lay there absolutely still, together in the same bed, sharing their bodies' heat. Neither of them spoke. Neither had to move for her to know that they were growing further apart with every second that ticked by, and always with that silence pushing its way like steel between them.

She turned towards the window, desperate to feel alone. The heavy curtains were drawn against the winter darkness. She listened for a long time to the sound of birds already singing, deceived by the pre-dawn, artificial glow of the street lamps. When, at last, she felt Rob throw off the duvet and head for the shower, she thought she would be relieved. Then, too late, she wanted him to fold himself around her and blow gently against her neck and whisper stories to her of the happiness that had once been theirs. *Surely this will all be over soon*, she thought. *Surely he cannot endure this much longer, any more than I can.*

It had been easy once, this life, this marriage, back when Rob seemed to know instinctively how to stop her tears and make her laugh, and she would look at every other couple they knew and believe with absolute certainty that there was more between her and Rob than any of the rest of them would ever have. Now she barely understood herself, and he was utterly lost. She had grown used to the dragging at the edges of her mouth which made her every look a frown. She couldn't remember when she had last even smiled, knowing only that she had once, effortlessly and often enough to have the beginnings of lines around her mouth to prove it. All that must have been in that time that she called before, because everything was now divided for her between before and since, before and now.

Yet it was not so long ago, only a matter of weeks and months, that she had been in love, secure in the knowledge that Rob was going to be with her, beside her, forever. Their wedding vows had sounded as fresh in Claire's head as if they had spoken them days, not years ago. They were going to look after each other. That was what mattered. She did not have to make her way through the ups and downs of life on her own, there would be someone to share it all with her. Five years in which they had passed from the early uncertainty of nervous chatter and careful flirtation to the reassurance and relief of love, by way of sunsets watched from the slopes of vineyards, holidays at first in hostels and then in what were called boutique hotels, and fears and dreams shared in equal measure in a tangle of limbs.

Then Rob had let her down, when all she needed was for him to be there. His presence, that most simple of things, but too much to ask. The betrayal went so deep, was so red with blood, that now she was left only with a familiar feeling – one that she had thought she had cast off long ago – that she was stronger alone.

I'm trying so hard, he had said to her. *I know it isn't enough. I know I'm not getting it right, but I'm trying so hard. Nothing I say seems to help.*

Nothing can help. Nothing at all.

Just six months before, she would never have
believed that a baby, a baby that had never lived, that
she could have held in her cupped hands, could have
done all this to them, to two adults who were exactly
as happy as they should be after two years of marriage
and three years before that of living together. At just
the stage when friends, relatives and even strangers
felt entitled to ask, *Are you thinking about children yet?*

None of it was the baby's fault, the baby that she
had called Oliver and that the doctor had called a
foetus. Oliver had done nothing wrong. It was Rob's
fault. He was to blame. He was to blame, because if
he wasn't to blame then there could only be her.
She still felt raw inside, though that was just her
imagination, or so the nurse had told her before
saying quite firmly that her body had recovered
completely. Did she mean that there was nothing at
all to show that Oliver had ever been there? Claire
had asked. *Yes*, the nurse said, uncertainly. Looking
away.

Now she looked again at the painting that was
called *Noli me tangere*, and wondered what she had
hoped to see. The caption, in black writing on a
small piece of laminated white card, was short, written
so that people in a hurry could understand quickly
and then move on, almost without having to look
at the picture at all. It said that Mary Magdalene had
come to seek Christ after the resurrection and found
only an empty tomb. Then, while she was still

thinking that his body must have been stolen, she had recognised Jesus, in fact risen from the dead, in the guise of a gardener carrying a hoe.

The form of Jesus was unmistakable, smooth-chested and youthful, with a thin white drape around his loins and a winding sheet around his shoulders. He wore nothing else, and how anyone could have thought this slight, almost naked figure might be a gardener was a mystery to Claire. Still, his body was unblemished and free from gore, his side not split apart by the brutal strike of a soldier's spear. It was no crucifixion scene, and she was grateful for that.

She would not have known that the other figure was Mary Magdalene without reading Daisy's letter and the caption. She would have known only that here was a woman of exceptional beauty. She wore an almost transparent shirt and a swirling robe of rouge-red. A scarlet woman then, a prostitute, something like that, the kind of woman whom no one decent and upstanding would want to be seen with in a day as bright as that shown in the picture, whatever they might choose to do at night. The kind of woman that men would shrink away from in the street, but minutes later be beckoning towards them into the shadows. Mary Magdalene was an untouchable, yet she knew only touch, valued herself by nothing else. All she must have wanted was to be loved, and she had offered herself up into the grasp of men knowing that she meant nothing to them

– but still hoping, always hoping, that somewhere, sometime, she would mean everything. It had taken this almost boyish Jesus to prove that someone cared, maybe just a little but even a little was enough. He had allowed her to touch him, in full sight of anyone who cared to watch, to wash his feet with her tears as the tears began to fall, to anoint them with oil and to wipe them with her hair. That was as much of the story as she remembered from school RE lessons, though she was surprised even by that, at how the knowledge could still come back suddenly, unthought of for years, but waiting for the time when it might finally matter. In the painting, Mary's hair tumbled down around her in golden wisps as she knelt on the rough ground, not caring that her robes were crumpled across bare earth, because she was prepared to dirty her robes and her hair with the dust of the road, all for the sake of a touch that would say what she wanted to hear. *You are one of us. You count for something*.

She reaches out to Jesus, a jar of ointment in her hand, ready.

Then Jesus draws away and tells her, *Do not touch me*.

There could be no other words with so deep a power to injure. Claire knew that. She had seen their effect. She knew too how she would feel if Rob turned them against her. Destroyed. So now she scanned Mary's face, looking for the sharp sting of rejection, the absolute horror, that she thought should have been there. She searched for desperation in the lines of the delicate hands that reached out for Jesus, for the utter, gut-wrenching pain of rejection as here, out in the open, Mary became untouchable once more. Here she was, this outcast, this woman who could not stroke a man's hand as they passed in the marketplace, or feel a man's arm around her shoulder in the street, without knowing exactly what it meant, now left alone, unloved, untouched, once again. At the very least Claire wanted to see simple embarrassment in Mary's face, at the assumption she had made in bringing the ointment with her — this physical proof right there in her hand that there had been something special and important in what had happened between them before. All of this and more she must surely have felt, just as Rob must feel it, pulling away at his insides every time she used those terrible words. *Don't touch me.*

But there was none of this in the painting. Mary was not trying to cling on. She was not wailing, or even sobbing. She kept her distance and so did Jesus. She did not touch him despite the desperation she must feel, despite the fact that there was so little space between them that she could easily have reached out for him, even if only to brush the edge of his winding sheet. It was enough for her just to be there with him. She did not ask for more. A picture of Rob came into Claire's head, wearing that awful look of resignation that was now stamped permanently on his face and had never been there before. Time and again she had wanted to shout at him that he was pathetic for keeping his distance, for obeying her so silently, for somehow lacking the courage to do anything at all. *Just touch him*, she wanted to say to Mary, *just do it and see what happens. How bad can it be?* But no. Mary, like Rob, was prepared to listen and comply and little by little move further away. Claire would never have done the same. She would have disobeyed the command and stretched out impulsively just because she could. Knowing this turned Mary's benign expression into a personal rebuke, the painting made into a mirror to show up Claire's flaws, hardly a picture at all.

In her dreams, when she slept, sometimes Oliver was there, newly born with wrinkled hands and scrunched feet, lying right next to her in the bed, his eyes still shut against the world. She would reach out for him just with her fingers, because that was how close he was to her. Then, suddenly, he was no longer there and she would be left grabbing out for him hysterically across an empty space, her hands bereft, screaming, *Give me back my son!* The words were still there when she sat up in the darkness, drenched with sweat and feeling for the switch of the bedside lamp and the relief of light.

Just one touch, that's all I want. Just to feel his lips and press his nose and count his fingers, one by one. Just to feel his weight against me, his legs wriggling, his arms reaching out to me, knowing that I am his mother. Had Titian too known what it was to be pushed away like this, to want nothing more than to touch some woman, some wife or mistress who had been snatched away by death, some baby, a son or daughter, who had fallen unknowing into the feverish grasp of disease? Had he lived with the fear ever after, like that which haunted Claire, that he could have done something, somehow made a difference? If that was what Titian was portraying here, then he must have been able to endure pain in a way that Claire could not. But then she looked again at the card on the wall and saw that it gave the year of his birth as around 1490, the year of his death as 1576, and the year of the painting as 1514. He would still have been a young man in 1514. All the disappointment and despair of a long, long life was still to come for him, and the form it would take still hidden away.

Touch him, she urged Mary silently. *You might not get another chance. Look at me. I didn't get any chance at all.* She leant forward, wanting to put her hand out to this woman who existed only in paint worked over and over by an artist desperate to capture some truth. Out of the corner of her eye she saw the room attendant begin to move forward and shape his mouth into a warning. She pulled her hand away and looked straight at the man, challenging him to say the words, *Don't touch.* But his eyes could not hold hers, not when there was such despair in them. He turned away, ashamed and not even knowing why.

She felt a wave of grief rise up inside her, and gave way as it pushed her down into a space that had become free on a varnished wooden bench. She did not expect to feel happy, not these days, but she wanted at least to feel something other than this unshifting hopelessness. She wanted to feel that there was something in her being that was still alive. Suddenly she felt simply alone, solitary amongst a crowd that seemed all couples, or women with children in buggies, or pushing school groups, their clothes fraying at the edges and carrying with them the smell of adolescent boredom. None of them seemed at all interested in *Noli me tangere*. They swept past, these strangers, without giving it a sideways glance, lured away by the bigger, more dramatic paintings on each side or, mostly, just passing through on the way to the gift shop. It made Claire feel sorry for the painting in some stupid way, so she took a deep breath and dragged her gaze back to it. She had come especially to see it, after all. She shouldn't leave just yet.

Through the centre of the painting a tree stretched up, laden with green-black and burnished brass leaves but still reaching out for a sky across which clouds scudded, grey but hiding a golden light that surely promised heaven. The tree cut firmly between the figures of Jesus and Mary, dividing the painting in two. In the distance, there was a farmhouse and a man, or a boy perhaps, coming downhill along a stony road, a dog at his heels and no idea what was going on up ahead. Then, towards the edge of the painting, the bright green of the land melted into the startling blue of sea. At least that was how it looked, but perhaps the effect was simply the result of the tears in her eyes. She reached into her pocket for a tissue, and as she did so, she felt the crumple of Daisy's letter against her hand, picked up that morning as she left the flat, written over sixty years ago but the words as fresh as the present day.

November, 1942
Dear Elizabeth,

I've been thinking an awful lot recently about those art classes your mother arranged for us at Edenside. We did love them, although I'm not sure we learnt a thing. Only four years ago, but it seems a lot longer. Still, some things still seem like yesterday; like meeting Charles that same summer and the two of us chasing after him just because he was two years older than us – and look where that got me! Well and truly caught! We were still almost children then, weren't we? We certainly acted like it. I know I did. And to think that now you've got a child of your own.

Three years since I saw you off at Liverpool, and your precious Nicky is already six months old. It

*seems beyond belief. I used to wish I'd come with
you when I had the chance. Now even if I could
make the crossing, I wouldn't. I'm determined to
keep my chin up and see the war through here like
everyone else. Still, there are plenty of times when I
wouldn't much mind being in your shoes and away
from it all! Don't think you're missing anything.
Believe me, it is tedious these days. It's nothing but
grumbling and dying, and struggling to get by. I
daresay you are as tired of hearing about it as I am
of living it. That must be what has got me thinking
about those grand times we used to have. It is a
comfort to look back from time to time, instead of
always having to worry about today or tomorrow or
next year.*

*I've got myself a new project, to cheer myself up
a bit, and that's really why I'm writing. It has
absolutely nothing to do with the war effort – and
thank heaven, that's what I say. We're completely
starved of art in London these days, of course.
Anything decent was stashed away by the authorities
years ago, and I suppose one can't blame them. It's
one thing for civilians to get themselves killed but
quite another for the nation's treasures to be blown
to smithereens. Still, there's been a lot of muttering
about it recently – letters to* The Times, *no less!
– because everyone is simply longing for something to
take their minds off this war madness (it's not just
me) and it doesn't seem fair any more to hide all the*

good stuff away. We haven't had a really bad raid in
London for months and months. What's been decided
is that the National Gallery is going to dust off one
masterpiece each month, put it on display, and allow
us masses to trail in front of it. It's meant to be good
for morale (like everything else). Well, to hell with
morale, I just want to see something that isn't brown,
khaki or camouflage green.

I've promised myself solemnly that I will go along
each month to see whichever painting it is that has
been chosen, then write and tell you all about it. It's
a reason to get through to the next month, and to
keep in touch with you besides, and that is all to the
good. So, what do you think? It must be better than
knitting socks for sailors or collecting old tin to turn
into Spitfires. I've done quite enough of that sort of
thing, for all the good it'll do. It'll keep my mind off
Charles, too, as I don't see any too much of him
these days. He's forever off with his unit somewhere
or other, a week here, a month there, trampling over
the countryside and banging away at rabbits and
foxes in the name of training. But I won't complain.
It's become normal in this ridiculous world we live in
not to see those we care about. You don't need me to
tell you that, with Bill posted God knows where.

I've already started my visits, as a matter of fact.
I saw the first painting last Wednesday in my lunch
break. I'm doing typing work at the moment, at one
of the Ministries in Whitehall. It's important typing,

*that's what they tell me, but typing all the same. I
don't mind it. It's better than being sent to Coventry
to work in a munitions factory.*

*Even getting to the National Gallery is a bind
these days. First you have to dodge all the earnest
ladies that blow around Trafalgar Square handing out
leaflets about how to make cake from potatoes and
what not to do with the American soldiers. I'd rather
know what to do with an American soldier, truth be
told. I haven't even spoken to one yet. Charles
wouldn't like it. As for Nelson, he's still watching on
in the usual way, except now there's a banner draped
around his column telling us all to Join the Crusade,
for what that's worth. It's something to do with
making us all buy Government war bonds, I expect;
most things are.*

*After all that chaos, the gallery itself seems very
quiet. It was rather sad, actually, going there after so
long. It was once such a marvellous place and there's
nothing much there any more, or not in the way of
art in any event. There's the painting of the month
now, at least, and the occasional special exhibition,
but the only other big draw is the concerts that are
put on every lunchtime – you'll have heard about
them, I expect. They get some quite famous people
performing. They are men who should be musicians
really, but they're playing their instruments in
uniform now. That still leaves most of the rooms
empty. I glanced into some of them as I walked by*

and they were piled high with gold frames stripped of their paintings and left lying on the floor looking wretched. The walls are covered with depressing pale patches too, like shadows that got left behind when the pictures went. The windows are sandbagged practically bottom to top, which just adds to the gloom without managing to hide all the cracked glass that's still there, waiting to fall out on an unlucky passer-by.

The room where they are displaying the painting of the month wasn't quiet at all, of course. It just shows how long it is since any of us have had anything decent to look at, doesn't it, that we're going quite crazy at the thought of seeing a picture we've never even heard of (I hadn't heard of it in any event). It isn't any old thing, though. It's by Titian, so it must be something special. He is one of the best known Italian artists after all. Even I know that much. One of the Medici set, I think.

The painting shows Jesus and Mary Magdalene, and they call it Noli me tangere. That takes me back to my Latin lessons! Pompous, though. I don't know why they have to give it a Latin name.

You'll think it's silly, I daresay, but the very first thing I noticed was what Mary was wearing. I always notice what women are wearing these days – and then I add up in my head how many clothing coupons they must have used. She is wrapped in a tunic affair with swathes of red fabric billowing *around her, and an equally flapping white shirt underneath. I can't remember when I last saw a woman wearing quite so much of anything, there is simply masses of it. We're banned from pleats and pockets these days, for heaven's sake, which shows where we've come to. My own wedding dress won't have much billow about it. Even if we could afford a flashy number, it wouldn't be thought quite decent in these ghastly, straitened times. Now don't ask. We haven't fixed on a date yet. Charles is barely here for one thing. When we do you'll be the first to know about it.*

I rather admire Mary for her sheer femininity, too, with all those folds of fabric gathered around her breasts and draping down to the ground. There's something magnificent about it. No one looks like that now, not in London anyway. It's all wearing slacks and trying to show we're as tough as the boys. I expect most men find it rather alarming.

So, we have Mary kneeling on the ground and reaching out to Jesus, and I do just wonder whether a tiny bit of him is flinching away — without meaning it badly, but because she's not meant to touch him. You see, that's how the story goes. No one can touch him because he isn't really a normal person any more, he's dead and resurrected, on his way up to heaven which is more than most of us can hope for, I should think. I suppose if Mary were to touch him, something would go wrong with the whole process and that wouldn't do, would it? Next to the painting they've hung up an X-ray of it. It shows that Titian painted another version first which showed Jesus definitely turning and starting to walk away. The final version is more subtle, I suppose, but the message is the same. Keep away.

I don't know, Elizabeth, it all seems a bit much when you think about it, all that not touching. Morals aren't what they used to be these days, put it that way, not in London anyway. There is plenty of touching going on, what with all these soldiers skulking around on leave, and not all of it welcome. One never knows who's going to try and have a quick feel when the lights go out.

Still, there's something about the helpless look on Mary's face that spoke to me. I can completely understand why she is just desperate to cling on to Jesus. There she was in utter despair, thinking that this man she is mad about was dead, for heaven's sake, and now he turns out to be alive after all, and not a mark on his body. It's the miracle of all miracles, but that's the world I live in these days, a world of miracles. Just think for a moment what it's like here, every single time there's a raid. You are stuck wherever you happened to be when the siren went off for as long as it takes, usually with a load of utter strangers and just praying all will be well. As soon as the all clear goes everyone rushes off to try to account for their loved ones. The worst stories, but the best ones too, are where people make it home only to find the place has been flattened – but then their son or daughter or wife is dragged out of the rubble still breathing, or comes running round the corner right as rain. Then there are all the boys who get trapped behind enemy lines, missing presumed dead, and turn up in Dover months later after making their way through practically the whole of France. Just think how you would hold on to them when you found them! Imagine how alive they would feel when you had been picturing them dead and gone! You would never want to let go.

The papers are full of these kinds of stories. They cheer people up a bit. I'm not sure I altogether approve. I call it feeding false hopes. We all know that for anyone who turns up alive there are thousands more who won't. Better to be strong and believe the worst, that's what I think, and I know what I'm talking about after all. When Mother was so ill I clung on to her like my life depended on it, as well as hers, but it didn't stop her dying. I couldn't pull her back for all that I tried. But one day, Elizabeth, one day perhaps I will find her, sitting in a garden surrounded with roses and warm to the touch again.

I'm sorry, Elizabeth. All this sad talk. I'll get back to the painting and tell you about Jesus. Do you know what he reminds me of? A new recruit lining up for his army medical, all scrawny and awkward. They put photographs of that sort of thing on recruitment posters sometimes. God knows why. Who is there left to recruit anyway? It's all conscription these days, even for the girls. I'm afraid our boys do look puny sometimes. I feel rather sorry for them. They're not a bit like the Americans, who are always so damned smart. They don't have that tired look our lot have. Our boys are jealous of them too, and one can't blame them the way some of the girls carry on. Molly, she's the girl I sit next to at work and she's not one to mince words, says it's not the Yanks you need to watch out for but the Canadians. She says they're too fast for well brought up girls. You'll know all about that, of course. You married one, after all. Let me know if it's true, or if I need to put Molly right!

I don't think this Jesus would have lasted long in the forces. He doesn't look strong enough. I can imagine him being a conchy, though, that would be about right – or maybe a padre, even better. They like to give people jobs that aren't so far away from what they did in real life. Charles didn't do much in real life, but they've made him an officer anyway. I think it's because he was at Eton. Apparently he's quite a good shot, which only goes to show that all those hours spent going after pheasants wasn't quite the waste of time I always said it was.

The setting of the painting was rather wonderful, I thought – green rolling hills and a fresh blue sea,

*and, best of all, practically deserted. I've quite
forgotten what it feels like to be standing in the
middle of fields, with the sea in the distance, and
only one or two people to be seen anywhere. One
can't get away from the crowds here from morning to
night, and come to that sometimes you're with them
all night as well. Soldiers, refugees, evacuees who've
had enough of the country and are making their way
home – the lot! One would feel quite cosmopolitan if
it weren't for the fact that there's a war on.*

*Write back, and let me know that you're thinking
of me just as I'm thinking of you. In the meantime,
I'll make sure I ask every Canadian I meet if they
know Bill. Until next month, and the next painting.*

So long,

Daisy

'You got a parcel today,' she had said to Rob at
supper. That was how it all began. She had let the
words come out abruptly, as if she didn't care. They
were sitting on the sofa in the living room, eating
pasta in organic tomato sauce out of bowls that had
been given to them by someone (she couldn't
remember who) as a wedding present. 'The people
downstairs must have let the postman in. It's too big
to have come through the letter box. I put it on the
kitchen table.'

'Thanks.'

His gaze did not flicker from the television screen.

Once she would have allowed him to be tired like this after too many hours at the office. She would have leant back into his arms and let him hold her and stroke her hair. She would have listened as he told her about people he worked with that she would never meet, about the deals done and the deals fallen apart, the praise given, the offence taken. How soon, since Oliver, had her patience ebbed away.

'Aren't you going to open it?'

'No rush.'

'It could be important.'

'It probably isn't.'

She turned back to the television herself. The noise of a pointless show full of people shouting with laughter about nothing drowned out the rushing sound in her ears. Slowly, the images on the screen filled her mind, the racket rasping away a little at the edges of an anger that was always there now, lurking not far from the surface. Rob only needed to look at her sometimes to make her want to scream.

When the programme finally ended, he picked up the television guide that had come with the Sunday paper and flicked through it.

'There's nothing on. Just the usual rubbish,' he said through a yawn. He turned off the television without asking her if there was anything she might like to watch. Then he threw the guide on the carpet, where it fell unhelpfully, fluttering into separate pages as it went. He did not move to gather them up.

Good, thought Claire, feeling the anger rise up. Now she had a reason for irritation, to tut loudly as she collected them up herself and wait for him not to thank her.

'I'm off to bed, sweetheart,' he said once she had finished scrabbling around on the floor. 'I have to be up early. I've got a meeting first thing. I need to get ready for it.'

It was barely ten o'clock. Even her parents would still be up.

'How early?'

'Around six. Six-thirty, maybe.'

'OK,' she said, her voice sharp, although what she wanted to say was *Not again*, or *Do you have to work so hard?*, or *Why can't you stay and have breakfast with me?*, the kind of things she couldn't say without a childish whine slipping into her voice. If she had actually come out with all that, she wondered what on earth he would have said. *If you want me here, when will you stop driving me away?* But no, that was not his voice. He would never say out loud what they both knew, which was that he had not worked this hard before it had all happened. Before, he had wanted to come home in the evenings as early as he could just to be with her, so they could eat together, have a glass of wine, sometimes make love, often talk about the future. Now the simple fact was that it was easier for him to pass the hours at home in sleep. It was her doing. She could not deny it. Nor could she stop it.

But there were times when she awoke in the night to the memory of watching her baby starting to bleed slowly, hopelessly out of her into a dirty public toilet; and then she thought, *Why should I stop it, why shouldn't I be this way? I have reason enough.*

She stood up and went into the kitchen, where the saucepan and the chopping board still lay on the counter, with the rest of the washing-up stacked up alongside. She turned on the tap over the sink and put her hand under the water that gushed out, waiting for it to become warm.

Rob called out from the bedroom. 'Why don't you leave it for now, Claire? You can do it tomorrow, before work, if you really want to.'

'I don't want to do it tonight or tomorrow, but someone's got to,' she shouted back. Emotion, the kind that came from grief, from thinking about Oliver, made her voice shake and hit her straight in the stomach, but Rob would have heard only the tight frustration. He would not have picked up on the misery that lay below it, or maybe he had just had enough of misery for one week. Certainly he did not reply. She turned off the tap anyway, pulled out the plug and waited for the water to drain. It wasn't hot enough. They had needed to get the boiler sorted out for a long time, but she couldn't face it and Rob never had the time. She collapsed on to one of the fold-up wooden chairs that were the only kind that would fit into the room, determined not to start crying. That was the cycle. Anger. Frustration. Despair. Tears. Over and over again. She could feel herself coming to the final stage now, but this time at least she managed to fight back the tears, clenching her fists so she could feel her nails sharp against her palms. It was getting too late for another predictable scene.

Seeking distraction, she picked up the parcel from the table. It was about the size of a shoebox, but not as heavy as it looked and not even full. She shook it, and listened to the dull thud that came from inside. Rob was wrong not to be interested. Parcels were always interesting. She had thought that for as long as she could remember, ever since she had known to wait by the door for the postman on her birthday, ever since she had found out about charity mail order catalogues and learnt how to buy a postal order and send off for Christmas presents. The postmark was Toronto, which was interesting enough in itself. Toronto was where Rob's grandmother had lived ever since her marriage half a century before. Her husband had drowned in a boating accident on Lake Ontario ten years ago and she herself had died at the beginning of the year after a heart attack, quickly and without inconvenience to Rob's father and his uncle Brian, both of whom had lived in Britain since the sixties. Her death had severed any lingering connection Rob might have with Canada, or so Claire had thought.

Their address was typed, not handwritten, and there was a return address label on the back: Jenkyns, Simpson & Strand LLP, Attorneys. She would ask Rob whether he had heard of them when she got into bed. She put the parcel back on the table and headed to the bathroom, then watched herself in the mirror as she brushed her teeth. No doubt about it: all of this had made her old. She opened the bathroom cupboard to put away the toothpaste. A bottle of pills had fallen over inside and now rolled towards the edge of the shelf. She set it upright. Folic acid. She had no need for that any more. She threw the bottle more vigorously than she intended into the bin, where it clattered against the metal. Then she pulled on a pair of faded pyjamas that she would never have let Rob see her wearing before they were married and retreated into the darkness of the bedroom. Rob was already asleep, or pretending to be. In the street-light orange that strayed through a gap in the curtains, which he had pulled to, but not enough for them to meet in the middle, she saw that the tension in his face had begun to disappear into dreams. She was relieved. She lay down beside him and put an arm around his warm body, drowning in pity for him and shame for herself. She did not know if he could feel her. Outside, even though it was nearly midnight, the birds still sang.

For three days the parcel had been left on the kitchen table, unopened, balanced precariously on top of the pile of letters and bills that Claire never fully succeeded in filing away and Rob did not even seem to notice. It attracted more crumbs and splatters of orange juice with every breakfast and always Claire's eyes were drawn towards it. *Open it. Open it. Open it.* The words ran through her head, going quicker and quicker, making her head spin, unheard by Rob.

'They're Grandma's lawyers,' he had told her when she asked about the firm of solicitors. 'Dad told me they might be in touch. They've been sorting out her will. She left me something, some papers I think. That'll be what's in the parcel.' He was straightening his tie in the bedroom mirror at the time, and Claire was still in bed, propped up against the pillows. She liked seeing him this way, she always had, just for those early morning minutes when he had to stand still, work his fingers round the knot of the tie and check that his shirt was tucked in and the cufflinks matched. It made her proud of him again, seeing him so smart, knowing that he was successful, then sending him off with a kiss, even though the kisses had trailed off since. Since Oliver.

It was too early for her to have to get up. She didn't have to be at work till nine thirty, and more often than not she was late these days for the job that had seemed unbelievable when she first got it, because who didn't want to work for an international children's charity? Now, however, just when there were no jobs anywhere for anyone, the last thing she wanted was to be confronted every day with posters on the walls of rescued, smiling girls and boys. She longed to escape.

'So how long is it going to sit there, waiting for you to do something about it?' She tried to make her voice light, although that wasn't how it sounded, even to her. *Open it. Open it. Open it.*

'Please, sweetheart, I'm running late.' His voice rang with annoyance poorly concealed. 'There's nothing I can do about it today. I don't want to rush it. Can't it wait till the weekend? It's *my* grandmother. It's *my* bequest. It's *my* name on the parcel. It really doesn't have anything to do with you.'

'But we're married,' she said. 'It is to do with me.' Oh God, and she could already feel the tears coursing down her cheeks, along paths that were becoming well worn. She was surprised that they could still have any effect on Rob, he had seen so many of them, but his voice softened when he saw her crumpled face reflected in the mirror, and he turned away from it to face her.

'Claire, darling. No more crying now, OK? I really do have to get to work. Listen, why don't you take a look, if it matters so much? I don't mind.'

'Really?'

'Really,' he replied. Well, she could still read him even if he couldn't read her, and what she saw in his face told her he was lying. He *did* want to be the one to tear off the paper, to see what was inside.

He *did* think it was his right. Yet he was prepared to let her have the pleasure of it. Too bloody decent, as always.

She could not stop herself taking both of them by surprise by getting out of bed and kissing him firmly on the lips, her arms feeling around his dark grey suit to meet behind his back, his arms automatically moving around her. For a moment, the old feelings actually came back, in that odd, unbalanced intimacy. She broke away and wiped her face dry with the duvet cover, then leant forward to kiss him again, but it was too late. She could tell that some thought or other of the day to come had taken its chance and crept into his head, and then he was picking up his briefcase and the front door was slamming behind him. The skin on her cheeks tightened where the tears had been.

She showered and dressed without lingering over any of it, even though she didn't have to leave the flat for more than an hour. Excitement drove her, an excitement that she had not felt since before that day.

The day of the miscarriage.

That was what it was.

Just say it, she told herself. *It's just a word.*

But still it repulsed her. It was too long, too ugly, too medical. Yet it was not the worst of the words that had been used at the hospital. There had also been ERPC, or evacuation of retained products of conception, D and C, lactation suppression and more. She could still picture the doctor's mouth forming the shape of these things, and remember how she had not understood any of them, not then, although she had come to. She shuddered violently, pushing the thoughts away, not wanting them to take root, then braved the November-cold kitchen floor. Only then did she hesitate, allowing the anticipation to build, doing nothing while the kettle boiled and she made herself a forlorn cup of tea, waiting for the tea bag to float to the surface of the scale-scummed water before she sent it back under with a flurry of milk, then watching the liquids swirl together. That done, she grabbed the parcel from the table greedily, as if she were snatching it from someone who wasn't there. She pulled away at the brown paper covering it, ripping Rob's name, Mr Robert Dawson, clean in half as she did so. Inside there was a cardboard box, a proper one that had been bought specially, not just a shoebox that had been reused. She lifted off the lid.

The first thing she saw was a silver frame, heavy with curlicues and swirls, and dark spots that had not been polished away. In it, a black-and-white photograph of a man and a woman. The man was young, maybe in his mid-twenties, maybe even thirty. There were lines around his eyes but she thought that was only because he was squinting into sunshine. He wore a tweed jacket and an open-necked shirt that might have been white. The woman was younger, in her early twenties probably, wearing a flower-flecked dress that skittered up in the breeze around smooth, bare legs. She was looking straight into the camera. The man had his arm firmly around her waist, and they were close together, with hardly any space between them. There was something intimate about it, and carefree. They made what her mother would call an attractive couple as they leant back together against the iron railings of a promenade somewhere, with beach and sea behind them.

The man and the woman were what Claire noticed first. Then she took in the rest. A section of the beach, to the left, that was swathed in rolls of barbed wire and a complicated arrangement of scaffolding poles that jutted out of the sand like shattered pipes. A sign that was blurred but she thought said Danger Mines. She was sure she had seen a picture before that had looked just like this one, in a GCSE coursebook probably. Britain's coastal defences in the Second World War, that was what it showed. So the photograph must have been taken sometime after the outbreak of war in 1939, or perhaps just before, and the couple must be Rob's grandparents. There was surely the look of Rob's father in the girl's lively eyes. That would make sense. Rob's grandmother Elizabeth had been born in England, she remembered that much. It was his grandfather who was the Canadian one. He was the reason why she had moved to Toronto, but she had met him over here. Yes, that was it. If Claire had ever known his name it had slipped from her mind. She was sorry, now she was looking at his face in the photo. Rob had told her the story of their meeting once. His grandfather had come over to England to study for a year or so, carrying a letter of introduction to Elizabeth's family from an old schoolfriend, as people still used to do in those days. He had been invited to lunch and, on a walk around the garden afterwards, had pulled a bee sting from Elizabeth's finger. People fell in love over that kind of thing back then.

She propped up the frame on the kitchen table, where it looked all wrong, its rich burnish making the table appear as cheap as it was. She took it into the living room instead, where she put it next to a vase of pink, blushing tulips that Rob had bought for her a week ago and were now hanging limply down, scattering pollen on the top of the bookshelf. She should throw the flowers away, really, but she had hoped that if she left them there long enough he might buy her some fresh ones. God, what games she played these days, and mostly with herself. Wanting his flowers but not wanting him. Demanding his love and giving none in return. Hating him but needing him. It had all become so complicated.

She concentrated on the photograph. Now here was love at its simplest, caught in a split second without any of the difficulties of real life pressing in. Both the man and the woman were smiling, more than smiling really, because the woman had been caught in laughter and the man was beginning to respond. On the far wall, Rob had hung one of their own smiling-faced black-and-white photographs, showing them fresh from the ski slopes in Switzerland, with their arms around each other, looking straight at the camera. Love must always begin this way, she thought, with open faces and enclosing arms, and who could ever know where it would end?

She went back to the kitchen and turned her attention to the rest of the contents of the box. A bundle of papers tied round with a silk ribbon that might once have been blue, and a letter on thick, cream, watermarked paper written by someone who was not important enough to be either Jenkyns, Simpson or Strand.

Dear Mr Dawson,

Re the estate of Elizabeth Julia Dawson (deceased).

As you may know, we have been acting for the executors in this matter and are now able to distribute certain specific bequests. Please therefore find enclosed the following items which have been left to you.

- *One black and white photograph in silver frame (hall-marked) of Mrs Dawson and her late husband.*

- *One bundle of letters written to Mrs Dawson by her cousin Mrs (?) Daisy Milton, when she lived in London in the early 1940s.*

  I had the good fortune to meet Mrs Dawson before she died. She told me that she was very fond of Mrs Milton when they were both girls and, since you and your wife now lived in London yourselves, she hoped that you might both find the correspondence they had during this period interesting.

  I would be grateful if you could acknowledge safe receipt of these enclosures in writing to me at the above address.

  Yours sincerely.

You might both find the correspondence interesting. That was what the lawyer said, that was what Rob's grandmother had thought. *Yes,* she was already thinking to herself, *I think I might.* There was something about it that had her intrigued already. The date alone was enough. The early 1940s. That meant the Second World War, and picking up the bundle she knew that she was holding history right there in her hands. And letters – letters, like parcels, were always special, or at least they had been when she was growing up.

That was before they all became bills and bank statements, back in the days when every morning meant the possibility – too rarely realised – of a postcard from her long-gone father that began with darling and ended with love.

She pulled carefully at the ribbon and felt it come loose, slipping smoothly through her fingers as if it might have been tied and untied many times over the years. Then she picked up the first letter from the top of the pile, just the first. There was something incredibly, unforgettably powerful about that moment as she turned the envelope over in her hands, feeling its soft creases and seeing a king, George the Sixth, she supposed, George the something anyway, on its pale purple stamp. She imagined opening the flap, pulling out the letter and finding the bomb-dust of London still held in its creases, falling out like sand through her fingers. She told herself to be careful. The paper might crumble apart in her hands after all those years.

She wondered only briefly whether it would be better to wait for Rob. It was his history, after all. His grandmother, not hers. He had said exactly that himself. It all added up to nothing to do with her. But he had also said that she could open the box, hadn't he? And his grandmother had said it was for both of them . . . In the end she could not stop herself. She was only going to read one now, anyhow. Otherwise she would be late for work again.

The date at the top was the first thing she saw. November 1942, more than sixty-five years ago. There was no address. The ink was brown, but must once have been black.

Dear Elizabeth, it began. *I've been thinking* . . .

She read it once through, from that 'Dear' to the confident, clear 'Daisy' at the bottom, and then she read it again, slowly, afraid that every turn of the page would pull the fibres of the paper apart. The feel of the paper against her fingers alone, so much thinner and more fragile than that straightforward lawyer's letter, was like a door into another world – but there was more to it than that. There was also the thought of the person writing it.

Daisy.

Daisy.

Sitting somewhere with a pen in her hand and a piece of blotting paper nearby, running her fingers carefully along the page, there was someone called Daisy.

It was a pretty name, one that made Claire think of the sun shining over a meadow, when there had still been meadows, and spreading flowers picked by small fingers and carefully turned into necklaces. She had never heard Rob mention anyone by that name, nor his parents, nor even his grandmother on the one occasion when they had met, for long enough for her to leave an impression on Claire of kindness and the experience of long life but no more. She knew who the Nicky in the letter must be. Rob's father, who everyone these days called Nick. He would have been a baby in 1942. And Bill, that was it. That was what his grandfather was called. A reliable, steady sort of name.

That night, Rob came home later than she wanted him to and didn't ask how her day had been. She told him anyway, that she hadn't got to work till nearly ten because there was a problem on the Victoria line, that she had had lunch with a friend and, finally, saving it until last, about the pile of letters tied with the blue ribbon, and the photograph on the bookshelf in the living room which he had not noticed until she pointed it out to him. She saw a spark of interest in his eyes, and knew that her own eyes, which had been dull a long time, were reflecting it.

'Have you read them?' he asked. She knew he would be disappointed if she said yes, if she hadn't waited for him.

'Of course not. I haven't had time,' and then, still honest, 'I just read one. Just the first one.'

Then she found herself telling him about the painting of the month and Daisy's job, and his father being just a baby, and he paid attention all the while. It began to feel like a real conversation, one that flowed without either of them having to make any effort, without anything caustic coming out of Claire's mouth, or any sighs slipping from Rob's. They were sitting at the kitchen table, and now their hands strayed closer together across its scratched pine, though they did not touch.

'I'm going to go and see all of those paintings, every one that she saw,' she said. 'I've decided. It'll give me something to do. Your mother told you I needed to take my mind off things. Well, maybe she's right. I'm going to read one letter at the beginning of each month, then go and look at the picture, just like Daisy did.'

She had had the idea in the office, while she was putting together a long and tedious analysis of donations and charitable spending that she knew everyone in the team would be pleased with but no one would actually read. It was the kind of task she was often given these days, out of compassion, because she could do it without always having to think about the living, breathing children behind the money. What was it that Daisy had written? Seeing the paintings would give her a reason to get through the next month. Well, that was what she needed too, a reason. Already, she felt the tense, unfamiliar burning of adventure in her stomach, and it was different to the dull weight of grief and the sickness of panic.

She didn't look at Rob as she was telling him what she was going to do. She didn't want to see him asking even with his eyes what the point was. She didn't want him to say that she knew nothing about art, even though that was true, or that the paintings might not be in the National Gallery any more. She didn't want to hear her own doubts voiced. She had gone through them enough times while she was at work, turning over everything that she could remember from the letter as if she still held it in her hand. In fact, he said none of those things. He asked only when she was going to begin.

'Tomorrow. I've got nothing else planned.' Except, she thought, being with you, reading the newspaper together but in silence, wondering what you are thinking, hidden behind those rustling, endless pages of print and unchanging news. 'The first letter is dated November. If I begin now I'll even be seeing them in the same month as Daisy.' Already she was calling her Daisy, as if she was someone that Claire knew and Rob did not.

'You know that if you want me to come with you I will?'

Had he wanted to say instead *Can I come?*, or was he just being polite? There had been a time when they had both always said what they meant, but that was in the time before. Before they were forever picking through the shattered glass of that unspoken future hope. She did not ask him to make it clearer.

'I know,' was all that she said. She did not add, *But I want to do it on my own. I can do it on my own.* She did not need to.

From the disappointment wrought across his face it was clear that he heard the unspoken words.

This was what had brought her in front of *Noli me tangere* and left her sitting on a wooden bench, looking at a painting that was half a millennium old and longing only for someone to hold her hand and make it alright. She shut her eyes and tried to imagine Daisy coming here to the gallery and seeing it too, but it was impossible. She had no sense of who Daisy was, or what she looked like, let alone what she thought. That would come in time as she read more of the letters, she was sure of it. More than that, she was determined to make it happen. She might not be able to bring Oliver back from that awful darkness that had engulfed them both, but, if imagination could do it, by God she would breathe life into this Daisy.

She wondered who Charles was. His shape was even more indistinct than Daisy's. He seemed to be her fiancé, because she seemed certain that they would get married. He wasn't very keen on her being in London, or that was the impression Claire got. Maybe it was a new thing for someone like Daisy to be going out to work rather than straight into marriage, and the idea of it made him nervous. It still did make some men nervous, even now. Anyway, marriage could be work too, Claire knew that well enough. She had watched her own parents reel through it until her father finally stormed out the day before she turned five, the scent of baking in the air transformed into burning as her birthday cake slowly dried and crisped in the oven. *Don't be silly, Claire*, her older sister Laura used to say to her. *You can't possibly remember the rows. You were too young.* But Laura was wrong. She remembered it all. The shouting, then the long silences. The loneliness that became normal. Her fierce determination that she would not repeat the pattern, would fly in the face of her mother, who had asked her anxiously, repeatedly, if she was quite sure the moment she had announced her engagement to Rob. That determination had not slipped until now – until Oliver, until a loss and a love that had challenged everything she ever held dear.

She got to her feet now and went right up to the painting once more, wanting to find some final secret in its very brushstrokes, but she could not even tell them apart. She left after that, walking out through the grand entrance of the National Gallery and down the steps, into the grey of Trafalgar Square. Daisy would have come the same way, she supposed. There were crowds here even now, too many of them, but different from the ones Daisy had described. They were tourists mainly, clothed in their own uniform of jeans and T-shirts, and brightly coloured waterproof jackets worn against the threatening sky. She wondered what brought them here. The buskers maybe, or the wretched pigeons with their gnarled feet, or perhaps just the pull towards other people the same as them. She found herself wondering whether Daisy might have come here on VE Day with all those thousands of others, fuelled by an exhilaration that was utterly unimaginable to Claire, unimaginable to anyone who had not been through half a decade of war to be left only with an uncertain future. The noise there must have been, all that love and hope, mingled with violence and fear, becoming cheers and yells. Her mind far away, she looked down too late to see that her foot had scuffed the edge of a freshly chalked pavement drawing. It showed a yellow sun shining high above fields of impossible colours.

'I'm sorry,' she said to the artist, who was squatting nearby, a box of mixed coins, not all of them British, by his side. 'I didn't mean to.'

He ignored her and she felt the ridiculous rise of tears once again, together with the thoughts that crept up alongside them so often these days, of being alone and empty, literally empty. There was no one to notice that she was upset, to put an arm around her shoulder in compassion, because this was London and who would ever have done a thing like that? Only Rob, and he was not there because she had told him she did not want him to be. She stood there uncertain, not knowing where to go now. Then the rain began to fall, forcing her to move away from the street artist and his too obvious pictures. She strode quickly away through the rivulets of coloured chalk that now found paths through the paving slabs, glad that there would soon be nothing left but blank, foot-roughened stone. Around her, small children who had been happy enough to splash their hands in the cold water of the fountains ran crying back through the drizzle into the arms of their parents. Claire turned her eyes away from them and looked up instead, towards the elaborate, elegant buildings of Westminster. Daisy must have worked somewhere around there, off to the right where the broad oulevard of Pall Mall branched off the square. She wondered if she could find out where. Just thinking about it, about Daisy, held close between the pages of her letters, warmed her, despite the chilling breeze.

She took a bus back to the flat, sitting on the top deck and watching the familiar sights of London pass slowly by, darkened by the pressing sky. The bus juddered its way through Piccadilly Circus, then up Regent Street and along Oxford Street, where Saturday shoppers, concealed beneath umbrellas held up against what was now just a smattering of rain, moved more quickly than the road traffic. She looked down at them through the blur of grease left on the window by someone's tired, desperate head, watching them seethe and swell against each other, pushing in and out of endless shops in search of nothing important. Finally the road cleared and she knew that she was on the way home, home to Kentish Town, home to Rob who would make her a cup of tea without her having to ask, in just the way she would once have done the same for him. He would pass it to her so that the tips of their fingers touched, and she would feel guilty with every sip that she would allow him no more. It would have been quicker to take the Tube, but she did not want Rob asking why she was back so soon. She did not want to admit that the outing had upset her so much. But perhaps that did not matter. She sat herself more upright on the seat. It was just the beginning, after all. There would be other paintings. That was what she had to hang on to. She would not give up, not yet. She was not ready for another failure.

2

The Mystic Nativity – Botticelli

Christmas this year meant Rob's family, his parents Priscilla and Nick, not her own. Her mother was away on a painting course, something to fill the time, meant to be fun but nonetheless portrayed to Claire as a form of martyrdom. 'I don't want to impose on you and Rob,' her mother had said, in a voice lacking conviction, when Claire had tried to invite her to stay. 'You've got your own life to lead now. Now don't you go worrying about me being lonely. The course organiser says there will be plenty of other people around my age.' In the past, Claire would have tried to talk her out of it, putting in the endless hours of work and reassurance needed to overcome once and for all her mother's 'Are you really sure I won't be in the way?' Now she did not have the energy to prop up anyone other than herself, and had simply said, 'Fine. Enjoy yourself. Call me if you want to talk.' When they had last spoken, her mother had been at a Christmas market in Munich with the rest of the painting class, chattering about ice-skating in the platz and warm gingerbread, but made emotional enough by Glühwein to be unable to conceal the fact she would rather have been with Claire.

She wondered sometimes whether her mother had become so needy *because* her father had left, or whether that was *why* he had left. He had always seemed loving and generous, at least where his daughters were concerned – albeit with his gifts more than his time, she had come to understand with age. But how could he in reality ever have had time again? Soon enough he had acquired a second wife who resented the first, and three children over and above the two he had only ever wanted. Claire and her sister had been pushed forever to the margins of his life, mere annotations, and never able to do a thing about it.

The night before they left, Claire knew she wouldn't be able to sleep as soon as she pulled the duvet over herself and felt an unmistakable panic grip her. She found herself counting through the endless hours, listening to Rob's steady breathing and waiting for him to stir, willing him to feel her anxiety and respond. Finally she could stand it no longer and began to nudge him into wakefulness, carefully at first, then more vigorously, until he rolled over and took her into his arms. At once, the tension started to wane, and she knew that he still had the power to calm her, here in the depths of the night when nothing else could intrude on their togetherness and she could allow herself to forget what had happened that awful night when Oliver had slipped away from her.

'I don't want to go,' she whispered, quietly because she wasn't sure that he was actually awake. 'I want to stay here with you.'

She told herself that she would forgive him everything if he said, 'If that's what you want, we'll do it' – but only because she knew that it was a test he would fail. Now she felt his arms hold her all the tighter and hugged them herself in response. His own whisper followed, slow with sleep. She had to struggle to hear what he said.

'Don't be silly, sweetheart. It's Christmas. We can't change everything now. My parents are expecting us, we have to go down. I thought we'd both decided what we were going to do. I thought you didn't mind.'

'I do mind, Rob,' she said, a catch in her voice.

'So why didn't you say anything earlier?' His voice was louder now and she knew he was fully awake. In the dark, she felt his arms pull away so he could check the time on the alarm clock. Two o'clock. Three o'clock. Four o'clock. Sometime around there, too late or too early.

'Because I didn't want your mother saying that I made you choose me over her. I didn't want you saying that I was being unreasonable.'

There was a pause, and she felt him beginning to pull away. 'I'm sorry,' she said. 'I can't help it. I'm sorry. It's the thought of no one knowing what to say to us. Or being insensitive, or even just trying to be kind. They'll all be wanting to know when we're going to try again. They'll think it, even if they don't say it. It's the thought of having to listen to it all when . . .'

When all I want to do is scream and say, Why don't you save your sympathy and ask Rob what happened instead? Why don't you ask him how it felt to pick me up from the ground and say, Are you hurt, Claire? Are you hurt? Let him tell that story. Except you can't ask Rob because he wasn't there. Why wasn't he there? Weren't you meant to be meeting him? Yes. Yes, I was. Didn't he tell you how it was? I was waiting for him just where we agreed. I got a text message to say he was running late. A quick drink with a client but he was about to leave. So I stayed where I was, standing in the cold, feeling my baby, my Oliver, kick, thinking that Rob was surely on the next underground train, or the next one, or the next one, that he was bound to be just around the corner by now. But he wasn't, so I gave up in the end, turned to go, and ran into a bunch of thugs who pushed me to the ground, who stole my bag and left me face down on the pavement, which was when my mobile beeped in my coat pocket with a message that said Sorry, drinks have turned into dinner, I'll call you later. The mobile switched off. The client too important. And me on the floor praying that my grazed knees were the worst of it, yet unable to take my hands away from my stomach. Saying I'm fine, I'm fine, to the strangers who pulled me up. Waiting for the police. Still cold, another stranger's coat around my shoulders. The police station. Then the hospital. The empty scan. Oliver's heartbeat silenced, inside me his body still. Knowing that there might be milk in my breasts and no baby to hold there. How is that for a Christmas story? Do you wonder that I'm angry? Do you wonder that I would rather blame him than myself?

Rob had flicked on the lamp on his bedside table, and she shielded her eyes from its brightness. The hate had come back in the sharp spark of light, and when she began to cry there was anger behind the tears, not grief. Rob put his arms back around her and now she was the one who tried to wriggle away, nearer to the edge of the bed. He did not let go. Instead, he began to stroke her gently, running his hands up and down her side to soothe her in the old way. When he tried to hold his hand around the curve of her belly, where Oliver should have been, shifting and hiccuping and waiting to be born, she tossed back the covers and left the room, leaving him, white with sleep, to fall back in frustration. She sat on one of the wooden chairs at the table in the living room, stubbornly refusing to accept the comfort of the sofa. In front of her was the silver frame with its black-and-white photograph, and those two smiling faces. *What reason could they possibly have had to be so happy,* she thought, *and why can't I have it too?* Next to it was Daisy's second letter. She had read it so many times she knew already what it said, but she picked it up now, then rubbed the tiredness away from her reddened eyes, knowing that reading it again would take her somewhere other than this flat, this life, this endless pain.

December, 1942

Dear Elizabeth,

We have been told not to send Christmas cards this year (again!), so you shall just have to make do with a letter instead – and believe me even this dreadful paper is difficult enough to come by these days. I had a gaggle of WVS women knocking on my door the other day asking me if I had any old books to donate to the war effort. It's pretty beastly to think that while Hitler's burning books in Germany, we're turning them into pulp here. So all in all I am quite determined not to be made to feel guilty about writing to you – I will just write very small instead, and having to do that's bad enough.

Remember the good old Christmases, with everyone in their best clothes bringing round properly wrapped presents and having a glass of sherry or two, and the church bells ringing out? Well, things aren't like that now, and no church bells is the least of it. It's dark and freezing cold and no one's got the ingredients to make even a mince pie. There's

virtually nothing in the shops either, for all that
Oxford Street is still crammed with people. Grown
men are reduced to fighting each other over the
tiniest, most overpriced dolls. How dreadful that a
father can't even buy his little girl something to
remember him by if — well, if the worst happens. The
only sorts of toys one can buy aplenty are grotesque
things like tanks and aeroplanes — even little
uniforms in children's sizes! It's all they play at now,
war games. You can't blame them. Some people are
making an effort, of course, and putting up a few
decorations — tinsel on the anti-aircraft guns and that
sort of thing — but I think you'll agree it's hardly
the same. Tinsel on guns, for goodness' sake!
Christmas trees cut short so they will fit in the
shelters! Where will it all end?

The National Gallery clearly thought we needed
some festive cheer, because the picture on display this
month is called The Mystic Nativity. It's by
Botticelli. It's a strange sort of picture, actually, but
there is a brightness about it that made me feel a
little less gloomy. It is very crowded for one thing.
That was the first thing I noticed. There are angels
practically swarming around the infant Jesus, three of
them on the roof of the stable alone, and a whole lot
more pressing in from the sides and circling around
above, brandishing olive branches for peace — as if
there were any chance of that any time soon. They're
wearing pink, yellow and green robes and the overall

effect is rather gaudy. Isn't it odd to think that it might have been easier for Botticelli to find a decent yellow paint all those hundreds of years ago than for an artist these days? Shortages, shortages, shortages. It's all anyone talks about. It's not just the paper shortage. There's an everything shortage. How tedious it all is.

As well as the angels, the shepherds and the three kings make an appearance, as do the usual stable animals. There is a particularly good ass, and also an ox which brought a smile to my face. The ass is practically standing on the manger to get a better look at the reason for all the excitement, but the ox doesn't seem to give two hoots about what's going on. It's just chewing away, with a rather bored expression on its face. There's not much that will impress a cow, is there?

To think that this frenzy of activity is over a tiny little baby that is weeks away from even being able to muster a smile! One would expect Mary to be pretty thrilled by the whole thing, I suppose. She is his mother, after all. In fact she is worshipping the baby with just the kind of look I imagine you gave Nicky when he was first born, although I don't expect you also had your hands clasped in prayer. But as for all those others! That's babies for you. Once they arrive everything in the entire world just has to stop for them and it's all fuss fuss fuss forever after. Every single new infant seems to be treated like

*a god in the making and I'm afraid I can't
understand for a moment why. I despair for Mary,
truth be told. Do you think she realises yet just how
much her life is going to change? What a dreadful
prospect. I daresay you'll be chuckling away over all
this, Elizabeth, and telling yourself that one day I'll
know better, but I'm honestly not sure that I will.
I'm afraid I've seen too many of our old friends
utterly disappear once the babies start coming along.*

*Don't think I don't know what I'm talking
about. I know plenty, believe you me. For one thing,
Mary looks nothing like a woman who has just
given birth. She is far too serene. A bit more sweat
and tears, and some blood too, that's what's really
needed. I called on Mrs Jones upstairs the day after
she had her third boy and let me tell you she looked
an absolute wreck, and not much better even now
come to think about it. Whenever I am feeling utterly
worn out, I must confess I do call her to mind and
comfort myself with the thought that it could be
worse. As for the rest of it, where's the bucket of dirty
nappies? Here's Jesus actually lying naked on a
white sheet, and no mother I know would risk that.
The baby's far too clean, of course, particularly given
they're all stuck in a stable, and a stable that's not
really much more than a cave when one looks closely
at the painting. It would be downright impossible to
keep the baby creamy-cheeked and sparkling in that
sort of place – yet Jesus looks fresh from the tub.*

Where are the tear stains and the snotty nose? That's what I want to know.

Poor old Joseph, he seems to be exhausted by the whole business, and I don't blame him. He's sitting slumped on the ground with his head in his hands, acting like it's the end of the world. He looks like an old man, not a new husband.

In the sky above the stable, there's gold. I expect it's meant to be heaven, but when I saw it, all I thought was, I wonder if it's real. It could be, couldn't it? It could be gold leaf. I asked one of the guards, but he didn't have a clue. There are two of them on duty the whole time, just in case there's a raid. If there is, it's their job to grab the painting and run hell for leather down to the shelter in the basement. I wonder if they'd let the general public (i.e. me) in first, or if we'd have to wait. Wait, I expect. Still, they have to be careful with the nation's treasures, I suppose, and the gallery has been hit enough times already for them to be worried about that sort of thing.

At the very bottom of the picture, there are all sorts of creatures scrabbling about in the mud and falling into holes in the ground. They look like rather grotesque, hairy monsters. Some of them have got scaly wings and cockerel's feet, or else tiny horns like goats. I couldn't think what the inelegant little beasts were, so I plucked up my courage and asked a man next to me if he had any idea. He was one of those

*people who one could tell just to look at knew what
he was talking about, or at least would sound as if
he knew. It was something about the cut of his suit,
I think, or maybe how he was standing.*

*Distinguished, that's what I mean. He told me that
they were devils, being seen off by the angels, which
seems like as good an explanation as any. Then he
asked if I liked the painting, and I said I thought so,
especially the ox(!), and he laughed and said he was
pleased, because he had helped choose it. Of course I
didn't twig at the time who he was, but that evening
I saw a picture of him in the paper and realised it
was Sir Kenneth Clark. He's Director of the
National Gallery, if you don't already know. Well,
you can imagine how thrilled I was to have spoken
to him. I expect he thought my question was very
stupid.*

*Charles came with me on my visit, which was
decent of him although he did rather hang around at
the back of the room. He found himself with twenty-
four hours' leave quite out of the blue, and used it to
come to see me, even though it meant the most
atrocious journey to get to London, like all journeys
are these days. I'm not too sure he liked the picture,
but it gave us something to talk about, which I
expect he was as pleased about as I was. It is hard,
seeing him so little. By the time I'm accustomed to
having him around again, he's already gone. I miss
him for a while, then before I know it I'm used to*

being on my own all over again. Sometimes I think it would be easier not to see him at all, and just put the business of trying to be in love on hold till the whole damn thing's over. Forgive me, Elizabeth. You must think I'm being unutterably selfish when you and Nicky are stuck on your own and in a foreign country to boot! I only hope they are good to you there.

Seeing The Mystic Nativity *started Charles off talking about settling down and having a family. I can't tell you how my heart sank. Poor Charles. He has far too much time to mull these things over, that's the difficulty. First off, I told him I thought we should wait at least another year before the wedding. Then it slipped out that I didn't know that I wanted children straight after that. He doesn't take that sort of thing too well, I'm afraid. It's not the first time we've had this sort of discussion (or should I just come straight out and call it a good old-fashioned row?). He can't understand that it doesn't mean I don't want him, it just means that I'm not ready for that sort of life yet. Can you understand any better? I'm not sure you will, but if you were still living over here and you'd never met Bill, I think you would.*

Anyway, I hold Botticelli entirely responsible for the whole business. A mere glance at the nativity scene was enough to leave me thinking that it's not for me, not yet. The whole idea of holding a baby in my arms is terrifying as far as I'm concerned, and that's not just because of seeing Mrs Jones practically on her labour-bed. It's because everything's different now, and I like it. I'm out working with all the other women. We aren't having babies, we're running the country, or that's how it feels sometimes. I see girls my age and younger – and much older too – doing everything these days. Rattling out tickets on the buses, hefting stretchers around, driving mobile canteens, working on the railways, everything. I feel as if I'm a part of it, even if I am just doing the typing. I have my own life, and it's a good one for the most part. I don't want to throw it away, not yet, not for a baby that's going to cry day and night for months on end, an endless stream of washing and a husband stuck out on manoeuvres. Not a chance, and I told Charles so.

Charles says I never used to talk like this before the war, and he's quite right. He says that if it weren't for Hitler, we'd be married by now. He's right again. We would be. I wouldn't have had anything else to do. I'm not saying that there wasn't a time when all I wanted was a decent man, a pretty house with a garden, and just enough money to be able to have one or two children and bring them up in just the way we were – but I've changed somewhere along the line and Charles can't help but notice it.

Charles isn't the only one who thinks I need to settle down. I saw Daddy last week and he was quite firm with me. He thinks I'm running wild in London, and that twenty-two is already practically on the shelf. At the same time, he still sees me as his little girl in a smocking dress with her hair in two plaits with red ribbons at the end. Poor Daddy. He has never had a clue how to deal with me, not since Mother died. Poor Charles too. I feel sorry for him, I really do, and that's no good. Nothing is worse than feeling sorry for a man. Whenever he's in London, he always seems out of his depth. He doesn't know his way around, or where he should take me out. He's not used to it, not like me. It's not his fault, but doesn't it seem incredible that here I was actually listening to bombs whistling down night after night and month after month and thinking that there was every chance I might not wake up in the morning, and all that time he was safe in a warm billet, with three meals a day cooked for him and not a thing to keep him from sleeping! I've seen more of this war than he has, that's the truth of it, and it makes him ashamed.

I didn't like sending him off with all this bickering still between us. It leaves a bad taste when he just wants someone to smile and wave goodbye to him as his train pulls out, but that's how it is these days when a man can't even hope for more than a day or two's leave at a time. When does anyone have the time to kiss and make up? He's gone now, and I don't know when I'll next be seeing him. It is rather

depressing, so write back when you can, with some
cheery news. In the meantime, I hope to goodness
you have a better Christmas there than we will
have here.
    With love,
    Daisy

'Robert! It is simply wonderful to see you.' As soon
as Rob opened the taxi door, and before he could
help Claire out, Priscilla was striding around the edge
of the house in her wellingtons to meet them – or,
more accurately, thought Claire, to meet him.

'How was your journey? No delays, I hope,' she
said, pulling him into her arms and kissing him
determinedly on the cheek. Her own cheeks were
red from the cold and her lips were chapped. She
must have been outside waiting for the sound of the
car drawing up, waiting for Rob, passing the time
doing whatever gardening could be done in the
middle of winter.

'No problem at all. It's good to see you, Mum!'
Already, he had his arm around her, and they had
turned to walk up the drive together, towards the
elegant Hertfordshire farmhouse where he had lived
since he was six and which had not been a farm in
generations. At once they were mother and son, united
again, held close by that particular, peculiar bond that
had been so cruelly ripped from Claire. She stayed
unremembered on the gravel with the bags.

'That'll be eighteen pounds, love,' came the driver's voice, impatient, and she realised that this was the second time he had asked her for the fare.

'I'm sorry,' she replied, looking down, fumbling in her wallet for the twenty-pound note that she had been sure was there and suddenly was not.

'I'll get that.' She looked up in relief at the sound of Nick's voice. He still spoke with a trace of the accent he had grown up with, and that Rob had never had. It betrayed him as Canadian, even forty years in Hertfordshire and a British passport later.

'You don't have to.' She was still scrabbling in her bag. Then, looking up and catching the smile on his face, she gave up. 'OK. Thanks, Nick. It's kind of you.'

'It's no trouble. Anything for my favourite daughter-in-law.'

'You've only got one daughter-in-law!'

'That's right, and she's my favourite. Now come on into the house and let's start with a gin and tonic. I bet you could do with one.'

Now she found herself smiling in return, just a little, and thinking that here was a chance to try and find out more about Daisy. She and Elizabeth had been cousins; the lawyer had said so in his letter. Nick must know all about her. The visit needn't be wasted.

She said as much to Rob later that night, as they shuddered beneath the freezing bedclothes and waited for the electric blanket to make a difference, which it didn't. She had never felt warm in this house, not even in the height of summer. There was a chill to the place that sat itself, unshifting, in her bones as soon as the front door shut behind her. She wanted to rile Rob, she must have done, or else she wouldn't have said it at all. She would just have muttered an offhand goodnight, then tried to sleep away the cold.

'Why is it a waste of time for you to see my family, and not for me to see yours?' he said.

'Because your family don't really care about me. Why should they? At least my family like you. Anyway, I don't exactly make you see much of them. I hardly see them myself. You're forever trying to get me down here.'

'It's a beautiful house. You're the one who's always saying you want to get out of London and into the countryside, and here we are. You're my wife, Claire, remember. That makes you a part of my family. You should be able to feel at home.'

'No, Rob. I'm just a guest. Anyway, maybe I don't want it to feel like home.'

A pause. She knew what was coming next. He did not disappoint her. 'If this is about my mother, I wish you'd just give her a chance. There must be plenty you could find to talk about if you bothered to make the effort.'

'Why should I? She doesn't try with me.' Yet

that wasn't quite true, she knew. Priscilla had tried, properly, to find the common ground between them when she had first been told about the baby, and Claire had found herself responding, grateful at the shift away from being the woman who had taken the son from his mother to the woman who would give her a grandchild. Still, that was all over with now.

There was something effortless about the argument they were falling into. It was one of those rows they must have had a hundred times before, and both were familiar with its pattern. The words tumbled out as easily as if they had been talking about the weather. It was no more than a distraction from the bigger things that they should have been fighting over but were easier ignored. Rob ended it the simplest way, by rolling over, away from her, and sending a cold draught of air down the middle of the bed. Claire lay back. God, what an absolute waste of time it all was. She thought again of Daisy, unable to stop herself telling this unknown Charles that she didn't want to be his wife, not yet, nor did she want his children. What on earth had she wanted to achieve? Surely Charles would, like Rob, have heard only insult and rejection. But then Claire knew well enough that it was sometimes impossible to hold back the most hurtful things – sometimes you thought to hell with it, and let it all out, only afterwards realising that a silence, however awkward, would have been better. She felt a small rush of sympathy and understanding for Daisy, and the feeling somehow helped her sleep.

She had gone on her second trip to the National Gallery on the Wednesday before Christmas, which was late-night opening. She had got away from the office early, like most people did at that time of year, but Rob was still at work, and she knew that even when he came home it would be with the problems of the day etched on his brow, or else the problems of the evening to come. She had stopped complaining about his absence. She knew it suited them both.

The gallery was practically empty, which came as no surprise. Most people would be out doing last-minute shopping, well into the final phase of grab-bing and buying that always set in at this time of year. Much better doing that than going round a lot of old paintings, that was probably what they thought. She had come through Covent Garden to get there, and every single one of the endless shops around the piazza had been making money, even those that were usually empty. Each time a door swung open, waves of heat and tinny carols were released into the crisp air followed by crowds of people trailing bags, scarves and wallets getting lighter. It felt like a kind of madness to Claire, looking through the plate-glass windows and seeing all those notes and coins, mostly notes, changing hands – yet it seemed to be making people happy, at least until they got home and started to add up in their heads how much they had spent and wonder who they had even been buying for. There was nothing wrong with being happy, Claire had never thought that there was, even if she had herself lost the capacity for it. She bought a polystyrene cup of mulled wine on impulse, from a man standing behind a wooden cart, and strode on smartly, leaving the crowds hovering around the bright Christmas decorations as foolish as moths.

The streets became quieter now, and gloomier. She shivered inside her coat, even though it was thick and she was wearing a hat and scarf as well, and held the cup in her hands to keep her fingers warm. She sipped from it carefully, not wanting the red stickiness to drip down the sides. It would have been much darker than this in Daisy's day, virtually impossible to get around in the blackout without even the light from a street lamp, let alone a shop, to help her home, just the faint glow of a covered torch bulb maybe. Even here in the alleyways where the street lamps were dim, Claire could not come close to imagining what that nightly near-blindness must have felt like, into which might come only the sound of whistling or footsteps, or the touch of a stranger's arm upon Daisy's coat, making her jump more than the cry of the air-raid sirens. Claire had rarely experienced darkness like that, except perhaps on cloudy evenings out in the countryside. On these occasions, she had felt its weight upon her, choking her, and found nothing appealing about its embrace. The winter days must have felt very short then, as Daisy joined the rush to get home before nightfall, and the evenings that followed an eternity. She wondered if Daisy had got any presents at all that year. She hoped so. Charles would have come up with something, surely. He seemed a reliable type; perhaps a bit too reliable for Daisy.

She took the steps up to the entrance of the gallery at a run, driven on by swift gusts of wind that were tugging the Christmas tree in the middle of Trafalgar Square so fiercely back and forth that its lights were set to rattling. Inside, thank God, she felt her body relax immediately into the warmth and clung on to the sensation, wanting to make the pleasure of it last. The woman at the information desk directed her to *The Mystic Nativity* and gave her a map, which she followed carefully, head down, to avoid making eye contact with the room attendants. She could feel their eyes on her anyway as she walked alone through all of those deserted rooms and they wondered why she was there and not at Selfridges or John Lewis or at home with her husband, writing cards and wrapping presents. The electric lighting was a warm orange, but as she passed beneath the gallery's glass dome, she could feel the darkness above trying to crawl inside and wrap itself around her. She shook herself and moved on.

It amazed her that Daisy had seen these paintings more than fifty years ago, and they were still hanging in the National Gallery. Here, now, was *The Mystic Nativity*, just as Daisy had described it, with Mary, Joseph and Jesus forming the central group and angels crowding round on all sides. She noticed something at once that Daisy had not, or had not mentioned in her letter anyway, which was that the three main figures were over-large compared to the rest. Presumably this was to make them look more important, which they were, of course, this family of God on earth. She felt pleased with herself for having the idea, and hoped she was right.

Mary was beautiful, of course – how could she be anything else? – dressed in a pink robe and hooded in blue, colours that were picked up in the wing tips of the barefoot angels that flocked about, swirling in a circle in the sky and pressing in from all sides. She reminded Claire, in the shape of her face and the colour of her hair, of the woman in another Botticelli painting she had seen years ago at the Uffizi Gallery in Florence when she had been inter-railing around Europe. At first she had resented the entrance fee, but not once she had found herself, with everyone else, in front of *The Birth of Venus*, with its portrayal of a natural, yet modest nude, balanced elegantly on a scallop shell and drifting across the sea to shore.

In fact she was sufficiently impressed by it to spend yet more money, along with everyone else, on a poster reproduction in the shop, which the very next day she accidentally left behind her in a luggage rack on the slow train to Rome.

Then there was Joseph, in a blue robe with a yellow cloak, his head bald like a monk's and edged with grey curling hair. Daisy had said he looked exhausted. She herself, looking closely, wondered whether in fact he was in despair, at the thought that this child, the child that he knew wasn't his, had finally been born and must now be brought up. But no, that couldn't be it, not in Botticelli's day anyway. No one would have seen it that way. Now it was different. Now people lived in a world of splintered families, which you were meant to call blended, and joint custody, a world where it had become almost normal to end up bringing up a child that, however much you might pretend otherwise, was not quite your own.

Perhaps Joseph's despair came simply from the realisation read too clearly in Mary's eyes that from now on her life would no longer revolve around him but also – or only – around the baby, and the little boy, then the man the baby would become, while the father was consigned to the background and left to grow old in silence. Claire had seen it happen again and again, because every woman she knew seemed to be having a baby just as she was losing her own. The couple so much in love, certain that all they wanted was a child to complete their happiness, suddenly not a couple at all but a mother and a father with this strange thing always there to hold them together but also push them apart. The husband soon enough treated like an extra child, getting in the way, useful only as an extra pair of hands whenever his wife felt like calling on him, and gradually retreating rather than be told yet again that he was doing it all wrong. Desperately trying to recapture the spark there had once been between them and that his wife now acknowledged only once her thoughts turned to a second child.

Was that what would have happened to Rob? When she was pregnant she had sworn she would do things differently and never once tell him that his way was wrong just because it was not hers. Yet God knows how she would have prevented it. No other woman she knew had managed to. It was work all week then rush home on a Friday to read the baby a bedtime story, and spend the weekends walking it round the park, always before a woman's critical eye and constant imperatives. *Don't do that. Be careful. Support his head. Change his nappy. Pick him up. Put him down. Let him sleep. Wake him up. Don't be so rough.* She had heard and seen it all before. Perhaps Joseph had simply understood his lot early on, and known that the safest place for him from now on was on the margins.

Still, when she looked properly at the baby, which she did last of all, wanting to stave off for as long as possible the feelings that she knew would follow, she understood it all just as she had known she would, as soon as she followed Mary's gaze down to her baby's face and found that she, like Mary, could not tear her eyes away.

For all that the baby looked far from newborn, with nothing red and crumpled about him as he lay calmly on the white sheet, the image pulled at her so much that it felt like a real pain, that awful pain, tearing at her with tiny nails. Of course it was right that the baby should be the centre of Mary's universe, everything else fallen into darkness around his shining face. How could it be any other way? He would change every minute of her day, fill every turn of her thoughts. What place could there be for anything or anyone else outside that? Claire knew deep down that she might have welcomed the intensity of it with open arms, as careless of Rob as Mary seemed to be of Joseph.

To think that this Christmas, she and Rob should have been practising folding and unfolding the new pushchair and laughing over it as they struggled, buying a first pack of newborn nappies and discussing the best way to get the baby home from the hospital. She should have been wearing something in a red, stretchy velvet-lycra blend bought from the maternity-wear section of a big department store, not the same black dress as last year. People should have been saying, *Better watch out, it might come early*, or, *Wouldn't it be nice to have a Christmas baby?*, not hovering nervously around the sherry, reluctant to offer her anything to drink – just in case she was pregnant again and it was too early to say.

To think that, come January, it should have been her surrounded by crowding figures, showing off their little boy (though she would think of him secretly only as hers), telling everyone that she had never felt so proud in her life, asking her friends if they wanted to have a hold of the baby while hoping they would say no, unafraid that her absent father and difficult mother might run into each other in the hospital corridors because now she had a family all of her own to worry about, and anyway how could they both fail to be united in joy once they saw Oliver?

To think that none of it was going to happen, that those emotions could only be imagined, and not felt at all.

Yet Daisy had shied away from the mere idea of a child! Claire could scarcely comprehend it. It was because she knew no better, she realised, because Daisy still had no idea what it was like to want a baby, let alone to lose a baby. There was nothing like losing a baby to make you want one even more than you ever thought you did. Losing a baby. How she hated that phrase, even though it was what people said, because they had to say something. Some words were needed. But to her it still sounded ridiculous, as if she had somehow misplaced Oliver, and he might still somehow turn up, handed in at the bus station or returned by the police.

She forced herself to focus on something else, and it was Daisy who came back to mind: full of enthusiasm for the changing order of things and writing with such excitement about jobs that these days most women tried hard to avoid. Claire couldn't hold back a wry laugh, not caring that a passing security guard gave her a curious glance. After all, here she herself was, the product of it all, sitting reluctantly behind a desk five days a week with a mortgage that needed two incomes to pay it off, and there was Charles, offering Daisy a country cottage with a garden and a family, especially a family, and Daisy was wishing it away. But then Daisy was younger than Claire – twenty-two, according to her letter – and that made a difference. By the time she was thirty, like Claire, she wouldn't still be thinking that way. She would want a house and someone to share it with, and would be terrified of being left alone.

A sudden eagerness took hold of her to be in the flat, which she and Rob had chosen together, and everything in it as well, all of it, walls, furniture, every spoon, book and vase, melding over time into something called home. She turned away from the painting and left the room. Her heels clattered across the wooden floor in her rush, ringing louder when the floor turned to marble. Then she was in the open air again and moving even faster through the deepening cold.

As soon as she turned the key in the lock, she knew that Rob wasn't home. Only then did she decide that she had wanted him to be there, desperately. She had wanted to find a bottle of red wine already open and pick up the scent of chicken under the grill as she came up the stairs. She called his work number and when he answered, after five rings, he sounded as if he had just been laughing, with someone who wasn't her. *Stop enjoying yourself there when you could be here*, she wanted to say. *That's not your home. It's only where you work.* Instead, she said she hoped he wouldn't be too late, and that she'd try to wait up for him. There was no reason to cook just for herself, and Rob would have eaten in the office, which catered for late nights, so she poured out a bowl of cereal for herself, realising too late that it meant there would be no milk left for breakfast tomorrow. There was nothing that could be done about it now. She fell down on the sofa, pulled a blanket around her and turned on the television. Then, with just Daisy's letters for company, she waited for the noise and colour to push everything else away.

Christmas Day now.

Only two more days to go: two more days of insincere conversation and tepid bath-water. Rob woke her up with a present wrapped in shiny paper decorated with red-nosed reindeer that he had borrowed from his mother. It was a heavy book about art that he must have carried all the way down with him on the train, and would now have to carry all the way back. It was well chosen, a sort of encyclopaedia, with sections on all the famous artists. There was an entry for Titian, of course, and Botticelli too, and she read them both. She wondered who was going to come next. Nearly time for January's letter, not long to wait. The thought pleased her and when Rob came out of the bathroom it was easy to kiss him.

'Let's go to the early morning church service this time, not to the family one,' she said. It was another test, she knew, but it was also a chance for them to be on their own. It might be enough to get her through the rest of the day.

He responded to her mood, saying nothing about the previous night, only kissing her lightly on the forehead as if she were a child, not his wife, and saying, 'I don't mind what we do. Just try and keep cheerful today, for me.'

Did she try? She thought she did, as much as could be expected. But by the time they sat down to breakfast, things were already going wrong.

'Katie and James can't wait to see you,' said Priscilla, as she fussed around Rob with the coffee pot and a toast rack. 'They're desperate to show off little Joy. She's such a sweet little thing. Hardly ever cries.'

Claire couldn't have cared less about Katie and James, just a couple in the village whom they knew slightly. Once there would have been something there – the shared experience of birth and children which bound unlikely people into endless conversations and lifelong friendship – but as it was, they had nothing in common. And the last thing she wanted was to see their baby, Priscilla must surely realise that. They would know about Oliver, like everyone else. She had been five months pregnant when it happened, and had no longer even needed to tell people that she was expecting a baby. There was no hiding that he was there and she wouldn't have wanted to hide it anyway. She wanted to tell the world. Priscilla had been as happy spreading the word as Claire herself. Then, too soon afterwards, the hushed whisper would have filtered up and down the village streets, growing louder as it went, that she was not, not any more – not now. Priscilla would not be a grandmother yet. Because Claire would not be a mother. They would all know. Of course they would. They would all look, and wonder if they should say something. She concentrated on her bowl of cereal.

'I've told them you'll be up at the church for the family service, so you can look out for them there.'

'Actually, Mum,' Rob was saying, 'we thought we might go to the early service for once. It'll be quieter.' Claire knew immediately that he had not spoken definitely enough. Priscilla would have heard the gaps in his resolve as easily as she did.

'Nonsense, Robert. That won't work at all. Even if you left now you wouldn't get there before it started, and you surely don't want to have to burst in halfway through. Anyway, where would it leave your father and me? We can't go to the family service on our own, not without both of you. It would be such a shame for your friends if they didn't get the chance to say hello. They'll all be there.'

We don't have any friends here, Claire wanted Rob to say. He had told her plenty of times that he had been more than ready to get away from everyone he grew up with. There was a pause while she and Priscilla both waited in silence. Until the kettle screamed on top of the hob, the only sound was of their own breathing, short and tense, preparing for battle.

'Well, I don't suppose it really matters when we go, does it?' he said finally. 'Claire, what do you reckon?'

She said nothing. It was his mother who responded instead. 'Do come with us, Robert. You're here so rarely these days. When else am I going to get to show you off?'

Here so rarely because of Claire, that was what lay beneath Priscilla's words. Before she was on the scene, he was always going to visit his parents.

Now, of course, everyone was looking at her, Nick

78

too. There were only two things that could be done. Cause a scene right there in their Shaker-style kitchen, or do what she always did, which was to act as though she didn't care and say, *OK. Let's all go together. Nick can drive. We can sit in the back of the car, along with the maps and the broken umbrellas. Let's do what you want. Let's not think about me.*

'OK,' she said.

They trooped into the church together, channelled by the narrow entrance into a tight little group as if they really were a family. The place was a heaving mass of children. Everywhere Claire looked, they were racing up and down the aisles, dragging in their wake presents opened hours before and now just about ready to be discarded. The girls wore either velvet dresses with big ribbons or pink silk with sequins, finished off in both cases with sparkly shoes. The church cleaning woman would be sweeping glitter out of the aisle for weeks to come. The boys, from toddlers upwards, wore striped shirts tucked into beige trousers, exactly what they would still be wearing in twenty or thirty or forty years' time. They were all either laughing, shouting or crying. Sometimes it was hard to tell which. The hymns, when they finally began, were badly sung by parents preoccupied by their young, and the music did not come close to drowning out the din. It wouldn't have mattered if they had had children of their own, or if Claire was pregnant, as she was meant to be.

Then she would have looked on and thought, *This is me. I am part of this.* As it was, she felt like screaming. *Please,* she thought, *can someone tell them all to be quiet?* But no one did, and why should they? Of course she couldn't be expected to understand, she didn't have children of her own.

She managed to bear it until the sermon. In an odd wave of silence, of the type that sometimes rolls unbidden over black-tie dinners and cocktail parties, the vicar's voice came loud and clear. He was talking about forgiveness.

Forgive our trespasses as we forgive those who trespass against us.

The Lord said be kind and compassionate, forgive one another.

Do not take revenge or exact punishment.

Rob. Rob. Rob. He was all she could see and she could take it no more. At the worst possible moment, just as the vicar was asking anyone under the age of ten to come forward and claim a mini chocolate bar — even though Christmas was not, he added with a false-sounding laugh, really about the presents — she felt her legs forcing her up. The pews around had emptied, the main aisle was filled with children and their parents, and she was pushing through them in the opposite direction, towards the heavy oak door of the ancient church. She struggled with the massive latch and eventually got it open, escaping into the morning frost, which still lay thick across the graveyard. She left the door ajar, wanting to pour coldness into all that damn warmth.

Forgive him. If only she could. But it hurt too much.

She had tried at first, when she was still in shock from it all, still lying in a hospital bed with the gel from the ultrasound sticky underneath her clothes. Then, it had seemed simple.

'I'm sorry,' he had said, his face in his hands, then his hands on her aching stomach, his lips still stained red from wine. 'I should have been there. I should have told the client I had to meet you. I shouldn't have turned off my phone. I didn't think. Will you ever forgive me?'

'Of course I forgive you. You couldn't have known what would happen. No one could have known. I love you, don't I?'

Did she? Was she asking him to tell her? The words had come out as if she meant them. But she had loved her unborn child as well, with a violent, angry love that had arrived only when it was too late. Once the shock had waned into grief, she learnt that she had not forgiven him at all. She had not even come close to it. It gave her a power in their marriage that she did not want. She didn't know how to redress the balance. Blaming Rob, criticising Rob. It had become so much easier than loving him.

Now, standing on the crisp grass, the dead of centuries lying deep beneath her feet, she felt the spider's web of a headache weaving itself around her brain. She held her hands to her temples in despair.

Rob came up behind her, his footsteps sharp against the frozen ground.

'I told you I didn't want to come,' she said, keeping her face turned away from him, staring blankly across the fields behind the church. 'Why didn't you listen to me?'

'We've been over all this. We had no choice.'

'And this morning? Didn't we have a choice then?'

'I'm sorry.' He said that all the time these days. She was always making him apologise for something. The word no longer meant anything to either of them.

'Why did you ask me to decide, when you already knew what I wanted? They're your parents. If there's something we don't want to do, it's up to you to tell them. Why couldn't you have stood up for me for once?'

She turned around now and saw him standing behind her, running his hands through his hair, his face clouded with frustration. She waited for him to say, again, that he was sorry. But this time, he didn't.

'Because I can't do that all the time,' he said. 'Because I'm tired of it all. There's nothing more I can do to support you. Christ, Claire, when is this all going to be over?'

'I don't know,' she said, and the weight of the pain in her head dragged at her and made her collapse against him. Then, as he supported her yet again, the bells began to ring, the door of the church swung open and those endless children started to run madly out. She saw Katie and James. They were looking over to them with smiles of recognition and welcome. James was wearing a baby sling, with Joy's head, in a hand-knitted hat, emerging from inside it. Katie was holding a nappy bag, her handbag and the service sheet. She looked tired. As Claire watched, a square of stained muslin fell from her shoulder. She bent slowly down to pick it up.

Rob looked down at Claire and said, with some understanding at last, 'Come on, let's wait in the car.'

They were joined for the big Christmas lunch by the usual assortment of relatives. Nick's brother, Brian, and his wife. Their daughter Emma and her husband Mike, who were more or less Claire and Rob's age. Emma and Mike's three-year-old daughter Poppy. Emma's growing bump, which Claire could not take her eyes off and no one dared mention in front of her. Priscilla's decrepit mother, collected by Nick from the nursing home ten miles away where she lived. He had slipped off quietly and stayed away longer than it should have taken, long enough perhaps, Claire thought, for half a pint of beer for him and a glass of sherry for her in the nearest open pub. Now she had been deposited carefully in the corner of the living room like a piece of antique china and by and large overlooked. Eighty-six years old, and almost shrunken into nothingness inside her best dress. Daisy would be more or less that age now, if she were still alive, thought Claire, smiling at her but not knowing what to say. How would Daisy have aged?

Towards the end of the day, Claire came across Nick in the kitchen, making himself a turkey sandwich and escaping the family jokes and the organised jollity of board games. The room was dark, with only the lamp on the kitchen table lit, casting odd shadows that seemed to creep across the beams. They both jumped when they saw each other.

'Would you like one?' he asked, brandishing the carving knife at the carcass and a mangled loaf of bread.

'I'm fine, thanks.'

'You're not just being polite, are you? You don't need to be.'

'No sandwich, really.' A silence fell between them while Nick pottered around, putting the mayonnaise back in the fridge and tossing the knife into the sink where it fell with a splash into water that was no longer hot. It was a relief, this relative peace, after a day that had been so loud.

'Maybe I could ask you about something else instead,' she said, 'if you don't mind.'

Nick settled himself down on one of the kitchen chairs, which creaked beneath him. 'Go on.'

'I want to know about Daisy.'

He paused and thought, sandwich midway between plate and mouth. 'Daisy? Who's she? Not one of Rob's ex-girlfriends, surely? I can't remember there being anyone with that name. Anyway, you don't need to worry about them. They weren't up to much.'

Claire knew that she was meant to smile, but disappointment gripped her too tightly. She did not allow herself to walk away and tried again. 'No, it's nothing like that. Daisy was related to your mother; her surname was Milton. She wrote letters from London during the war, and your mother kept them. She left them to Rob. The lawyer said she was a cousin.'

'Ah, of course, that's it. The Daisy from her will. You got the letters, then? They said they would be sending them straight to Rob.'

'Yes, we got them. I wanted to find out more.'

She waited for him to ask why. *Because she's beginning to mean something to me*, was what she might have said. But he did not ask. He simply paused, chewed for a while, then spoke. 'Truthfully, I can't recall her ever mentioning any Daisy when she was alive. The first time I heard the name must have been when I went through the will with the attorney. As for being cousins, I didn't know she had any, so I'm not sure they were. I'm sure if they were that close I would have heard of her. Strange, wouldn't you say? She must have had the letters all those years, but she never showed them to me. It's the way life goes, isn't it, though? It's all about the here and now. That's what she used to tell me and she was dead right. What happened yesterday, this morning or last week, what you're doing next week, that's all most people care about or talk about. It was only after she died that I realised I'd hardly ever asked her about her life before I was born.'

'That's children for you. Selfish through and through,' said Claire, trying a smile.

'Well, that sort of thing never does interest children. Rob's just the same, doesn't give it a thought. It's only when you get as old as me that you start caring where you came from, and by then it's usually too late to find out. She told me a few things, of course, but I expect she didn't think I'd be interested. Anyway, I reckon that once she moved to Canada she pretty much lost touch with her own family. The world wasn't as small then as it is now, you have to remember that, and they were a long way off, not like my dad's family. Now they were practically next door. She was born in England but she didn't even come back to visit until Brian and I were both living over here. Think about that! I expect she would have written to people like Daisy for a while, and then gradually lost touch. She just hung on to the letters as a keep-sake, I suppose, from the old life.'

'Did she ever talk about the war?'

'Sometimes, but I know she felt guilty about not

being properly in it. She was out of danger, you see, even though my father wasn't. It was a time when people came together, and she missed out. She liked books about it all, I remember that much. I bought her a few of them, London in the Blitz, that kind of thing. I'm sorry – that's all there is.'

'It doesn't matter,' she said, looking out through the kitchen window into the utter darkness. Her face must have betrayed her.

'I don't know about that,' said Nick. 'It looks like it does. Why don't I see if I can find anything out? Would that help? It might take a while.'

'Yes. Please,' she said. 'I don't mind waiting. There was someone called Charles, too. I don't know his surname but I think he might have been important. Daisy writes about him. And a place called Edenside.'

'Well, that last one I can help you with. Edenside is the house where my mother grew up. Her parents bought it when she was just a little girl. It was a sprawling place up in the North and they must have rattled around in it. No brothers and sisters, you see. It was just her. The house is actually still there. We took Mum back to see it once when she visited. Boy, what a place! Surrounded by bungalows now, but you could still see it from the road and it was pretty grand. She told us they used to do a lot of entertaining, have shooting parties, the occasional dance. We can't even imagine that kind of thing nowadays. I'm not sure she liked all that so much, though. She didn't give that impression. She was keen enough to get away when she met my dad.'

'Bill, wasn't it?'

'That's right. I'm impressed.'

'It's in the letters. Daisy mentions his name.'

'Is it? Maybe I should read them sometime.'

Another silence fell. Claire idly crumpled a paper napkin decorated with holly leaves and edged with gold, willing him to come up with more. She was wondering, for the first time, how Elizabeth – married, a mother, and alone in a foreign country – might have felt receiving Daisy's letters. There must have been times when she would have given anything to be with Daisy, back in England, living through the war with everyone else, instead of sitting eternally on the sidelines praying for her husband's safe return and reading the papers every day for news of home. She might have been envious, in awe of Daisy's casual dismissal of marriage and children and everything else that made up Elizabeth's new world. She might even have been angry, reading the letters like a criticism of the choices that she herself had made. Perhaps that was what had made her put the letters away in the back of a drawer and leave Daisy to her life while she got on with her own.

Suddenly Nick was speaking again. 'Claire, I want you to know how sorry I am, how sorry we both are, about the baby. I can't imagine a more difficult and painful experience for you.' There was embarrassment in his voice, but conviction too. At least he meant what he had said. She could tell that he did.

'Well, these things happen,' she said. 'There's nothing anyone could have done about it.' She was used to saying the words. They came out easily enough. If only she could believe them.

'Rob told us what happened. I know he feels very bad about it all.'

So he should, Nick. So he should. She didn't need to say it out loud. The look on her face was enough to show how she felt.

'Priscilla had already bought some things for the baby, you know. A bear with a string you could pull to make it growl, and an outfit for the hospital, that kind of thing.'

'I'm sorry,' she said.

'You don't have to be. I just thought you should know that she cared.'

She couldn't look at him as she replied. 'I bought him an outfit too. It was white with a duck on the front. In the shop they wrapped it for me in tissue paper with blue hearts on. I threw it away, box and all. I couldn't bear to think about it lying there in the drawer.'

Nick leant out to put his arm around her, and she could not help but flinch away.

She went upstairs to bed before Rob, complaining about the headache that really did still linger and leaving him playing Scrabble, a game she hated, with his family. On her way there, she hesitated outside the room that had been made up for Poppy and her parents for the night. Through the half-open door she could hear the child's snuffling breathing, and the rustle as she shifted her position restlessly beneath stiff white sheets and blankets that had been bought when Rob was the same age or younger. In bed herself, thrusting goose-bumped legs down beneath the sheets, she thought of how warm and alive and small Poppy was, and all she wanted was to hold her in her arms.

3

A Woman and her Maid in a Courtyard – Pieter de Hooch

No.

I told you.

No.

In her dream, she was pushing him away, and then her eyes were open, she was suddenly awake and doing the same. Rob was lying on top of her, naked, kissing her, stroking her breasts. All she could feel was her body resisting, and her head screaming that one word. *No.* Then, in wakefulness, the words came out.

'No, Rob. I'm not ready. How many times do I have to tell you?'

For a second or two longer, she felt his weight on top of her, and found herself looking straight into inscrutable eyes. Then he rolled away, and she thought he must despise her.

'I thought you wanted a baby.'

'Yes, but . . .' She felt herself physically shrinking

away from him, right to the edge of the bed. A baby. Yes. A baby with Rob? Maybe. She wasn't sure. Not yet, not when she was eaten up with despair and he with frustration. How could a child born from that turn out right when even a child conceived with love could die?

'Come on, Claire. Don't you think we need to talk about this? How long is it going to be? I need to know.' He was leaning back against the pillows, his arms behind his head, staring up at the ceiling and the cheap paper lampshade that they kept meaning to replace. His nakedness made him look impossibly vulnerable. She pulled the duvet over him.

'I don't know. Soon.' She reached out to touch his far-off shoulder with her hand. He shook it away.

'Where have I heard that before? Last week and the week before and the week before that. In fact, now I think about it, I've been hearing it for quite some time.'

'You're rushing me. I don't like it.' There was an edge of hysteria creeping into her voice. It was true. The thought of him inside her, his body hard with rage, made her afraid. It was not how she wanted it to be.

'Well, if you do still want a child, this is hardly the way to go about it. Christ, when we were trying before you could hardly keep your hands off me.'

'Please don't make it sound that way.'

A pause. The hope that he would give it up and

just leave her alone. Then his voice again, echoing too loud around the magnolia-painted walls.

'Can you even remember when we last made love?'

'A while,' she said, because she didn't want to say what they both knew, which was that it had been four months, more, the time it took for the lingering heat of summer to roll into the depths of winter. She had still been pregnant, and they had been starting to joke about how they would manage it when she got properly big. 'The doctor said we should wait three months.'

'Don't make me out to be a fool, Claire,' he replied. 'The doctor said we should wait three months before trying for a baby. He didn't mean three months before we fucked. Anyway, we both know it's been much longer than that already.'

'Don't talk about it that way. You know I don't like it. The doctor said we should be patient, remember? He said we shouldn't hurry the grieving process. He said it could take a while, sometimes. You couldn't tell. It depended on the person.'

'I just think it's time for you to start trying harder.'

'Try harder to do what? To want you?'

'Yes.' His voice sounded hopeless now, deflated.

'If I don't want you, isn't that your fault?' She could hear her voice becoming more frantic.

When he spoke again, the words came out ordered and careful, as if he had practised the speech in his head countless times, and this was the first time he was hearing how it sounded out loud.

'I know you feel like I let you down, Claire. I was thoughtless and stupid, I know that. But I've tried everything I can to make it up to you. I've let you treat me just as badly as you wanted, month after month, and none of it has made a blind bit of difference. I don't think it's made you any happier, and it's destroying me. There's nothing more I can do. You have to decide. If you plan on blaming me forever, that's up to you, but . . .' Now he was the one to trail off. He had reached the difficult part, the part he had probably always stumbled over even in his head, in the silent rehearsals.

'But what?' she said.

'We both need to accept that we won't stay together. Not forever.'

So much of her had wanted to hear those words, to have him acknowledge that what had happened was enough to destroy their whole life together. Yet now she found herself suddenly gasping for breath. Unexpectedly, a vision of herself in her wedding dress came into her mind. The church, with its wooden pews and stone floor worn down by faithful steps. The vows. The rings. Her father, tall and proud as he gave her away. Her mother, sitting further back, her hat and dress too gaudy, an attempt at confidence that her face could not match, eyeing the door in case the second wife, invited but the invitation tactfully refused, decided to make an appearance after all. Friends, a lot of them back then, generating goodwill. Rob, beaming ridiculously in a rented morning suit, holding her hand, then afterwards kissing her among the late daffodils and early tulips. The flower girls tumbling down the slope in the lawn, streaking their silk dresses with grass stains and scattering fruit cake and royal icing as they went.

'Is that what you want?' she said at last, quietly and almost calm.

'No. You know that. I still want to need you, Claire. I still want to love you. But I can see it might come to that. And what about you? You need to love me too. This isn't going to work otherwise.'

Now those sunlit wedding memories were replaced by other ones. The doctor running the probe of the sonograph across her belly, again and again, just to be sure. The words that she knew were coming. *I'm sorry. There's nothing there.* Knowing the sickening truth that she would never again feel Oliver and there was nothing left inside her but despair.

Rob must have known what had come into her head. 'You don't need to think that I've forgotten, Claire. I haven't. I'd think about it every day even if you weren't here to remind me. Why didn't I leave when I'd said I would, why didn't I let you know sooner that I wasn't coming? God, we've been over it together enough times. But it happened that way. I can't change it now. If that day had been a different day, a normal day, none of it would have mattered. You would have been annoyed, and rightly so, but nothing more. I've tried damn hard to accept what happened and you just can't. But you've got to, Claire. You've got to work out some way of putting it behind you. It was inevitable, don't you remember the doctor saying that? An inevitable miscarriage. It couldn't be stopped.'

'No,' she said. 'Don't use that word. It was only inevitable because you weren't there. You weren't there to protect either of us. If you'd been there, it wouldn't have happened.'

He was angry now, angry like she was sometimes, often, but he never was – until now. She could feel the tautness of his body beside her. 'I let you down, for Christ's sake. I know I did. People do it the whole time. It happens. How could either of us have had the slightest idea of the consequences? If I had, do you think for a second I would have done things the same way? I would have dropped everything to be there with you. But it doesn't mean it was all my fault. What about those kids who snatched your bag? The one that punched you in the stomach, or the one that pushed you down? If you have to blame someone, can't you blame them? What if it was going to happen anyway and it was nothing to do with me or them at all? Have you thought about that? Things happen in life, good things and bad things and coincidences, things you could never predict. How do you think *I* feel about it? Turning on my mobile. All those messages. Knowing you were hurt. Finding you in that hospital bed. You're my wife and all I ever wanted was to keep you safe. So yes, I feel guilty. Is that what you want me to say? Yes, I feel responsible. Yes, yes, yes. But I will not have you acting like I killed our child.'

All she wanted was to pick something up and throw it at him and make him feel the agonising pain inside her that she couldn't get rid of and he didn't understand. But there was nothing to throw, so instead she struck out with her hands, pushing at his naked body, trying to get it away from her. She thought he was almost made afraid by the onslaught. But she would have hurt herself if she could have, knowing that she was the one who had decided they should meet that evening, even though she'd known that it would be difficult for him to be there on time; it was she who had not let go of her bag as quickly as she should have done when she was attacked, instinct making her hang on. And it was she who had had Oliver in her care and let him go, just let him go without ever realising how easy it could be and how fragile he was. But she could not bring herself to say any of this so instead the words became flailing arms, anger and tears.

That was how they welcomed each other into the New Year.

January, 1943

Dear Elizabeth,

Happy New Year, and here's to 1943. Thank you ever so much for the sugared plums. They arrived yesterday and not at all battered. I'm trying to make them last, although I must confess I sent a few on to Charles. They're a luxury item these days, and it doesn't do to be selfish.

There are a lot of people here saying that this will be the last year of the war, but we've all heard that before. I don't believe it for a minute. I wish I could, but I don't. Not that things have been going too badly recently − encouraging reports, that's what Charles calls them − but it's not enough. For every advance we make, all I can think about is the men it has cost.

It's on my mind more than usual, all of this, because Charles is being shipped out at long last. I expect he's off to North Africa. I don't think that's any great secret, is it? That's where they all seem to go. I won't be seeing him for a long time, probably not until it's all over, however long that might be. I'm writing to him far too often, because I feel guilty about secretly wanting it that way. I've no idea how long it will take a letter to reach him, let alone the plums. As a matter of fact, I don't suppose he'll ever get those. The odds are they'll end up rotting in the corner of a warehouse somewhere, attracting the rats. Still, it's worth a try. Poor Charles. I'm sure he's

*going to be as miserable as anything. He couldn't be
worse suited to the desert. He won't even walk on
the beach barefoot, and as for the sun – he can't bear
it. I can't help imagining him trying endlessly to
keep all that desert sand out of his boots.*

*Just walking up the steps into the gallery this
month reminded me that last time I was there, so
was Charles, with his arm linked through mine and
the two of us having a grand old time. Then, of
course, I remembered that by the time we walked
back down the steps and into Trafalgar Square, we
were rowing about our entire future together. I always
remember the bad bits, that's what Charles says. I
wish I could be like him. He says he only ever
remembers the good.*

*The painting of the month is by Pieter de Hooch,
a Dutch artist from the seventeenth century, or so the
caption says. I hope I've spelt his name right – you
can look him up in an encyclopaedia if you want to
check. It is called* A Woman and her Maid in a
Courtyard *and that's just what it shows. The maid,
who is wearing a long green-grey dress with a white
collar, and a white cap over brown hair, is crouching
over a platter on the ground which has a fish in it.
Beside her there's a metal pump, with water shooting
out into a stone basin, then a bucket and a brush,
one of those ones made of twigs around a wooden
pole like a witch's broomstick. Standing above her
with one hand pointing, clearly issuing orders, is the*

99

girl's mistress, in a sharp black jacket trimmed all round in white, and a grey skirt that reaches almost down to the ground. She has the matronly look of a woman with grown-up children. Big hips, that's what I mean, and an air of authority about her. It all adds up to hard work for the poor maid, or that's what it looks like to me.

Still, I know plenty about that. We lead a tough life these days. Work, work, work. It seems like that's all there is for us now. It doesn't stop when I leave the office. There's always more one could be doing. The latest thing is turning old blankets into new coats. Imagine that! All the girls — me included — prancing along Piccadilly dressed in their picnic rugs as if it's the latest Paris fashion. Make do and mend, that's what they call it. Never throw a thing away just in case there's something useful to be done with it. I'm already planning ahead for Molly's birthday next week, which means turning a whole lot of carrots and potatoes — and this week's ration egg of course — into something that might just pass as a cake. I sometimes feel rather hard done by about it all, thinking back to how life used to be, when we didn't have a care in the world and could while away the evenings sitting on the terrace at Edenside with flowers in our hair and a glass of lemonade in our hands. It's selfish, I know, but I can't help it. Still, looking at this painting did pull me up a bit. It showed me that life has always been a slog and I'm

*no worse off than women have ever been, and a lot
better off than most.*

*Although at first glance it looked as though there
were only women in the picture, when I looked again
I saw another figure there, a man approaching the
entrance to the courtyard, though still a good way off.
He is dressed all in black, even to his tall hat, except
for a white collar around his neck. Now that's why
they're both working so hard, I thought to myself.
They're rushing to get ready for the master of the
house. While the women hurry frantically about, he is
sauntering casually along, hands behind his back,
without a care in the world. I don't expect the
women have even realised he is there yet but you can
be sure that they know he must be on his way, and
as soon as they hear his footsteps at the entrance
they'll be snapping to attention. That's domestic life
for you, after all. Making sure everything's just so for
the moment the man walks through the door. The
apron on, supper ready to put on the plate, the
evening paper neatly folded, and the children's toys
swept into a corner – all in return for a nod of
approval. The ridiculous thing is that the women in
this painting are doing perfectly well on their own,
yet without the master one can't help but feel that
there is something missing.*

*It's always about the men, isn't it, even with them
all gone away? Everything we're doing is to help the
men on the front or look after them once they are*

back. *Show me a woman who isn't waiting for that knock on the door or footfall on the floorboards that means that the man she's thinking about has come home! Here we all are trying to carry on as normal – but mostly it's simply filling the time, and always with that nervous waiting feeling inside. There are some women who think that, as long as they don't let their man out of their thoughts for a second, they can keep death away by strength of mind alone. They're wrong. When it comes to dying, what will happen, will happen, that's the only lesson I've learnt from any of this madness.*

De Hooch wouldn't have had anything like this on his mind when he painted the women in his picture, of course. For all I know, the mistress is hoping the master won't be home for hours. It's just that there isn't anything that doesn't remind me of this awful war. Still, it's an interesting painting, and not a religious one, which makes a change. All the colours are bright and clean – no dust anywhere, no plaster hanging off the walls, no cracked bricks. Was London like that once? It's a mass of ruins these days, although the authorities try to tidy everything up when they get the chance.

Next to the painting they are displaying photographs of other de Hooch works, which means there's more than usual to look at. It's to give us visitors some context, or so the notes say. So I now know that de Hooch painted a lot of courtyard scenes and the maid appears in a number of them, always a maid, allowed to clean and polish the trappings of wealth but not have it. That's another part of life that's gone for good, I'd say. There won't be parlourmaids and housemaids and that sort of thing again, or not like there used to be. Women won't stand for a life in service nowadays, not now they can work in a factory and have a home of their own instead of just a single bed in someone else's.

What other news? It is shockingly cold and I try not to be outside a minute longer than I can help. Even in my rooms I am careful as anything with the heating — more than one bar of the electric fire and one feels ridiculously guilty about being wasteful. You are well off out of it. There was a hard frost last night. I came home late and it was the clearest of nights. The moon lit up everything so I didn't even need my torch. And the quiet! I had the street to myself, just me and that eerie white light to guide me to my front door. It made the bomb crater at the corner of my road almost beautiful and for once I didn't just pass by thinking, when are they going to clear that mess up? The smallest things can buck me up these days, as you can probably tell. Of course once I was inside common sense got the better of me and all I could think was how this would make a perfect night for a raid. I slept in my clothes just in case, although it turned out quiet. Like I said, you can never forget this damn war.

*Should I try and get myself sent after Charles, do
you think? Women are gadding about all over the
place these days, you know. I don't need to be stuck
in London, just waiting, do I? I could be off
somewhere more exciting. But I wouldn't leave my
father. I know he hates it enough that I'm here and
not at home with him. He is alone enough as it is,
without me being any further away. Anyway, I have
a life here, of sorts, even if does sometimes feel as if
I'm only marking time. Or is it that deep down I
simply lack the courage?*

    All my love,

    Daisy

Claire left the flat much too early, while Rob was
still in the shower. She called out her goodbye over
the sound of the water, knowing that even if he
heard her and wanted to kiss her goodbye, by the
time he emerged she would already be gone. In fact
there was no response, no kiss even attempted, just
a slammed door between them. She was in Trafalgar
Square by quarter to ten. It meant that the National
Gallery was not even open, its blank façade blanker
than ever and its metal, bank-vault doors still firmly
secured.

She made herself walk slowly towards the main
entrance, weaving her way across the paving stones,
killing the remaining, dragging minutes and trying
to ignore the cold. There had been fog outside when

she awoke and it still hung in the air, though lighter now than when she had drawn back the bedroom curtains and looked out into smoky nothingness. She glanced up, past the almost-lost figure of Nelson on top of his column and into the grey, thinking about all those planes that wouldn't now be taking off from Heathrow, all those angry people who would be crawling like worker bees around the terminals. Then she focused back down towards the ground, on Trafalgar Square's lions in front of her, bedewed with water but still, as always, perfectly and grandly at ease, resting on their enormous paws and free for a while from the frantic clinging, then slipping, grasp of passers-by. The National Gallery loomed above everything else, its Grecian pillars pushing outwards into the open space. Claire realised that she was looking at it properly for the first time. At the very centre, its cupola rose up, a perfect round amid the sharp squares and triangles, decorated with a pattern like peacock feathers, and with its finer details etched in dirt. Impressive, and functional too, but not quite beautiful, not for her anyway.

She glanced at her watch, decided that the doors must be about to open and walked the rest of the way with resolve. She was looking forward to this painting, which Daisy seemed to like. She wanted to be the first inside. Still the Gallery was shut and she joined the straggling crowd that had already gathered at the top of the steps, ready for the first tourist attraction of a long day. She took up a position right by the door and spent the last few seconds scuffing her leather boots impatiently against the black-and-white mosaic floor and counting up the wads of discarded chewing gum – some old and ingrained, some still creamy and fresh – that decorated it. Black and white. But things were never that way, that was what her mother had told her when she was a child and everything was always unfair. Things were always somewhere in between. She remembered Rob's accusation: *You're acting like I killed our child*. Was that really what she thought, that he was a murderer? No, of course not, not really, not when her head was clear and she was thinking straight. It was the grief speaking. It could do strange things, grief. She had not known that until now. She had never had to know. It had brought with it this desperate, physical need to blame someone, someone who would be right there when she had to lash out – Rob. The only person who was always there.

Claire, like Daisy, noticed first that this was a woman's world, just like Daisy's had become. The scene that de Hooch had painted was organised and controlled. There was no rush or panic in it, no mess or clutter, just clean, tidy lines and the maid doing what she was told. If there had been men in the courtyard, Claire thought, they would have been lounging around, getting in the way. There would have been broken bits and pieces strewn on the floor, waiting to be fixed, which the women were not allowed simply to throw away. It seemed to Claire sometimes that men carried a kind of casual careless-ness around with them like a badge of honour, just to drive women slowly mad. On her way to the gallery that morning, she had watched as the man sitting opposite her on the tube cut his fingernails on to the carriage floor, ignoring the glances she cast him over the top of her newspaper, as if it didn't matter. Long after he had got off the train, carrying a bunch of flowers for a girlfriend or a wife, as if that made up for it, Claire sat staring at the jagged, dirty clippings, unable to get the unpleasant rasping sound of the nail scissors out of her head. A woman would not have done that. No, women were almost always neater and more careful than men.

The strange thing was that men didn't seem to be at all bothered about this. She remembered one occasion when she had been clattering around the kitchen wiping surfaces, flipping on the kettle, wondering how to get rid of the limescale round the taps and whether they had paid the gas bill, while all the time Rob simply looked on. When she confronted him, laughing, because it had been a long time ago, he had said to her that he didn't mind one bit that he couldn't multitask. Most of the tasks she insisted on doing didn't need to be done in the first place. Now, she knew, she would not laugh. She would probably shout. She had lost her sense of humour, somewhere along the line between the hospital and here.

Looking at these women in the painting doing everything – running the home, keeping it clean, doing the cooking – she felt the acid taste of resentment building up inside her. Things hadn't changed. Life was still like that for most women, and still there was usually a man behind it all, dropping in when the work was done, just as the master was doing here, sometimes grateful, sometimes not, but always assuming that things would be ready for his return. Almost without thinking about it, she pulled out her mobile phone and texted Rob, to ask him if he had unloaded the dishwasher yet, of all things. She knew he wouldn't have, because he never did that sort of thing till the last minute, when he heard her key in the lock and knew she would come and take over and do it herself. Nevertheless, she immediately regretted sending the message, knowing it too well to be no more than pathetic sniping of the type she had once despised.

She put the phone back quickly inside her bag, as deep as possible, wanting to avoid Rob's response, but at the same time wondering whether his silence would be worse. In front of her, the women were still there, trapped inside their courtyard and then within a gold frame, the rest of life for evermore held just out of reach. The mistress and her servant must have shared a camaraderie of sorts, yet any tentative overtures of companionship would no doubt have been swept briskly away into the gutters at the end of each day, together with the grit from the floor.

This narrow life was one that Claire could not imagine Daisy accepting, so far removed from the energy that seeped out of every London street, with the boredom of the same walls from morning till night slowly dulling her mind. Daisy must surely have been drawn to the city in the hope of some-thing different, and maybe even someone different. She must have realised that it was in her hands to change everything that her life was meant to be, with the consequences still hidden far away. Claire had heard that said about the war, not just this one but the one before, that while the men had been off fighting some distant enemy, women like Daisy had fought their own war, one that the men did not even realise was going on, and thereby won their liberty, or some liberty at least.

She wondered whether Daisy was wrong about the other figure in the painting, this man dressed almost entirely in black and coming steadily closer. Perhaps he was not the master, but a messenger bearing the bad news hinted at by the angry dark-ness in the sky, while the women were unaware that something might be about to happen that would change their lives – for better, for worse, who could possibly know which? These women, with their lives spent within the confines of brick walls, could not know what dangers were hidden around the corner, any more than did Claire herself, who had a freedom that the servant and her mistress could neither have dreamt of nor probably even understood.

A sudden clatter behind her made her start and turn, but there was only an elderly woman there, who had dropped her reading glasses on the floor. Claire picked them up and handed them to her. She found herself wondering, not for the first time, if Daisy were still alive: in her late eighties, getting through the days, dropping her glasses and hoping they hadn't broken, remembering when she was young. Wondering whatever happened to Elizabeth, and why they lost touch. Maybe. More likely not. People didn't live forever, after all, however much they might want to – not that most of them really did, not once they were frail and fearful of incontinence, and all the old friends were long gone. Look at her own grandparents. None of them had managed to trudge even very far into their seventies, which she knew was hardly promising for her own longevity.

She tried to imagine the two of them meeting, Daisy and herself, old and young, talking about the paintings, and about what Daisy's life had been like back then. They might even come to the National Gallery together. For a moment a picture of her smiling self came into her head, pushing a fragile, still elegant old woman in a grey-framed wheelchair collected from the information desk across the endless wooden floors. The glances from other visitors said, *Isn't that nice? She's taking her gran out. I wonder if it's a special occasion?* But no, Daisy must be dead by now. Nick would have known more about her otherwise. There would have been a Christmas card every year, the occasional birthday card or even a letter or a present when an old memory was unlocked and nostalgia trickled out.

Looking back at the painting, she focussed now on the elaborate, careful detail. On the right-hand side, the building to which the pump was attached looked like a stable, with a roof made roughly from struts layered with twigs and a wooden door that had swung open. Its walls were carefully whitewashed but less clean where they reached the ground, which was paved with bricks and no longer perfectly flat. Behind the women was a low wall, a cloth draped roughly over it, and beyond that a house of several floors, red-roofed, with darkened windows and outbuildings of its own. Not much of it could be seen because this place was part of the outside world, the one through which the master of the house could wander untrammelled by concerns while the women stayed at home busying themselves with endless domestic tasks. Only a glimpse – that was all these women could get – into a separate existence, empty of people other than the approaching man, but full of promise almost because so little of it could be seen; and the less one knew of something, Claire had always found, the more alluring it became.

That must have been how the world once was, she thought, but not now, when women were everywhere, and you could hardly get away from them. She agreed with Daisy that both of the women in the painting were waiting, whether they realised it or not. Weren't women always waiting for something, unable to accept the present moment because the next thing was already on their minds? Weren't they always pressed on one side by the hope that what happened next would be better, but on the other by the fear that it might just be worse?

She wondered afterwards if she would ever have met Dominic if she and Rob had not argued yet again that morning. What if they had stayed in bed and made love to each other? She would have arrived at the National Gallery later, after a breakfast made by her husband, or she might not have gone there at all that day. What if she had liked the painting less, and turned away sooner, or more and stayed longer? Then Dominic would most likely not have been there. All traces of him would have disappeared into the humidity-controlled air.

She didn't have to go into the crowded café next to the shop after seeing the painting. She didn't have to stand in the long queue, her back aching from the slow, hesitant pace that went with galleries and museums, waiting to order a latte. But she did do those things. She could also have replied 'Yes' when the Polish girl behind the till in the crisp white shirt and long black apron asked her if she wanted to take it away. But instead she said 'No', and that was how she found herself standing by the till holding an over-hot china mug, looking round in frustration at the crowded tables full of people who were friends or family, and then saying to a stranger sitting on his own, 'Do you mind if I share this table?'

He looked up. Eyes blue, welcoming. 'Of course not. No problem. Here, let me move my paper.' He folded it up neatly and slipped it into the shoulder bag that was lying by his seat on the polished granite floor.

'Thank you. But I don't want to interrupt.'

'It's fine.'

'Well, thank you.'

She cupped the mug in her hands and felt the steam that rose up from it against her face, reminding her of a long-ago facial, the kind of thing she didn't bother with these days. She blew across the foaming surface to cool the coffee. She knew that he was still looking at her because she could feel it, even through her half-closed eye lids. It gave her a sharp pinch of anxiety, but it was too late and awkward to move somewhere else. So she stayed, keeping her eyes down and focussed on the pale wooden tables with their gold-coloured metal trim.

'Are you here to see the Botticelli exhibition?' His voice was distinctive and confident. It was a voice that already told her boarding school, then Oxbridge or perhaps St Andrew's or Durham. She knew that his bath and grass would have a long 'a', like a satisfied sigh exhaled, not a short one. He did not seem to notice that he was breaking the rules about sharing tables, which after all no one normal ever really wanted to do. The rules said that you must both ignore the other person, by pretending to read a book or check a diary or, these days, by sending an email on some electronic device or other. You must always feel slightly uncomfortable, not make direct eye contact and then feel obliged to leave as soon as possible – far more quickly than if you had been sitting alone.

The question meant that Claire in fact had to look up to meet his gaze, out of politeness as much as anything else, she told herself. He had brown, rough hair that was almost too long around the ears, an effect (and it was effective) no doubt only achieved with some effort. Those eyes, so inviting, unthreatening but still challenging. Some stubble, but not too much, and it was a Saturday, after all. He was wearing a T-shirt with an exploding volcano on the front of it that would have come from a clothes rail with a sign above it saying Retro, if it didn't say

Vintage. It looked freshly ironed, as did his jeans. He did not look like a lawyer. She was not sure what he looked like.

She answered him at last. 'No. Is there one?'

He looked rueful. 'Well, I thought there was. But I got the dates wrong. It ended last week. There are some Botticellis in the public galleries, though. I'm going to look round those instead.'

Claire was meant to say only 'Ah,' or 'Hmm.' Nothing more. Then he would have returned to his newspaper or gone in search of his paintings and at the very worst looked disappointed at her failure to respond to his friendliness, which wouldn't have mattered because he was just a stranger. Instead she said, 'I saw one myself, actually, a month ago.'

'Which one?'

'It's called *The Mystic Nativity*.'

'An interesting choice, if you don't mind me saying so. *The Mystic Nativity*'s rather unusual.'

'Is it? It seemed like a good thing to see before Christmas.' It was all she could think of to say. What was it that Daisy had written in her letter to Elizabeth? And where were all those other thoughts that had come into her head when she was standing in front of it? They had felt important at the time. There was something difficult about discussing art, or perhaps it was this man who was making it difficult. He already sounded as if he knew what he was talking about, rather like that man Daisy had run into, Sir Kenneth Clark. People like that had an air about them that crackled with authority – and something else that was harder to put a finger on.

'Did you know that it's the only piece Botticelli ever actually signed?' he was saying. 'So at least the art historians can be sure it's by him. They're always arguing about that sort of thing – which artist produced which paintings, what's happened to the ones that have gone missing. It can get people quite worked up, believe it or not.'

'Is that what you are, an art historian?' she asked.

He laughed. 'No, not these days. I did study art history when I was younger, but then I realised that I was spending so much time reading about art I could no longer actually enjoy it. I'm still involved in that world, though. I work in an auction house. How about you?'

'I'm just getting into art,' she said, and because she didn't want him to think that she knew nothing at all about it, she found herself telling him something that she didn't think even Rob knew – because they couldn't know absolutely everything about each other, people never did, even after years of togetherness when it sometimes felt as though there were no memories left that had not already been shared. 'At school, for a while, I used to paint. But once I started A levels, I never went into the art room again. You know, when I think about it, I haven't held a paintbrush in my hand for nearly fifteen years.'

'Not even to redecorate your bedroom?' A smile. A direct look. Seeing her own blue eyes reflected in his.

'No,' she said. 'My husband does all that. He's good with practical things. You know, painting, wallpaper, that kind of thing. When he's not being a lawyer.'

There was a pause. It went on for too long. Claire found herself looking down self-consciously at her wedding ring, and the engagement ring beside it, both of them too new to have worn thin from rubbing against each other. The solitaire diamond was still shining, albeit more dully than when Rob had first slipped it on to her finger, his hands shaking as much as hers as he had pushed it into place, and she had said, without a second's hesitation and with him hardly having to say a word, 'Yes, I will. Of course I'll marry you.' She had been meaning to get it cleaned. She twisted the two rings around together. Then she glanced at his hands, guiltily. They were bare. She continued, speaking rapidly. 'I've decided to come to the National Gallery once a month, and see what I can teach myself. It's something new to do.' She did not mention Daisy.

The man was still looking at her carefully, and she concentrated on her coffee. It was now unpleasantly cold.

'That Botticelli painting you saw,' he said at last. 'It's not just about the birth of Jesus, like most nativity scenes. Botticelli thought the apocalypse was coming when he painted it, and that the whole world was going to be destroyed before too long. He was trying to show that side of things as well.'

'Oh,' she said. 'I didn't know that. I would never even have guessed.' She felt disappointed, embarrassed even, as if she had missed something obvious. She wondered whether Daisy, caught up in a real war, had known that she was looking at a picture that foretold utter destruction. Surely not. If she had, she would certainly not have thought it such a good choice for the painting of the month.

'He was wrong, of course. The world's still going strong.' *Is it?* she thought. *I'm not so sure.*

'I'm Dominic, by the way.'

'I'm Claire.'

Down at her feet, she felt her mobile phone vibrate in her handbag. It would be Rob. Hardly anyone else ever called it, because she so rarely picked it up.

'Would you like another coffee, Claire?'

'Yes,' she said. The phone had stopped ringing. 'That would be nice, Dominic.'

Only when she was outside her front door, fumbling in her bag for the keys, did she check her mobile phone. There was a voicemail and a text.

She listened to the voicemail right there on the pavement, with the wind whipping the sharp grit of the street against her legs. It was from Sarah, who was meant to be coming round for dinner that night with her husband David and another couple. She was saying that David was ill and wouldn't be able to make it, and anyway he had a lot of papers from work to read over the weekend. Sarah herself would still be there, of course, but on her own, if that was OK, and leaving early so it wasn't too late when she got home – so, really, thought Claire, hardly there at all. She wondered if the excuses were lies and knew that she was meant to call Sarah back and say that she quite understood, and shouldn't Sarah really just stay at home too. She didn't. It was easier to have someone there than no one. Anyway, Sarah and the other guests were meant to be friends, real friends, people that she and Rob had known at university and with whom they had once been able to spend endless hours that somehow expanded into days, discussing everything under the sun. After Oliver, she had released her grip on the ties that bound them to each other and watched them spin away. Some had hung bravely on, for the sake of memories that told them that once (if not now) Claire had been good company, once she had danced at parties, been the first to suggest the next outing and talked about her job too much because she couldn't help loving it. In the end their concern, pulling on her like quicksand, had become as choking as grief and she strove even harder to keep them far away. Oliver was enough for her. None of them could understand that. Nothing had come close to filling the little emotional space she had left – not until this unreal Daisy, who came to Claire only when Claire called on her yet was somehow building more room for herself by the day.

The text was from Rob and said: *Done. Shopping too.* She was confused for a second or two, until she remembered. It was the dishwasher he meant – now, clearly, unloaded. It was odd, but talking to Dominic had made her forget all about it. In fact she had forgotten about most things, talking to him. In the unpromising surroundings of the cramped café, he had somehow managed to take her away from everything that usually filled her head, the tiny things like paying the council tax and buying a new TV licence, and the enormous things like Oliver – and Rob. He hadn't asked her outright what she did, like most acquaintances. Nor had he asked, in a careful, concerned voice, how she was, like most friends. Instead, they had discussed exhibitions, books and the latest films, just like the people sitting at the tables all around them were doing, and like she and Rob had done at one time, before they were married and when they still sometimes got up early to escape flat-shares they had outgrown and have breakfast together.

Claire had read the arts section of one of the Saturday newspapers on the way in to town. She had found it thrown down in a tube carriage, and baulked slightly at picking it up. Now she was pleased she had.

It made her feel knowledgeable and impressive, even though she had no reason to impress a stranger, and still less reason to give a stranger her mobile phone number, which she had done, and agree, gladly, when he said, 'Let's do this again.' Not that he was a stranger now. He was an auctioneer called Dominic who knew about Botticelli, no doubt Titian too, and even knew how to draw, sometimes visiting the National Gallery to sketch paintings from its collection, badly or so he said. She was glad that the only thing he really knew about her was that she was married. She was glad that she had not taken his number. She was glad that none of it really mattered because she would not see him again. Still, it had felt like a miracle for a while, to be made to feel so different, as if she and what she had to say was all that mattered, nothing else.

His message came through just as she stepped into her home and the weight of normality crashed down around her shoulders. It sat in the inbox of her mobile phone next to Rob's. *It was nice to meet you. Keep in touch. Dominic x.* So now she had his number after all. *It was good to meet you too.* That was the response she tapped out, the door of the flat still held open. No x. It was guilt about the immediacy of her reply, and not about the shopping or the dishwasher or the argument, that made her rush into Rob's arms when she finally went inside and kiss him softly, properly, on the lips.

'This is a surprise,' he said, smiling. His eyes

betrayed more complex emotions. Uncertainty. Shock. Wondering how long this new mood would last. Claire did not see any happiness in them. She kissed him again, hoping to find some shadow of relief at least.

'I should do this more often,' she said. 'Like I used to.'

When I used to kiss you ten times, twenty, thirty, more, before we even got up. When I used to say 'I love you' every morning as you left for work and mean it. When I never imagined how easy it could be for you to betray me, or me to betray you.

'There's no rush, you know. This morning, I didn't mean to put pressure on you. I wouldn't do that, not intentionally. I understand that it's going to take time.' He meant it as a reward for that kiss, that simple gesture, but it felt like more than that. It felt like a reprieve. Already, even as she said 'Thank you' and leant her head into his chest, she knew he was allowing her to stretch out their separateness for longer.

He stroked her hair as she hid her face against him. 'You smell of coffee and cake,' he said, 'and I'm hungry.'

He might as well have said Dominic's name, as it was Dominic who had bought her the final coffee, and then, after that, a slice of Victoria sponge, the stickiness of which still lingered on the tips of Claire's fingers. She broke away immediately.

'Did you like the painting?' he asked, and she knew that he was trying to hold on to the almost accidental intimacy she had offered him.

'Yes', she began to say, but then found that all she could remember of it was the rolling grey of that ominous sky billowing down on the two women below. She shrugged her shoulders with almost a shiver and went on, 'It was fine. Now come on. We've got to get everything ready for tonight.' They were in the kitchen and she scanned the food that he had laid out on one of the surfaces. 'Did you remember to get the lemons for the cheesecake?'

He paused, then groaned. 'I'm sorry. I knew there was something else.'

'I'll go and buy some now. The shop round the corner will have plenty.' Normally, well, the recent normal anyway, she would have made a fuss. In the old days, she would have just smiled and made things right, and they would have gone back to the shops together, hand in hand, while she told him about her morning in far more detail than he really wanted to know. Today, she simply turned around, her coat still on, and left the flat knowing that even though she had not shouted or cried, Rob would have felt her disappointment and crumbled away just a little more inside.

She read both Dominic's message to her and hers in response more than once before she went to bed that night, and checked more than once to see if he had texted again, which he did not. She saved his number too, under D for Dominic because she didn't know his surname, and because already something told her she would use it again.

4

Apollo and Daphne – Pollaiuolo

'Let's do something together today,' Rob was saying. 'Go to Kew Gardens or Richmond.'

They had visited both places together before, and wandered intertwined through their prettiness, stopping somewhere along the way for tea, taking photographs which they would never get round to printing out and buying each other a present to remember the day. *So many times like that, once*, thought Claire, and it made her hesitate, halfway out of bed, legs on the ground. She had woken up early and abruptly, with an impatience pulling at her limbs, but then lain there still, rather than break the silence with movement. A woodpecker was beating rhythmically against one of the trees in the communal garden. The sound felt like the beginnings of a headache.

'I'm sorry Rob, but I can't,' she said at last, waiting long enough surely for him to have known already that the answer was no. 'I told you last night. I'm going to see Daisy's next picture this morning.'

'So go tomorrow instead. The Gallery's open on Sundays. You're not doing anything else, are you?'

'No, but I promised myself I'd go today. It's the first of February today. It's the February picture I'm going to see.'

'That means you've got the whole month to see it. Nothing's going to happen if you're not there today, is it? The letter will still be there. So will the painting. The world won't end.'

He said it lightly, trying to make her laugh, but she wouldn't. When she replied, her voice was tense. 'It's my project, Rob. I've decided how I want to do it. I don't want you stopping me from finishing it.'

'I'm not saying you should stop. I just thought you might want to spend some time with your husband for once, just the two of us, somewhere that isn't this flat. Is that such a terrible idea?'

He was still trying, too hard, and Claire wondered how he could possibly manage to keep his voice sounding so patient. She knew she would not have. 'No, of course not,' she said. 'But can't we leave it for now and decide on something later?'

'Yes, of course. I suppose we could.'

Then she knew he was going to let her have her way. It made her give him a proper smile, one that was hardly forced at all.

'Thanks, Rob. You know it means a lot.'

'I know,' he said, and then, more quietly, 'I'm just not sure why.' Did he think she hadn't heard, or did he not want her to hear? She did not bother to find out. She didn't have time for arguments, not today. She had told Dominic that she was visiting the National Gallery every month and it was exactly a month since her visit to the de Hooch painting. That was why she had to go there again today. If he wanted to see her, he would know where to find her. The thrill that ran through her at the idea of it was almost shocking. She did not try to understand the emotion, because things felt dangerous enough already, and the more she thought about it, the quicker she knew she would be drawn in. Her mother, her own failed marriage now long behind her, had decided to give Claire some final words of wisdom before she set off down the aisle towards Rob. She had not wanted to believe them at the time. 'Just because you're married,' her mother had said, 'it doesn't mean the attraction to other people goes away. It's the way you deal with it that has to change.' And then, desperately, 'Try and do better than we did.' *I could hardly do worse*, Claire had thought then, but that was before she knew what it was to live with the images of the life she should have had, images that seemed much stronger somehow than reality, constantly playing out against her closed eyes, before she knew how deep the desire to escape could run. Despair had been too strong for happiness, it had destroyed it in a single blow.

She threw aside the duvet and left her husband lying alone in bed, with the warmth of the night disappearing in a moment. From the doorway, she watched him as he fell back on the pillows and closed his eyes in what she hoped was sleep.

She had breakfast in a place down the road, not wanting to eat to the sound of the toddler downstairs crying, which he did every day at around this time. Claire had been friends with his mother for a while, at the beginning. They had chatted about what she should expect next with her own pregnancy, and talked about going on trips together to the park once Claire's baby came. She had pictured them there, Oliver asleep in the buggy while this older child lurched higher and higher on the swings. They had not really spoken since the miscarriage. Whatever words the woman could have used, all Claire would have heard was her saying, *I have my child and you have lost yours. Here is my son, where is yours?* There had been a time when the little boy used to crawl, then stagger, then finally run into Claire's open arms, but that too had changed. He had become wary when she came near, as if he understood better than his mother what had gone from inside her.

She sat in the café on a cheap plastic chair which was meant to look as if it was made of wicker, with a cup of tea in front of her, watching people of every kind walking endlessly past the plate-glass windows on which the special offers were written in luminous green, back-to-front so they could be read from outside. Up in one corner of the window, a butterfly was fluttering inelegantly across the condensation generated by the customers and the constant steam from the coffee machine. The more it flapped its wings, the wetter and heavier they became, and the wider its frantic trail across the glass. She did not think it was going to get out, not without help, so when she left, she stood on tiptoes and caught it up in her empty polystyrene cup and took it out on to the ugly street where she released it, tipping it on to the pavement. Stupid, really. It wasn't going to live, she could see that. At first it couldn't even fly away. It was going to freeze to death, most likely — whoever had heard of butterflies in February? But better for it to freeze, having escaped, than for it to die trapped in the heat of human sweat. She had always hated feeling trapped more than anything else. Even as a little girl she had found it difficult to play hide and seek, shying away from wardrobes and the dark spaces behind doors and under beds.

She threw the cup into a bin and headed down into the underground. Just as she was going down the escalator, her phone beeped. There was a text, from Dominic.

Am going to gallery today. Are you?

She hesitated. Should she reply? She decided against it: she wanted to know what it felt like to be in charge, to be the one who was asked, 'Did you get my message?' She had never been in charge with Rob. She had always let herself be blown along beside him, following where he led, right from the day they first met when she was reading English, rather half-heartedly, and he, in the same year as her, had already signed a training contract with a London law firm. He had been self-assured back then, knowing exactly what he wanted. Well, look where that had got them both. Now things were going to be different. She would take control. She would have the upper hand. Yet despite her resolve she could not help running down the rest of the length of the escalator and taking the first tube train that pulled into the plat-form, even though it was packed with shoppers heading to Oxford Street, and the next one was only a minute away. Normally she would have waited.

She was carrying Daisy's letter in her bag, put care-fully back into its original envelope. For the first time, the envelope had a large inked stamp on it which said *Opened by Examiner*. She supposed this was something to do with censorship. The letters were being sent out of the country to Canada, after all. It meant that she was not the first stranger to read it, that there had been someone else turning the pages long before her, and before Elizabeth even, looking for secrets just like Claire was. She had read the letter already, the night before in the flat, but she wanted to read it again, within view of the painting Daisy had described. There would be something special about doing that.

February, 1943

Dear Elizabeth,

February's painting of the month is another Italian one. The artist is called Pollaiuolo, which is something of a mouthful, don't you think? It's old, too. They think it dates from around 1470, and it is called Apollo and Daphne. *How many walls must it have hung on before it came here for me to look at? Dozens and dozens, I should think. And now I expect it will be owned by the National Gallery for the rest of time.*

It is a tiny painting. In fact it's so small I cannot fathom why it was chosen at all. I thought the National Gallery was meant to be showing art to the masses, but sometimes they don't make it easy. I could hardly get a decent look at it, what with everyone crowding round. Still, I daresay it made it easier to transport, and we take what we can get these days. You'll remember the story, I'm sure. Apollo is maddened with desire for a lovely nymph called Daphne. She is having none of it and calls upon her father to help (he, like all the characters in Greek mythology, is some sort of minor god). He saves her by turning her into a laurel tree. Thus Apollo is thwarted and Daphne escapes. Unrequited love, Elizabeth, and hasn't it just been around forever? How much energy we all spend chasing after what we can't quite get! It must be what keeps the world turning.

Mother used to say that there was never a perfect balance anywhere, not even in marriage. One person would always love the other just that little bit more. I didn't understand what she meant at the time, of course. I thought that love was the simplest thing of all, because loving her was so simple. I never realised that I would sometimes hate her once she had gone, just because she had left me behind when she died. As if there was a thing she could have done about it! I see that now, of course. And look at Charles. He might have got me in the end but I hardly made it easy, did I? One proposal wasn't enough for me, although I think two did the trick. Even now I'm making him wait.

The painting shows Apollo in a rather daring leather tunic that doesn't even reach halfway down his bare thighs, with golden locks flowing around his shoulders. He has thonged golden sandals on his feet, and a scarf streaming out behind him so one can tell how quickly he is moving. Frankly the only way on earth Daphne could have made her escape was with her father's help because already Apollo is reaching out to her, and his legs are more or less entwined with hers. She is barefoot and has long golden hair too, and what seems to me to be rather a doll-like face. She's more decently clad than Apollo in some ways. Her dark blue tunic reaches down to her ankles, but is then split somewhat invitingly up to the top of her thigh, revealing rather a lot of shapely leg. Around her waist is a thin brown girdle which would fall off in an instant if Apollo gave it a good tug.

The oddest thing about the painting is that Daphne is already turning into the famous laurel tree. Her arms are waving around above her head, but for the most part they aren't arms; they are branches and brown leaves and about the same size as the rest of her, for goodness' sake. I suppose it has to be that way, so it tells the story, but the poor girl does look rather absurd flapping these tennis racket-like wings around. I think you would at least have smiled if you'd been there, but I must say I laughed out loud. I just couldn't help myself. Truth be told, Apollo might have been quite a good catch for Daphne – and there is something about her face that made me wonder if she is thinking that he might not be such a bad proposition after all. Too late, Daphne, too late!

I was still laughing over it all when I felt a tap on my shoulder and turned round to find a rather handsome man right behind me holding a glove out as if he was a courtier and I was – perhaps not quite a princess, but certainly some minor figure in the royal household. He was practically bowing, and the effect was most charming, I must say. I reached out for the glove, which was mine, of course – I'd dropped it on the floor in my usual way, and naturally it was one with a hole in it, although they *all have holes in them these days, come to think of it. Then he said, 'You have the most beautiful hands. I would love to paint you.' Goodness, Elizabeth, can you imagine anything more splendid? It's the kind of thing one dreams about. I was awfully thrilled, as you can imagine, but couldn't help thinking he must be completely mad. He isn't, of course. He really is an artist.*

I'm not quite sure how it happened, but before I knew it I was having lunch with him bought from the canteen they've got going in the gallery. We each had a cup of scalding tea, and shared some ham and chutney sandwiches, sitting on the marble stairs and getting in everyone's way. He asked me if I was enjoying the paintings, and I explained how I was coming along every month and writing to tell you about it afterwards. He thought it was a tremendous idea, and asked whether I liked Apollo and Daphne. I'm afraid I hardly knew how to respond, with him being frightfully knowledgeable about such things, so I didn't say much, just that I didn't know a thing about art and I was only beginning to learn. He looked a bit disappointed at that, so then I told him that it had made me laugh, and why, and he began to laugh himself. What a difference it made to his face! Not nearly as serious as I thought at first. In fact, I think he might be good fun. Still, I wish I could have come out with something more impressive. Next time I'll try harder.

*He is working in London at the moment on
commissions for some committee. It's been set up to
make sure there's what he calls an artistic record of
the war — so we don't have just lists of dead people
and battles to remember the awfulness by. Well, this
committee has recruited any number of artists to paint
things of interest. I have no idea whatsoever how
they decide if something is interesting or not, but it
certainly all sounds very important. I told him that I
didn't think there could be much artistic merit in
something so dreadful and boring as this war, and
I'm afraid that upset him a little. But he says, if I'll
let him, he'll prove me wrong. He's called Richard,
by the way, Richard Dacre. I should have told you
his name earlier, but I don't suppose it matters.*

*I haven't had word from Charles, but I'm still
writing.*

No more news for now.

All love,

Daisy

Sitting on a wooden bench in front of Pollaiuolo's
Apollo and Daphne, Claire wasn't sure that Daisy had
got the painting right in every way. There was not
much to laugh about here so far as she could see.
She thought that the expression Daphne wore was
full of sadness, a face that was about to crumple into
tears. The sudden fear that had fallen upon her at
Apollo's approach, the panic of a naïve girl at the

slightest brush of a boy's lips against her own at her first school dance, might have melted away if she had only given it the chance. Instead she had called straight out to her father to save her, begging for escape, and been left only with the physical realisation creeping through her limbs that she had in fact succeeded in trapping herself for ever, at the very moment Apollo's legs pressed warm and strong against her own. She must have learnt then what she had given up. The love of a god, the love of a man, even the comfort of a parent's arms around her, now hidden away forever behind a screen of branches and leaves.

There was something desperate in Apollo's face too, as he tried helplessly to hold on to her, to pull her back from her fate, or at least commit her image to his memory. He was trying to save her, for himself but also from herself, clutching out to her as if he were still not prepared to give up the fight, not yet. All of it hopeless, the strength of the irate father too great for the amorous youth – but at least he was trying, trying as hard as she had wanted Rob to try. *If only*, she thought, *he had not given up on me. If only I could have told him that if he kept going just a bit longer everything would be alright between us again.* She could not be sure of it, though. There was a part of her that was afraid that she was already too different from the woman he had married ever to allow his approach again, let alone to attract it, her own metamorphosis complete. In that case there was no hope left for either of them. As for Daphne, it was a hard lesson she had learnt. Be careful what you wish for. Who knew how your wish would come true?

It was an uncomfortable thought, and like all uncomfortable thoughts better pushed away. So instead Claire thought about Daisy, and how she had come to this same place to look at the same picture that she was seeing now. She half-closed her eyes, almost expecting to open them and see Daisy coming towards her, holding out her hand and saying, 'So pleased to meet you. How good of you to come.' Was that how people spoke back then? She imagined her dressed smartly in a neat suit and hat, making an effort, and the two of them sitting there side by side, saying that they felt as though they'd known each other for years. There was something about that moment, she could feel it so strongly, that made her look up in welcome with a smile ready. But there was no Daisy, of course. How could there be? Instead, there was Dominic, and her smile had not been wasted.

'Claire! Hello! I saw you coming in,' he said. 'I hope you don't mind me following you up here? I didn't want to miss you. Did you get my message?'

'Yes. I'm sorry, I didn't have time to reply. I was already on my way. I was going to call you later.' She felt annoyed at hearing herself apologise when there was no need, embarrassed, too, that Dominic might have been watching her from the entrance to the room, wondering what held her before Pollaiuolo's strange painting and whether the tiny adjustments she had no doubt been making to her clothes and hair were for his benefit.

'It must be fate,' he said, and she thought for a second of Daphne's fate, and what that had meant for her. Then he came and sat down beside her, so close that their shoulders touched, there was no mistaking it, and said, 'It's great to see you again.'

'It's good to see you too,' she said, and felt almost ashamed at how true that was. She still had Daisy's letter held between her fingers, and only when she looked down did she realise how tightly she was gripping the delicate pages. She folded them carefully and slipped them into her bag together with the envelope. His quick eyes were following her hands, amused, but she offered no explanation.

'So what made you pick this room?' he asked. 'It's not one of their most popular ones.'

'A friend told me about this painting. She likes to tell me about unusual pictures, and then I like to come and visit them.' It didn't seem strange at all to be calling Daisy a friend. It didn't seem like a lie. It just felt right.

'It's an interesting choice. She must have excellent taste.'

'Perhaps,' she said, and the names of first Charles, and now Richard, flickered across her mind. 'Do you know anything about it?'

He shrugged his shoulders. 'Not much. There were a couple of Pollaiuolos, brothers, both of them artists in Florence. They were very well thought of in their day. They were part of the beginning of the Renaissance scene. You know the kind of thing – they didn't just paint, they could make jewellery and sculpt and all the rest of it. They aren't so famous now as they were then. Do you like it?'

He was looking at the painting appraisingly, and she too looked at it again. 'I'm not sure. It's nice enough, I suppose. How about you?'

'Oh, I think it's a bit of a joke really. Something about the arms just doesn't quite work. The laurel leaves wouldn't have been that odd colour at the time, of course. That's just something that's happened over the years. There must have been something in the paint the artist used that's turned the green to brown that way. Even so, for me there's something odd about the composition. Like I said, the way Daphne's arms are stuck up in the air just looks rather comical.'

'How funny! Daisy said something just like that.'

'Daisy? Is she the friend with the good taste?'

'Yes, in a way. She's more of a pen pal, really,' she said.

'Really? I didn't know people still had pen pals these days,' he replied.

It was to divert his attention from Daisy that her next words came out. 'Do you feel like a cup of coffee?' It was too late to stop them, even though it wasn't meant to be that way, Daphne could have told her that. It was Dominic who should have been asking her, and she who should have been saying, 'Not today. Maybe another time. I'll let you know.'

'It's almost lunchtime,' he said. 'Why don't we make it a sandwich instead?'

'Oh, I suppose that would be OK.' She could hear a nervousness in her voice that would not have been there if she were meeting up with one of her existing friends, a real friend who had been around for years.

'A coffee's fine,' he said. 'I don't want to cause any problems.'

'No, really, it's no problem. I'll have to phone my husband first, though, so he knows I'll be home later than I planned.'

'Of course. Go ahead,' he said, but there was something in the way he said it that made her feel foolish, that here she was a grown woman yet her husband kept tabs on her.

She called him on her mobile, with Dominic standing next to her, and there was no answer. Rob must have gone out. It was easier just leaving a message, but Dominic's presence made her self-conscious about calling him 'darling' and about what she said, which was simply that she wouldn't be home for lunch. Not that she was having lunch with someone else. Certainly not that she was having lunch with someone he'd never heard of who, by the way, was a man. She saw a trace of a smile curling round Dominic's lips as she spoke, and knew that he was laughing at her. When she hung up, she found herself laughing too, freely and easily with this still almost-stranger. It was an odd feeling, but an exhilarating one. A feeling she had long forgotten, which might just be happiness.

'How was the painting?' Rob asked, as soon as she got home. It was the same question that he had asked every time, after each painting, because he knew he should.

'I liked it,' she said. Dominic had kissed her on the cheek when they parted. His lips had fallen lightly against her fair, downy skin like a brushstroke on a painting, just too close to her mouth. Then she remembered Rob and added quickly, 'It was the story of a myth. Apollo and Daphne.'

'Really? The one about the laurel tree?'

'How on earth do you know that?' she said.

'I just do. Didn't you?'

'No,' she replied, knowing that she had let herself forget that there was more to him than his job and what he had done to her – and hardly caring, because she had just spent an hour, closer to two, with a man who she knew was attracted to her and didn't think to hide it. She closed her eyes and the image she called up was of Dominic. He had made her feel confident and beautiful, and it showed, in the lift of her shoulders and the colour of her cheeks, as if some of Dominic's sheen had transferred itself to her.

'Do you know how the story goes?' he said, his eyes searching. 'Apollo didn't just desire Daphne. He was tormented by her. He had been shot with an arrow that made him go mad over her. Then Daphne was shot with another arrow that made her just as desperate to get away. They say that when Daphne's father first turned her into a tree, she was still so determined to keep out of Apollo's reach that even her branches pulled away from him.'

But it was the image of Dominic, not the truth beneath Rob's words, that made her take a deep breath. 'It's been too long,' she said. 'Let's try again. Now, before I change my mind.'

He did not even understand at first, but, once he did, he didn't ask her if she was sure. He didn't ask her if she was ready. He just said, 'If you want to stop, tell me and we will.'

She nodded, took him by the hand and led him into the bedroom. Then she pulled the curtains, shutting out the sharp afternoon sunlight. It was cold in the room, but that was not what made her hands shake as she turned to him. She fumbled with his shirt buttons, then the belt of his jeans, then the jeans themselves, wanting to be quick, but realising too late that her hands weren't moving the way they should be. It didn't matter, because he was pulling at his clothes as well, and grappling with hers, and she didn't need to do a thing. Then she felt his desperate fingers, freezing against the warmth of her body, and she was naked, and so was he, the two of them lying on top of the duvet, not moving, as though neither could remember what happened next. Already she had goosebumps running up and down her arms and had utterly forgotten why she had wanted to do this. She began to say that it was enough, they should stop now. But the words did not come out, and Rob had started down the familiar road of their lovemaking. She could feel the eager-ness in his deep kisses, full on her mouth, in his laboured breathing and in his erection, which was pushing insistently against her legs. A feeling of panic came upon her, and her own breathing became shallow.

'It's OK, Claire,' he said, stroking her hair and looking straight into her eyes.

'It's not,' she said, but again the words stuck in her throat, and already he was inside her and thrusting her hard against the bed. She shut her eyes, just as she often used to, but now, for the first time, thought of Dominic.

Afterwards she lay there, cradling Rob's head in her arms, and hoping he would go to sleep, which he didn't. He was over-solicitous through gratitude, thanking her over and over, as if she had made him beg for sex, which perhaps she had, more or less.

She wanted to tell him to be quiet, it didn't mean a thing. She had not done it out of love, but out of guilt, and because of the feelings that another man had roused in her. It had happened with hardly a thought for her husband. She had managed it because she had other things to think about now, to distract her from thinking about how Rob felt and how she felt, and how they no longer understood each other. First there was Daisy, and now there was Dominic, and they had her caught up between them in a careful embrace. Rob should be grateful, she told herself. He had got what he wanted at last. She turned away from him, pulled his arm around her and pictured another man there instead.

'How was your lunch?'

His voice broke the silence and the warmth of the daydream. She eased herself away from him before she replied. 'Fine. I went to an Italian place. I felt like a change.'

'Sounds nice.'

'Yes,' she said. 'It was.'

'What kept you so long coming home?'

'Nothing much. Just the shops.' The deceit came more easily than she could have imagined possible. She eased herself away from his hold and left him in bed, just as she had that morning, which seemed a long time ago now. She stood once more in the doorway, feeling sorry for him. 'Would you like a cup of tea?' she said at last.

Her wallet was on the kitchen counter by the kettle, just where she had left it, tossing it down when she came in. The card that she had picked up as she left the restaurant with Dominic was sticking out of the top. She considered only briefly throwing it away.

'I didn't expect to see you again, you know,' she had said. They were sitting opposite each other in a little Italian restaurant, just round the back of Leicester Square yet still somehow out of reach of the tourists. Somewhere along the way, the sandwich had become a plate of pasta followed by a tiramisu, served with two spoons so they could share it. As they had eaten she had been aware that they were subconsciously falling into each other's gestures – a hand swept through hair, reaching out at the same time to the bread basket, spoons laid down together – and even when she tried to break away, soon after they went back into the same pattern. Psychologists, she knew, would call this mirroring. An article on how to find a man in a magazine would simply call it flirtation.

'I wasn't sure I'd see you either,' he replied.

As she licked the last of the tiramisu off her spoon, she wondered if they were both lying, or if it was just her. 'Well, it's a small world, I suppose,' she said. 'My sister always used to say to me, never have an affair in London. You're bound to run into someone you know at an incriminating moment.' Too late, she realised what she'd said and felt herself blushing, then trying to recover. 'She was joking, of course. I wasn't even married then, far from it. She doesn't say it now.'

'She sounds like a very sensible woman.' Dominic smiled, unconcerned. Smiling made him look older, she thought, but also more dignified. It showed up the lines around his mouth, which made his clothes look as though they didn't quite match the person inside them. She had thought, last time, that he was her age. Now, even though he was still in jeans and a T-shirt, she wasn't so sure.

'So, tell me about yourself, Claire,' he said.

Until then they had only chatted neutrally about things that were interesting but did not actually matter. She felt the change in atmosphere in an instant and knew that this was the point where she should say, 'I'm sorry, I've got to get home. My husband wouldn't like this.' Instead she told him, about her job at the charity, about where she lived, where she had grown up. Nothing too important, nothing that really meant anything, but still she was conscious that she was giving away the fact that she could no longer bear the job but couldn't find another one, and that the flat was smaller than she would like. Oliver she kept a secret. Daisy, she did not. She was afraid that she must sound dull, like people sometimes were when they had been with the same person a long time and life itself was no more than a routine. She knew that Daisy's story made her more interesting, and with Dominic there seemed to be nothing that she wanted so much as to be interesting. He sat through it all, opposite her, nodding in the right places and asking the right questions. He listened intently. He sounded intrigued. Above all, he made her feel like she mattered. He called it the Daisy Project, somehow managing to encapsulate everything she was trying to do in just two words.

She told herself that the uncomfortable feeling she had inside was simply because she wasn't used to being shown this kind of attention, not now her friends had mostly given up on her, as had her husband. It was not because she was doing anything wrong, at least not very wrong. Then she was blushing again, a guilty flush, and realising too late that he was telling her something significant, about his friend who worked at a film archive and was always longing for someone, anyone, to care about his old newsreels.

'Why don't you call by this afternoon?' he was saying. 'He's always there on a Saturday. Have you got anything else on?'

'No, but . . .'

'So let's call him. He's a great guy.'

The arrangements were made before she even had the chance to be sure that it was something she wanted to do. All she could do was leave another message, still to Rob's voicemail, saying that she would be home later than she thought. No more than that.

'So, now that's sorted we can have a coffee.'

She felt almost breathless with the energy of it all, and sat back in her seat and just listened while he told her more about the auction house, which was whole worlds more exciting than Rob's mergers and acquisitions, and that he rented a pied-à-terre down by the Thames, which was also several steps up from Kentish Town. 'And I have a daughter. Her name's Ruby and she's five years old.' That was how he ended, and Claire never saw it coming.

'Oh,' she said. 'I didn't realise. You didn't say, before.' It meant he was married too, or had been once, or something like it.

'Did I have to?'

'No, of course not.' Claire, uncertain, looked away from him and around the restaurant. It was empty apart from them, although she had hardly noticed till then. She had seen only Dominic, and an image of herself reflected in the window, vivacious and beautiful, almost unrecognisable. Looking like the woman she wanted to be. The waiters had kept their distance, hanging around the bar at the back, polishing cutlery in the hope that someone might come in and use it. It made it feel intimate. Surely Dominic must feel it too.

'Anyway, I didn't want to put you off.'

'What on earth do you mean? Put me off what?' she said, laughing.

'You know what I mean. It's a complication. Like a husband.'

For a moment, Claire couldn't reply. The words ran through her head again, then once more, as she tried to process them into something she was sure she understood. Had he really said something that meant, so definitively, that they were not going to be 'just friends'? And the way he had said it, so straightforwardly, still smiling, as if he were used to getting what he wanted. Rob had not sounded like that for a very long time. Dear God, so this was it, this was what it felt like to be offered the chance to have an affair. The image of Apollo and Daphne was suddenly there before her, and with it the realisation that Dominic believed her to be worth the chase. Six months ago, she would never have allowed herself to think of such a thing. She would never have got as far as the Italian restaurant. She would probably not even have been in the National Gallery on her own. She would have had eyes only for Rob, and daydreams only of her unborn baby. She would have fled headlong from the prospect of anything else. Now, though, she thought of the other thing, of the child called Ruby, and what she herself would give to be strolling through Hyde Park maybe on a weekday afternoon, with the firm, foamy feel of the pushchair's handle between her hands, or sitting on the grass in the dappled sunlight and making her baby gurgle and laugh as strangers walked past and smiled at the two of them together. Far from Daphne as she was, she didn't feel like running at all.

'I don't think a child is a complication,' she said. 'I think it's wonderful.'

'Well, I am pretty crazy about her actually,' he replied, and the truth she heard in his voice brought with it a picture of him swinging a laughing little girl around, her dress spinning up in a summer breeze, somewhere miles away from the clatter and clutter of central London.

'Where does she live?'

'With her mother, in the countryside in Suffolk. I just see her at weekends.' It meant he was divorced, or separated. That was what he was saying, for all that it mattered.

He called for the bill, which they did not split, and as they parted he kissed her on the cheek, more firmly than he had last time, and said, 'Let's do this again soon.'

Still picturing him with Ruby, being the father that Rob was not, she agreed without a second thought.

Claire had seen plenty of photographs of London during the war, but none of them had affected her as much as the newsreels she spent the rest of the afternoon watching. Maybe it was because of the way history was being given life through movement, or maybe it was because of Daisy, the simple fact of knowing someone who had been there, been through it, and carried on with her life.

The films showed a world of sturdy matriarchs flanked by children with scabbed knees and patched clothes. These were de Hooch's women, staunch and square, the weight of responsibility sloping their shoulders, women whose husbands might have found themselves fighting for the second time in a lifetime, and who knew that if it went on much longer like this the sons would be following right after the fathers. There were girls, too, lots of them, in their best dresses, foxtrotting with the soldiers or each other when there weren't enough boys to go around. Any one of the girls could have been a Daisy; any one of the soldiers a Charles, all of them with smiles fixed on their faces – through happiness, through fear, Claire could not tell.

Then there were the bombed out houses, all those stained, scarred buildings, ancient, grand or humble, their innards torn out just the same and scattered across the streets to get in the way of normal people on their way to a normal day's work. Some places she even recognised: St Paul's, lit up by flames like some grotesque son et lumière, but still standing, and John Lewis, its windows shattered but the tills operating and spotters on the roof looking out for planes coming overhead, to ensure that shoppers need not be disturbed by a raid until the last possible moment.

Hardest of all to watch were the newsreels where soldiers sent messages home from far away, messages that were full of longing and love, even when they couldn't find the words; some got no further than 'Cheerio and best of luck' and must have hoped their mother or wife or the girl next door would read the rest in their eyes. One clip finished with them all joining together to sing 'We'll Meet Again', and Claire wasn't the slightest bit ashamed to cry all the way through, because now she was beginning to understand how much the words must once have meant.

This was Daisy's world. She had seen it now, played out in black-and-white images reflected in her tears. It was a world that might have left Daisy bored and frustrated and in search of adventure, but it made Claire afraid.

5

Portrait of a Young Man –
Andrea del Sarto

Dear Miss Milton,
    Portrait of a Young Man – 2nd of March at
1 pm. Would you care to join me?
    Yours,
    Richard Dacre

It was a postcard, smaller than the ones you could buy these days, and tucked inside the envelope holding March's letter, sent on by Daisy to Elizabeth, Claire supposed, in the same way that, had they still been together at Edenside, she would have passed it with casual nonchalance across to her as they sat around the fire at teatime or, had they still at least both been in England, she might have read it out to her, giggling, over the telephone. It was written in fine, tall letters that ran close together and showed more care somehow than Daisy's rapid, clear sentences. There was no picture on the back, only an incomplete address for a Ministry on the Mall, but it must have been enough for it to reach Daisy one way or another, and to lead her across Trafalgar Square and up the gallery steps at the appointed time. It didn't take many words to make a new beginning; that was what Claire thought as she traced them out, because she could tell well enough that was what it must be.

March, 1943
Dear Elizabeth,

I saw Richard again, I should start with that — the artist Richard Dacre, the one from last month. It was at the National Gallery — yet again! To think I'd hardly stepped into the place before last year and now I feel I could walk around it blindfold. He sent me a note, asking me to go with him to the next painting. He addressed it care of the office, so I suppose I must have told him where I worked when we first met. Miss Johnson handed it over rather sniffily, I thought. It seems it's not appropriate to receive personal post at work. So that told me! Still, there wasn't much there to be ashamed of that I could tell. It was all rather formal, in fact, but nice nonetheless.

As soon as I bounced through the main door of the gallery there he was, leaning against one of the pillars waiting for me. Straight off, he asked me to lunch and I said yes. It was warm outside for a wonder so we took our sandwiches and sat in front

of the gallery on the lawns with everyone else. We
ate the same sandwiches as before. Ham and chutney.
We're all such creatures of habit, aren't we? How
quickly we establish our little routines! I would laugh
if it were someone else.

I think now I should tell you what he looks like.
What have you been picturing? Well, his hair is fair
and swept roughly back across his head. It sticks up
in places in the wind and flattens down in the rain.
He wears a battered old jacket all the time, and he's
got earnest-looking spectacles which he takes on and
off so often I suspect him of not really needing them.
His eyes are quick and clever and follow me around
the room. Oh, and I've seen him again between the
National Gallery and finding the time to write this
letter, but you'll have guessed that, I'm sure. He
knows about Charles, and don't think I've exactly
put him out of my mind either. I haven't. But it
raises my spirits to go about with a man, and such a
different sort of man at that. It's pleasant to be taken
out once in a while, even if it is just for a sandwich
or a drink, and I think I've a right to some fun,
haven't I? He took me to a place called the
Mandrake Club. It was crammed full of artistic types.
They all fussed over me and made me laugh. I could
never have gone somewhere like that on my own, or
with Charles come to that. Richard buys me flowers,
too, well, he has once, anyway. Only a couple of
blooms — you can't get much — but enough to fill a

jam jar on my window sill. During the day, they're soft purples and blues, then at night they become black shadows. Charles isn't one for that kind of thing, you know. He says we've known each other too long for him to go to the trouble. Richard doesn't reason about these things – he just does them.

He really does want to paint me, you know. He's gone to the war artists' committee, the one he told me about, and they've agreed to him doing some pictures of women in the workplace. I'm to be one of them. How extraordinary it sounds! It doesn't mean a thing to him, I know. It's just his work. But can there be an easier way to flatter a woman? If so, I can't think of one. 'Why me?' I said. 'You're a working woman, aren't you?' 'Yes, just like everyone else. So why me?' 'Because you're different,' he replied. 'I like the way you look.' Different, for goodness sake. He made it sound so much better than being beautiful that it never occurred to me that it might not be a compliment until he was long gone and who was I going to argue the point with? At the time I just blushed like a debutante. Three years of living in London and I'm not sophisticated yet!

I know what you're thinking, because I'm thinking it too, but you're not to write and tell me that I'm doing something wrong. I'm not, not yet. I swear it.

We did go and see the painting after our sandwiches, of course. I wasn't going to miss it, not

when I have you to tell about it! It was called
Portrait of a Young Man, *and it's by an Italian
artist called Andrea del Sarto. Now when is there
going to be something by a British artist? That's
what I'd like to know. Perhaps I'll write to Kenneth
Clark and ask. No one seems to hold it against the
National Gallery that Italy's the enemy. Richard says
it's because art transcends boundaries and battles and
all the rest of it. I think it's because all of these
artists are long gone. Del Sarto's been dead for four
hundred years, for heaven's sake. Who cares where he
came from?*

*The painting was different to the other ones so far.
It's a portrait for one thing, of a sculptor. It shows
just the head and shoulders of a young man. He is
sitting on a wooden chair working at a block of stone
or something of that sort and he has turned to look
up towards the artist. He's wearing a white
undershirt with enormous, billowing blue sleeves,
underneath a black doublet of some kind. His face
looks almost tired, and his expression is guarded
– what people call hawkish. I think that's the right
word. It's as if he's none too pleased to be put on
display like this. Del Sarto has cast shadows across
him, but not enough to hide the fact that he is rather
attractive. He has full lips and high cheekbones like
all the best aristocrats, with the sort of piercing gaze
that one only ever sees in people with power. I expect
he was the kind of man who in his day could have*

drawn a woman towards him in a second and probably discarded her just as fast. He would have been rich, too. Del Sarto wouldn't have gone to the bother of painting him if he weren't, and let's not pretend there isn't something pretty attractive about wealth. Still, to my mind he looks almost too strong. He makes me feel a little nervous.

That's what I thought, anyway. Richard told me a lot more about it all; for one thing, the reason that there wasn't much in the way of background was to make the man seem dignified. It has clearly worked, because he does have an unmistakably superior air. It's a dark painting, too, and he said that del Sarto was using dark against light to make the portrait feel melancholy. I could see for myself, once he had said it, that it is rather gloomy. The subject doesn't look happy. He doesn't seem to be enjoying the experience of being painted one bit. I read somewhere that there are tribal peoples who will not allow their snapshots to be taken because they believe the very making of an image will destroy their innermost selves. It's as if he feels that way too, that the artist and now we visitors are snatching something away from him and he wants to hang on to it.

We went to another exhibition after that. Richard insisted, and I couldn't say no even though my lunch break was well and truly over by then. He is too charming to refuse, I'm afraid. It was an exhibition of war art, set up in what would otherwise be yet

another empty room. He said he wanted to show me
that war art could be beautiful, even if the subject
matter wasn't. Well, when I walked into that room, I
couldn't believe how many paintings there were, for
one thing – and how many war artists there must be,
working away. There isn't anything they don't seem
to have painted already, from women rolling bandages
and making camouflage nets, to U-boats surrendering
and Messerschmitts being knocked out of the sky.
Endless pictures of London, of course, because there is
hardly a better subject, not since the Blitz. Lots of
them show the barrage balloons swinging back and
forth, with all that silk flapping and sagging in the
wind and the WAAF girls trying to keep everything
under control. Do you know why artists always
include the barrage balloons? Richard told me. It's
because they love to paint material and it's their way
of keeping doing it even now women don't wear vast
robes like Mary's in Noli me tangere. It takes a lot
of skill, you see, and they want to prove they can do
it. Just showing off, that's what Daddy would say,
but he never was one for artistic stuff, was he? Not
like Mother. I've still got one of her watercolours, the
one with the rowing boat on the lake and Edenside
in the background. It's hanging on a nail up on my
bedroom wall. It's not up to much, I know, but I
don't care one bit. I still remember how pleased she
was when she finished it. That's all that matters.

In truth I found some of these pictures rather too

realistic. They took me back to the sheer awfulness of the nightly raids for one thing. Believe me, it wasn't as much fun as they make it look in the pictures. Remember that when you next see one of those newsreels showing us all having a good old sing-song in the shelters. Most of the time it was bloody awful. Christ, I was frightened at times. People died, a lot of them, simply because they ran the wrong way when the sirens went or were in just the wrong place. Ridiculous, undignified deaths too. Heads cut clean in half by falling glass, or trapped in the lavatory when the house fell down. Why record that sort of thing? It's better just to let it go.

The only ones I liked were some drawings by Henry Moore, of Londoners just like me (yes, I suppose that's what I am these days) sheltering down in the underground at night and lying out along the tracks like corpses lined up for collection. There isn't much detail to the figures, but one can still see that they are people, and some are children, others are couples, others are old. He didn't sketch them as he found them, but ambled around taking notes and worked up the pictures later. He didn't want to disturb their privacy, Richard says. He knows that's the reason because Henry Moore himself told him. They met and talked just the once in a pub somewhere and Richard has never forgotten it. You might think that there is nothing less private than being crammed into a public shelter with hundreds of strangers and having to get yourself to a bed of some sort and then snort and snore in front of them all. But oddly enough there is a strange sort of solitude down there. People build invisible walls around themselves. I know, because I've done it myself. The only things Moore's drawings don't show are the rats and the mosquitoes. There are millions of both in the underground these days. Still, perhaps it's best that way.

Richard is desperate for one of his pictures to be put on display. A light comes into his eyes when he talks about it, and it makes him look not so terribly different to del Sarto's man. I said in that case he'd better make his painting of me a good one!

Miss J gave me a good ticking off when I got back to work. She made it sound as if we were going to lose the whole bloody show on account of me being half an hour late back from lunch. One is made to feel guilty about everything these days, even throwing away a piece of mouldy bread. It does get me down sometimes. Still, I'll be forgiven by tomorrow, that's what Molly said, and she'd know. She's always getting into trouble for one thing or the other. If not, I'll get myself another job. There are masses of them around these days. I wouldn't mind a change. Any kind of change would do.

All love,
Daisy

Del Sarto. Another artist that Claire had never heard of. She looked him up in the book that Rob had given her for Christmas, but there were only a few lines about him, so in the end she decided to go to the local library, which was just around the corner, to see if she could find out anything more. It was a Thursday night and Rob had left straight from work for an expensive stag weekend in Prague that had been arranged by someone he had never met for someone whom Claire had not thought he really liked. What happened to a few rounds of drinks at the local pub, she said to him, or a night out clubbing? But once he had shrugged the questions away she had not pressed the point. He was going because he needed to get away from her, but did not want to have to say it. He had arranged to see his parents the next weekend. Then, the weekend after that, there was the annual department conference in Geneva, other halves not invited.

She hadn't really expected the library to be open in the evening, but it was. It turned out that there was even a separate reference section upstairs, away from the DVDs and the paperbacks. When she was directed there she realised that there was a whole world concealed on the second floor, stuffy and lined with copies of law reports and unopened phone directories. It was a world inhabited by elderly men who shuffled up and down between narrow aisles, greeting each other wordlessly with pats on the back and eyeing anyone who turned on the photocopier or asked to use the computers with suspicion. Claire looked up and down the lines of wooden chairs, with their lonely occupants doing things that only they believed were important, and she thought, *We are all the same in here. None of us wants to go home.*

There was a section, called Art and Design, the shelves stacked tightly with books, none of which looked new. There were several on Italian artists. Del Sarto would surely be in there somewhere, she thought, and lugged the largest volume over to one of the desks, where a laminated note told her that if she left any graffiti behind, her library card might be confiscated. It hadn't been enough to deter previous visitors from digging their cheap biros into the soft wood and leaving misspelt messages of broken hearts and wishful-thinking sex scattered at random in thick blue ink. All those idle, wonderful hours of daydreaming that had gone on here, all those hidden hopes keeping readers from their revision. She had been that way once about Rob, years ago.

Del Sarto had his own section in the book, although it was not a long one, which was a relief because it was the type of book that Claire's university tutor would have described on a reading list as turgid. She discovered little more than what she already knew from her art book at home: he had been an important painter in Florence in the Renaissance and had lived from 1486 to 1530, so far as anyone could be absolutely sure. He had been popular in his day and was known for his careful, particular use of colours. *Portrait of a Young Man* was not singled out for particular attention, and there was no plate of it in the book. Perhaps it was not one of his best regarded works, for all that it mattered. It wasn't the point of the project, after all, to see the best paintings. The point was to follow Daisy. But how far? She thought again of Richard Dacre. He seemed an intense, impetuous sort of person from Daisy's latest letter, but she imagined that all artists were intense; it would be a disappointment if he were not. There was a serious quality to him as well, a foil for Daisy's light heart. Then she thought of Dominic.

She put the book firmly back on the shelf and, because there was no rush to get home, because there was no one there, she made her way to the History section, and pulled out a book about the Blitz. Daisy's description of the shelters had got her thinking, because whenever she had imagined them before, she had played out in her mind exactly the sort of images Daisy had talked about, of a group of chipper Cockneys having a knees-up while bombs whistled overhead and a commentator spoke of London's courage in adversity. It didn't take much reading to understand that it hadn't been like that at all, that most shelters, from the Underground to the concrete street shelters, the church crypts and the basements of the London department stores, had all, to varying degrees, been unpleasant places to be.

She thought of poor Daisy, on her own, lying somewhere night after night in the heart of the bombing, wrapped in a blanket, lined up with all the rest, someone's feet kicking her face, someone else's back to her own. With every hour that went by, the air would have grown thicker and thicker with the stench of overflowing toilet buckets and sweat. No, she realised now, there was no glamour or romance in any of it. The faces captured in the photographs in the book she had picked up, whether their expressions were happy, sad or showed no emotion at all, had one thing in common. They were shot through with exhaustion and strain. It was not an easy thing to be amongst strangers, to be getting through a war with family far away and so much tedium amidst the dangers. How much better it must have seemed to turn one of those strangers, this Richard Dacre, into a friend.

She had told Rob about Dominic, that was why he had suddenly been so keen to get away. She had used what she thought were the most neutral of tones, but he had seen the truth of it straightaway, a truth that she had denied unconvincingly, all the time unable to keep a sense of triumph out of her voice. Why had she mentioned it at all if not to bait him? Any fool could see that it would have been much better to keep quiet. But there was a canker inside her, corroding her inside, ulcer-like and spreading, always spreading. It made her want to wipe his smile away when it dared appear and remind him that she had not forgiven him. It made her want to see him angry. She wanted him to prove to her that he understood how she felt about Oliver, her baby, her son. How was he ever going to understand, unless he knew what it was to hurt like she had hurt?

'I'm sorry I wasn't home for lunch yesterday,' was how she had started, the day after they had slept together again, at last, and with Rob still looking happier than he had in months. A non sequitur, designed to throw him off-balance.

'It doesn't matter,' he replied, pulling her towards him and wrapping his arms around her. 'Where did you go?' She could feel his breath by her ear, and the tension in her shoulders.

'I told you already. An Italian place, just near the National Gallery.' A pause. A long pause. 'I went with someone I met at the gallery, last time, in the café. We got talking.'

He hesitated before replying, already warned by her voice that something was wrong, already moving away from her. 'Good. It's great to meet someone new, someone you can talk to if you feel you need to. You don't seem to see many of your friends these days, not like you used to.'

'I know,' she said, not really listening, only thinking ahead to what she was going to say next. 'Well, this time we met again and decided to go for lunch. He knows all about art, you see.'

'He?' Rob was jealous in a split second. It made his voice sound dangerous.

'He wanted to be an art historian once.'

'Who are you talking about, Claire? What's his name?' Now he was concentrating fully, his brow creased as if he had been looking at a legal document for too long, trying to work it out, and now had suddenly unravelled its meaning.

'Dominic.' She looked away, out of the window at the tiny pre-blossom buds on the trees, knowing that Rob's gaze was fixed firmly on her. 'You don't need to worry, Rob. He's got a daughter.'

'But has he got a wife or a girlfriend?'

Now she was the one who hesitated, uncertain, aware that she did not know the answer, because it was a question she had not asked. 'He's divorced, I think, or separated. One of the two. Does it matter?'

'Of course it matters, Claire. There's no way I want you having lunch with some man I don't know, however much he knows about art. Not without me.'

'Why not, Rob? You meet up with women sometimes. What about Julia? You're always meeting up with Julia. You went out with her, for God's sake.'

'Yes, but that was over ten years ago, and we're both married. This is completely different. You know it is.'

'And what about all those women you're friends with at work? There seem to be plenty of them.'

He waved her comment aside. 'They're colleagues, they're not friends. You know that.'

She was determined not to let him be right, even though she knew that he was. 'I thought you wanted me to get to know some new people. To try to put things behind me.'

Things indeed. God, that it had come to this, that she was using Oliver as a way of getting the better of her husband. She had not been like this before, she knew. She had been kind and loving. What was happening to her? Where had the sweetness which used to be there whenever Rob called her sweetheart gone?

'This isn't what I meant. I was thinking of a support group, some counselling maybe. Something to help you get things back in perspective. People who've gone through the same thing. People who have lost a child. I didn't mean picking up a stranger in a café who's ordering spaghetti carbonara for you before I know a thing about it.'

She clenched her fists, feeling her stomach turn, and spat out her response. 'Well, I'm very sorry but I didn't realise I was meant to give up all my social life on our wedding day.'

He groaned. 'You don't have to, you know that. But there was a reason we got married, wasn't there? To show that we were committed to each other. To be there for each other when we had problems, without needing to turn to someone else.'

She sighed impatiently. 'It's nothing, Rob. I can make a new friend, can't I? You can't talk about art with me, after all.'

'How do you know? You haven't even tried. And you were never interested before.'

She tried another swipe, one she was more confident with. 'Anyway, you're not even here half the time.'

'You know I can't help that. Don't blame me for it.'

Then the phone rang and Rob went into the bedroom to answer it, shutting the door behind him after the first greeting, so Claire knew that it was his mother who had called. She counted out the minutes that he was away until she ran out of patience and retreated to the living room. When he re-emerged, it was clear from the way his shoulders sagged, and his carefully averted eyes, that his appetite for the fight had disappeared. She was pretending to be engrossed in a black-and-white film, but inside her heart was still pounding.

'Claire,' he said, even as she willed him to say nothing. 'Claire, do you ever try to remember how things used to be? I do, all the time. I haven't forgotten any of it. Have you? Remember how we walked all the way round the outside of London Zoo, just so we could see the giraffes sticking their necks out over the fence. Remember the time we got lost in the maze at Hampton Court and we thought we'd get locked in at closing time.'

'Yes,' she said, although in truth she had forgotten those times until now. The memories had slipped away fast when she had no longer seen any reason to keep them. They came back now, though, together with all the fun and laughter and feeling young that had gone with them.

'We had some good times,' he said and then, with more difficulty, with the awful sound of tears in his voice, 'You were so easy to love then. I knew I would never love anyone else like I loved you. I still want to love you, more than anything. Why must you make things so difficult?'

'Because things are different now,' she said.

'I know. I just wish to God that they weren't. I wish to God it was all just the same.'

'It can't be, Rob. It's too late,' she said, knowing that she was also coming close to tears.

'It doesn't have to be too late, Claire. You don't have to let it be that way.'

Claire told herself that, if Rob had not been away, she would have delayed her next trip to the National Gallery and stayed in with him instead, the two of them carefully holding in their cupped hands the frail memories he had offered up to her; blowing life back into them, trying to make them feel real.

Yet she knew she was kidding herself. She would have gone all the same. Rob had not bargained on Dominic, neither of them had.

On the Friday evening she found herself in the flat on her own, bored beyond belief and lonely too, unable to bear watching any of the trash on television, yet knowing it was far too early to go to bed. She imagined Rob as part of a group of men drinking Budvar, laughing too loudly in some bar in Prague's old town. On the coffee table, her mobile phone seemed to gleam brighter and brighter, its metallic casing reflecting the light from the lamp in the corner like a beacon. All of a sudden she knew that she was going to pick it up and send a text to Dominic saying, *I'll be at the gallery tomorrow. Meet you by del Sarto at noon.*

There couldn't be many pictures by del Sarto, which meant that it wouldn't be difficult for him to find her — and even if it was, so much the better. It showed that she was worth the effort, worth seeking out. She felt a thrill of excitement run through her as her finger tapped away. Then, because she didn't want to answer if he called her back and so reveal herself to be sitting at home on her own, she called her sister Laura, who lived in Spain these days, running some sort of website for tourists and ex-pats just like every other English person in Andalucia seemed to do. She answered straightaway, and Claire fell back on the sofa and let her sister's chatter wash over her: about how hot it was (London was dark and rainy), how the garden was so big it was impossible to look after (Claire and Rob could not afford even a roof terrace) and how difficult the neighbours were (well, at least they were an acre away, not upstairs, downstairs and on both sides). There was a comfort to it, the familiar rhythms and topics, even if she was waiting for something better.

'So how are things with you?' her sister finally asked, not that the question itself registered. It was only the silence that came afterwards that told Claire she had missed something. She had been listening out too intently for something else, for the beep of another call, or a message at least, coming through from Dominic.

'How are you?' Laura was impatient, offering little comfort now.

'Fine,' she said. 'You know. The usual.'

'How's Rob?'

'Away.' Only now, when she had to say it out loud, did she feel ashamed that her husband had so easily left her behind.

'Why aren't you with him?'

She could picture Laura now sitting up on the wicker chair on the verandah, putting her plastic glass firmly down on the edge of the plunge-pool, swatting away a mosquito and actually concentrating.

'It's a stag weekend. Wives and girlfriends not invited.' She wished there was a way of keeping the defensiveness out of her voice.

'That's OK then. There's nothing wrong, is there?'

'No, of course not,' she said, then gave up trying. 'Not really. It's just . . .'

'It's just what, Claire?'

Just that there was this person, this man called Dominic who was interested in her, who made her feel special, whose lips she could still feel against her cheek – and who had a child, a real, warm child; who had so much that she did not. Which added up to, *There's someone else.* That was what people were meant to say, wasn't it? Those were the right words. But she knew she could not tell even her sister. Perhaps once, when they had been closer, but not now that Laura was so far away. All that growing up together, the whispered secrets, the anguished longings, didn't seem to count for much now. Was it because Laura already had a seven-year-old daughter and a five-year-old son, whose voices Claire could hear in the back ground, arguing shrilly against the last rays of the day's sun? Now Laura was telling them to keep it down, couldn't they see she was on the phone?

'Nothing,' she replied, instead of all she might have said. 'I'm just tired. I'll ring off now, see if there's anything on the TV. I can tell you're busy.'

'Are you sure you're OK? Really? I'm worried about you, these days. Why don't you call me more often? If I can help, you know that I will, don't you? You can always come and visit, if you want to get away from things.'

No doubt she'd be calling their mother next, telling her she needed to do something. The last thing Claire needed was for her mother to get involved, calling more often, offering advice that turned only into stories of how her own husband had let her down too, seemingly forgetting that this same husband was Claire's father. She mustered up enough energy to put Laura off, forcing a smile into her voice. 'I know. If I need you, I'll tell you. Now go on, get back to being a wife and mother.'

'OK, little sister, as long as you're sure. Do you want to say hello to your niece and nephew before you go?'

She knew she should say yes, but couldn't bear to. 'Not this time.'

'No other news then?' said Laura, and they both knew it was more of a statement than a question.

'No,' said Claire, and finished the call. No news. Nothing to gulf that immense distance that had grown up between her and her sister, her and everyone else.

By the time she heard her phone give its sharp, distinctive beep, it was after midnight and she had given up waiting for Dominic to respond. She dragged herself from something that was not quite sleep to read the message: *I love you. I miss you.* It came from Rob. Of course it came from Rob, drunk no doubt, reeling back to a three-star hotel. There they both were, lying in half-empty beds far apart, wishing that there was someone else beside them, but still she did not send a message back. Then another beep. Not Rob, Dominic.

I'll be there. Xx.

This time, she replied. Heart racing now, sleep pushed away.

Great. Xx.

When Claire saw the painting, it took her by surprise. Daisy had said it was melancholy, but Claire saw something different in it. She found it sinister. The subject of the portrait, the unknown man, looked out with something close to menace, a sexual menace almost, underlain with violence. There was something chilling about the way he was gazing out at her, back over his shoulder, keeping his body angled away and showing only his face straight on, as if to shield whatever he was doing. She wondered what it was that he did not want the casual onlooker to see. It was nothing he was ashamed of, that was clear. He did not look the type to feel shame. There was too much arrogance in those dark, unwelcoming eyes, in the tilt of his face, half-shadowed beneath a black tricorn hat. He looked like a man who liked to scheme, who was used to holding intrigues in his delicate hands. Daisy was right, he did not want to be there, exposed to an endless stream of passers-by trying to read the secrets in his eyes. The anonymity of the title of this painting suited its subject well.

At first Claire didn't understand what the art book had meant about del Sarto's use of colours. He had not used many of them here, though there was a boldness about the blue of the man's robe – just as there was a boldness in his face, and lingering even in his seated stance. He looked as if he were ready to pull out a dagger and flash its blade at anyone who came too close, and Claire wondered whether, hidden beneath the folds of his shirt, his arms were strong. She realised that restricting his palette had been deliberate on del Sarto's part. Blue, grey and black. They were the colours of evening and nightfall and things hidden in darkness. This was a man who avoided coming too openly into the light. His thoughts were deliberately veiled.

The caption said that he was now thought to be reading a book, although previous commentators had said he was sculpting; the paint was so faded it was difficult to tell one way or the other. It did not make much difference, or so it seemed to Claire. The message was the same. Danger. Watch your back. She gave a shudder and turned away, and there was Dominic, his arms open wide and his blue eyes alight, ready with a kiss direct on her lips that said, *You're mine now.*

'What do you think you're doing?' she said, feigning outrage.

'Just saying hello. Nothing special. It's no big deal, is it?' There was no pause for her to respond before he continued and she knew her moment to object and be credible was gone. 'Listen, I'm sorry I didn't get back to you till so late. I turn my mobile off most evenings. I don't like the distraction.'

'It doesn't matter.' A small untruth, fooling neither of them, and revealing more affront at the slowness of his response than at the assumption underlying his kiss.

'Now if you're finished, let's get out of here.'

'Hang on, I thought you were interested in art.'

'I am, but that doesn't mean I want to spend all my weekends in the National Gallery. I thought we could walk down to the Thames. The sun's shining. It's not too cold. It'll be beautiful down there on a day like this.'

'Fine,' she said, and side by side they joined the steady shuffle of shoes across the gallery's floors, formed largely from constantly swelling and contracting tour groups that made the pace just too slow for comfort. It was a relief when they finally reached the entrance and strode down the steps into Trafalgar Square. Claire inhaled the crisp air deeply, not tasting the pollution that she knew must be there. A swift breeze had sprung up, and the spray from the fountains swept in front of her and decorated the place with rainbows.

'Let's keep moving,' said Dominic. 'I don't want you getting soaked.' Before she knew it, his arm was around her shoulders and he was propelling her forward. She did not move away from him – and he kept his arm firmly where it was.

They walked together across the square, just like any other couple, then navigated their way awkwardly over the endless pedestrian crossings at the other side, their rhythm interrupted by buses, taxis and tourists. Claire rarely took this route, and although she knew the river was close, it was still a shock to find it suddenly there at the end of the street, swollen and muddy and busy with boats. They weaved through the traffic gridlocked along Victoria Embankment and then Dominic led her to the stone balustrade. They stood there together, leaning out over the water. Over to the right, she could see the white wheel of the London Eye, its shadows caught by the buildings behind, and then on towards the impossibly elaborate Houses of Parliament.

'Don't you find this place romantic? I always have,' said Dominic.

'Me too,' she replied, remembering that she had kissed Rob here once, years ago, soon after they had first moved to London. He had brought her this way after they had eaten a cheap meal in a Thai restaurant. He told her that he thought it was the most beautiful sight in the city, the Thames by night. She had thought so too, seeing it with him back then. The water had been lit up by the street lamps and the lights in the office buildings, like silver beaten bright. The rubbish that must have been floating scum-like at its edges had been hidden by darkness. The darkness had not hidden the flash of Rob's teeth as he smiled at it all in wonder, and it was his boundless enthusiasm that made her lean towards him and press her lips to his. Then he had lifted her up and swung her around, even though there had been other people nearby who had turned to look and she had protested that she was too heavy. She could remember even now the coldness of the air against her legs as her skirt, bought new for the occasion, flew up around her, and the mad dizziness when he put her down.

'When do you need to get home?' Dominic asked, cutting into the memories and laying the present bare, where those early kisses with another man had somehow led.

'Not yet. Rob's away this weekend.' That was a mistake. She had not wanted Dominic to know his name.

'That's where I live. Just over there, in that building,' he said, pointing to a tall, almost Gothic-looking apartment block behind them.

'Really?' she said. 'You really do live right here on the river?'

'That's right. It's not very big, just a one-bedroom place. It's enough for me. It's got a beautiful view.'

She didn't respond. They walked on together and she understood too late that he had been making her an invitation. She looked back at the entrance to the block and he followed her gaze and laughed. 'Don't worry,' he said. 'No pressure.'

Then he put his arm closer around her, and they carried on. She felt herself leaning into him, smelling a deodorant, or was it an aftershave, that was not Rob's. It was not difficult, walking this way. It made her wonder whether any man would have done, Rob or some other, if all she wanted was to be kept safe and warm and free from loneliness. It did not seem like much to ask.

The traffic from the road lining the river-bank eased once they got as far as Westminster, or else was diverted away, and then there were gardens between them and the remaining cars and vans, scattered with solitary people eating sandwiches and feeling cold. There was a café, and Dominic went to buy them hot chocolate while Claire sat on a bench and waited, watching the river and seeing her life slipping away from her out to sea. On either side of the bench were trees, laden down with pink blossom. Opposite, across the span of water, was the jumbled mess of old and new buildings that made up St Thomas' Hospital. She and Rob had talked about her going there to have the baby. It was not really close enough to their flat, but it was what an old school friend had done, sending round photographs afterwards showing the view of Big Ben from the window of the labour ward. It seemed a good start for a baby to have.

Maybe the next one.

She sat up straighter.

It was the first time she had allowed herself to have such a thought. Not a replacement for Oliver, but someone to come after him. It was a good sign, surely: one day things might get back to normal. But how? Because right then Dominic sat himself down beside her, very close, and handed her a cardboard cup that was almost too hot to touch, and she realised that none of this was normal.

'What is it?' he asked.

She blew carefully across the surface of her drink. The chocolate was so thick that it had a skin on it. It reminded her of the cooling custard that had been served endlessly at her primary school lunch-times. 'Just a friend of mine. She had her first child in the hospital over there. It happens so quickly, doesn't it? One minute you're all still going out for drinks after work on a Friday night. The next minute half your friends have to stay in to look after the baby.'

Dominic leant back against the bench. 'Ruby's mother and I were well ahead of the game. We were the first of our lot by a long way. I still remember all the presents we got when she was born – a ridiculous number, and most of them were utterly useless. None of our friends had any idea what a pair of clueless new parents might need and nor did we. It was like we were the only ones in this new world, and we didn't have a thing to talk about except sleepless nights and changing nappies.'

'Still, you had Ruby at least. You had your little girl.'

'Of course. It was all that mattered.' His face had lit up at the thought of his child.

'How is she?'

'She's great, just great. Right now she wants to be a princess living in a castle with a pony to ride. She wants me to buy her one. Can you believe that? Just the pony, she says, she knows she can't have the castle.'

'Well, some things never change,' Claire said, laughing. 'I was just like her at that age. My mother even signed me up for riding lessons. It took years to pluck up the courage to tell her how much I hated them as soon as I began.'

There was a pause. They both sipped from the cardboard cups, looking straight ahead at the river.

'You don't have a child yet, do you? You and Rob?'

She didn't like hearing Rob's name come from Dominic's lips, and the laughter left her, for that and all the other reasons.

'No. Did you think I might?' She could hear the pleading in every short word, wanting him to say yes.

'Yes,' he said. 'But only that first time. I thought you might be coming to look at the paintings to give yourself a bit of a break, while your husband stayed at home with the baby. People do, you know. They sometimes need to get away. Of course I knew before I even bought you that slice of cake that you didn't. A woman will always tell you straightaway about her family if she's got one, or a husband come to that. Usually then she'll start showing you photos from her wallet or on her mobile phone, always of the baby, never of the father. That's what happens when you have children, you see. It's all about them from then on.'

Claire had never heard resentment or bitterness in his voice before. She did now, but only as a background to all those feelings and thoughts of Oliver that came flooding in. She wanted to make a non-committal sort of sound and leave it at that, but she could feel her face falling and knew she was giving herself away. Dominic was still talking, and she tried hard to concentrate on what he was saying, but it was too late, and now he had noticed.

'What is it, Claire? Did I say something wrong?'

'No, nothing like that. It's just that I should have a child. But I don't.' She had to fight to get the words out.

'I'm sorry,' he said. 'Tell me about it.'

So she did, not about what had happened, but about what it felt like, to see everything she had dreamt of collapse into a nightmare, to have to tell everyone that her baby had gone, to find herself crying into the arms of colleagues that she did not even like.

'I called him Oliver,' she said at the end of it all. 'We knew we were going to have a boy. We'd had the second scan. I thought he deserved a name.'

Rob hadn't understood about the name. He thought it would make it harder for her to let go. He told her so, as soon as she first allowed herself to say the word, Oliver. 'Why did you have to give him a name?' he had said, way back at the start of the autumn, when the burnished finger leaves of the horse chestnuts were still dipping in the wind, and grief had made both of them cry, not just her. 'Because he was our baby!' she had screamed back. 'Because I don't *want* to forget him. I don't *want* to let him go.' She had decided then that Oliver had hardly even been a baby to Rob. *She* might have been dreaming already of the christening and the first birthday party, imagining the photo in the album of the cake with its one bold candle burning bright, and a shining faced, red-cheeked baby in a high chair behind, picturing a boy in shorts and a blazer running through the school gates. But for Rob, perhaps all Oliver had ever been was a shifting black-and-white ghost on a screen, a racing heartbeat, a complicated collection of cells that happened to have arms and legs and tiny toes and intricate ears.

'Of course he needs a name,' Dominic said, taking her cold hand firmly in his. 'Every child should have a name.'

She knew that, right then in that moment, she

was the only person in the world to him, and that this was the only conversation worth having. She could read it in his eyes. 'Thank you,' she replied. It was all she was able to say, before she found herself kissing him, as she had known she would as soon as she woke up that morning, in fact since she had said goodbye to him outside the Italian restaurant after they had seen *Apollo and Daphne* together. Dominic's smell, the shape of his mouth, his taste, his tongue, the roughness of his stubble against her cheek, the feel of his hair in her hands. The way he had understood so easily what she had tried to say. Everything about it felt different to kissing Rob. A scarcely remembered warmth grew inside her. For a long time, she could not bring herself to break away.

6

Madonna of the Basket – Correggio

As soon as she got home, a wave of exhaustion poured over her as if she were somehow sick rather than teetering on the edge of infidelity. It made her desperate to lie down and feel the cool of the pillows against her cheek. She had made an excuse to leave in the end, a poor one which Dominic had seen through.

'Don't worry, Claire,' he had said. 'It doesn't matter. No one needs to know. These things happen, believe me, especially to women as beautiful as you. I can't be the only man you know who wants you in this way.' *No*, she thought. *There's my husband too.*

He had seemed so calm, as he reached up and stroked a loose tendril of hair back behind her ear, his fingers too cold against her skin.

'Why don't you ask yourself if you're really happy with Rob?' he had said. 'You deserve to be happy.'

She had not replied, but her silence would have been enough for him to know it all, that she wasn't happy, that she hardly knew how to be, that if she had felt happy in recent times it was because of him, not Rob. Now that it was too late, she could hardly believe that she had allowed any of this, that she had not said that it was none of his business and that it had been a mistake, it would not happen again. Still, there was no point saying these things, not when she knew well enough that it was going to happen again because she was going to let it, because it was what she wanted. Even that feeling of wanting something was one that she had not felt for a long time. It made her desperate to grasp it.

He had leant in to kiss her once more, and it was then that she made herself stand up and say, 'I'm sorry, Dominic. I really do have to go. Now.'

'That's fine. I understand. But I don't want this to be the end of it. Do you?'

'No,' she said, meaning it. She touched him lightly on the cheek with her hand, and walked swiftly away. A chill breeze had sprung up, and when she looked back, she saw that blossom from the trees was blowing around him, like yesterday's confetti caught up in the wind.

'Till the next time,' he called out to her. She carried on walking.

Now, back in the flat, she retreated immediately to bed, drawing the duvet around her, struggling to keep out the cold draught that came in around the bedroom window frame. Her head was bursting with it all, shame battling with joy. She despised herself for responding to his touch, in a way she had not with Rob for a long time. Yet at least she *could* still respond, she had not shut down that side of herself completely.

Rob and I have grown apart. We just share a living space. We're not even friends now. He doesn't understand me any more.

The justifications came easily. She had been reading statements like these in magazines since she was a teenager, and thought only how pathetic they sounded. Now here she was calling them up, and almost convincing herself that she had done nothing very wrong after all. It was just a kiss. The truth was that she knew that she didn't feel guilty enough.

Then her mobile phone began to ring, shrill and insistent. Her heart pounded. She was certain it would be Rob or Dominic. Dominic or Rob. She did not answer, waiting instead for a message to be left that she would simply have to listen to. In fact, it turned out to have been her mother. *I'm no better than her. I'm turning into her, aren't I?*, ran a voice in her head. The needy mother, unable to be alone, the absent father. Now the difficult daughter and the absent husband, just a repeat of the same old pattern, the men unable to feel other than pushed away. The answer in her mother's tones, *Well, that's what happens to daughters, Claire, they all end like their mothers in the end. It's just a matter of time.*

She shuddered and rolled over to open the drawer

in her bedside table and bring out the neat pile of Daisy's letters. Starting from the beginning, she read them all through, up to March. Then she read them again, turning the pages carefully, one by one. By the second time round, finally, she was absolutely calm. The feeling she used to get as a little girl, when, as she sucked her thumb, the noise of the world slowly seemed to disappear, had crept over her. She made a cup of tea, got herself three chocolate digestives out of the biscuit tin, and took up the envelope that contained Daisy's next letter. *Dear Elizabeth*, it began, but in her head she read it as *Dear Claire*.

April, 1943
Dear Elizabeth,

Richard has started the painting of me. I feel important now when I go into work. I sit up straighter in my chair even when he isn't there and I'm forever checking that every hair is in place. All the others are wild with jealousy, of course, and keep asking if they can be in his next picture. They have no idea why he's chosen me instead of one of them – especially the ones who know how pretty they are. I daresay they've been talking about the whole thing behind my back. Sometimes when I go into the cloakroom they all go quiet – and normally they're like a crowd of twittering sparrows, gossip gossip gossip non-stop. But it's nice to be talked about for once. I've never given them any reason to before.

Richard leads them all on dreadfully, and they'll do anything for him just to get noticed. They know he's been commissioned to do a whole series, you see. It won't just be me, there'll be other women too. Well, since he told them that, you can imagine he never wants for a cup of tea even if it means everyone else going short at the morning break. Poor Miss Johnson is utterly bemused by the whole thing and flutters between annoyance at the disruption (loss of productivity is what she calls it, by which she means that we are spending too much time on chatter and blushing), and pride that someone thinks that the work her girls are doing is worthwhile. 'I told you, girls', she says, 'I told you this was important. We're winning the war right here in this room.' Whenever anyone from the Ministry drops by, she won't let them leave until she's introduced them to Richard. He's even told her that he might put her in the picture, somewhere in the background. When he said that she went as red as a tulip and started blustering dreadfully. She didn't say no, of course. No one would.

He came for the first time on a Wednesday, completely out of the blue, waving around all sorts of letters giving him permission to be there. Miss J spent a lot of time reading through them, and looking him up and down over the top of her glasses. I was on the edge of my seat as you can imagine. Then finally she said she supposed it looked alright and showed him around, giving everyone's names and explaining what we did. He did try to show interest, I'll give him that. Poor Richard! At the end of it all, he looked around the room in an appraising sort of way, and said, 'I'll start with that one over there,' and it was me of course! I haven't told a soul that Richard and I met months ago (already months ago! The time has flown) because they'd all start muttering about it not being fair. Anyway, it's a lot more fun pretending we don't know each other. I don't want anyone to find out that it was me that Richard chose, not this office. I'm soft at heart, that's what it is. I don't want to see Miss J disappointed.

At first I kept asking him what he wanted me to do and where he wanted me to look, but he said he just wanted to see me doing what I normally do. So I got down to work, and then he said 'Hold it there,' and I had to sit stock-still until he told me I could move again. It's harder work than typing, believe it or not, not moving a muscle.

He isn't coming every day, because apparently it's important to get the light right. Sometimes it's no good because it's cloudy or it's raining, or it's too early or too late. Still, when he is there I can't help enjoying having a man look at me the way he does. He is very intense, one can see it in his eyes, especially when he has a pencil in his hand. Sometimes I think I might as well be naked, the way he stares! He's used to painting nudes, he told

*me. Men or women. He's not bothered. He says they
don't need to be perfect. It's more interesting if they
aren't. I wonder what he thinks of my body. He
hasn't said and I'm certainly not going to ask. I
spend my time just looking right back at him, bold
as brass or so I think, watching him toss his hair in
the sunlight, or run his hands through it. Sometimes
he gets a wild look about him and presses so hard
on the pencil that the lead snaps. Then there are
other times when he steps back and smiles at me. I
always smile back. I can't help it. That makes him
frown. Like I said, I'm not meant to let my
expression change. He even left me a note on my
desk, putting me right on the point! He started by
telling me all about Correggio's* Madonna of the
Basket, *which is coming up at the National Gallery,
and then he told me straight that when he takes me
to see it I must note in particular how serene the
Madonna is and ask myself whether Correggio's
model can have been fidgeting around as if she'd
been bitten by a flea. He told me to make sure I
take it more seriously or I'd drive him quite mad.*

*Still, that wasn't all he said. The rest of the letter
made up for the dressing down. He also said he was
enjoying watching me all day, just as I'd been
hoping, and asked me if I was enjoying sitting for
him. Then he said that he knew I was! He says I
show it in a certain light in my eyes. I don't know
what he means! It seems you can't hide a thing*

from an artist. Richard says they learn how to read
faces early on.

At the moment he's working on what he calls his
preliminary sketches. He won't let me look at them,
and you can imagine how irate that makes me, but
he told me no, very firmly. He said it would ruin the
surprise. Some of the girls have had more luck,
because they are able to walk about behind him
while he's working whereas I have to stay put. They
say there isn't much there for all the time he's spent
over it, but I expect that's just the jealousy again.
Still, I'd like to see some of his other paintings, just
so I know whether he's any good. I don't want him
to make a mess of my picture. I want it to be so
good that it goes on display at the National Gallery
and people walk past it and say 'I can see why he
wanted to paint that woman. I wonder who she is?'
and then read my name on the label. If there's only
ever going to be one painting of me, and I can't
think that there would be more, I had better look
absolutely magnificent in it, don't you agree? I said
that to him. He told me not to interfere, he was
trying to concentrate.

I heard from Charles at last. Goodness, how long
has it been? Months and months, I should think. He
sounded well, better than I would have expected,
although it's always hard to be sure from a letter
– especially when a man's doing the writing. He has
received my letters, at least, some of them (no plums,

193

though!), but it takes an awfully long time for anything to get through. He says he can't wait to have a crack at the Jerries, but at the moment it's still just waiting. He also says he thinks about me all the time, and is looking forward to when it's all over and he can sweep me into church, then take me off to live in a little cottage in the countryside with honeysuckle climbing around the door and the nursery already set up and painted blue. There was a lot more of that sort of thing in his letter, pages of it – sentimental stuff, not like Charles at all. I expect that's what happens to all of them out in the desert, waiting around for the next orders to come in – daydreams start floating around like mirages. Still, if being out there is making a romantic of him, all I can say is it's about time! It doesn't sound so dreadful. He says that in the big towns the shops actually still have things displayed in the windows, and he's going to send me some stockings to show that he's thinking of me. And I'm thinking of him, too. Sometimes. Oh, God.

Now, I am not neglecting the National Gallery, I don't want you to think that. I like it more than ever, particularly now there's going to be a painting of me in there one day. As I said, this month's picture is Correggio's Madonna of the Basket *– yet another Italian, and I must admit I've never heard of him. The gallery seems to have an endless supply of paintings by Italian artists. Perhaps that's why they don't mind risking some of them in a raid. It's*

*a lovely piece, small, though. The name alone made
me smile. It's like me being called Daisy of the
Typewriter, that's what I told Richard. He says he
won't call me that. He says he'd rather picture me
miles and miles away from the clatter of keys and
jammed ribbons and carriage returns. He thinks I
deserve better, even if that is how he's painting me.*

*I met him in the gallery. I made my own way
there. I don't want to start tongues wagging; there's
no call for it. He arrived first as it turned out and
this time I was the one tapping him on the shoulder.
He turned around slowly, and for an odd moment
the look I saw in his face − complicated − made me
think of del Sarto's man. I'm learning to see these
things for the first time, I think. In the past I didn't
bother to look properly − not just at paintings, but at
people too. Now I do. With some people, there's
nothing to guess. Take Charles, for example. It's all
there, right on the surface. One knows exactly what
is going on inside. There's nothing wrong with that,
for goodness' sake. At least it makes things easy.
With Richard, what's on the surface is only the start
of it. I find it exciting. I can't help it. You know
where this is leading, don't you, Elizabeth? I expect
you worked it out before me. I feel as if I'm
stumbling, and Richard is the one who is going to be
there to catch me, and it's all because Charles is
stuck in a desert trying to keep the sandflies out of
his eyes and I started learning about art. It turns out*

Charles was right all along. He should have got me down the aisle months ago, and then none of this would be happening. Still, I'm not married yet, just you remember that.

This picture is set in Egypt, which of course made me think of Charles all the more, and feel even worse about being so bloody to him. It's of Jesus, Mary and Joseph (yes, another religious one; there do seem to be an awful lot of them about), but it might as well be of Charles, me and the baby that he wants and I don't. The baby's even blond and curly-haired, just like Charles was when he was tiny. He didn't tell me that. His mother did, when I met her for tea at Claridge's the last time she was up in town. She still carries around a snap of him at that age in her bag.

Mary and Jesus are sitting out in the open, with Joseph off to the side, working with a lathe. Mary is wearing a dusky pink robe, with a diaphanous drape around her shoulders. Diaphanous drapes are all the rage with artists, I've learnt over the months. They're always cropping up. It is pure showing off, because the effect is tricky to achieve, or so Richard tells me, and I can believe it. Mary is trying to put a blue jacket on to this wriggling baby and although her hair is mostly swept back, just a curl or two has come loose with all the effort. Oh, Elizabeth. She looks so tender about it. You'll know exactly how she feels, I expect, even if I don't. The painting is clearly meant to be all about Mary and her little boy – the

*background doesn't seem particularly important.
Wouldn't Charles just love our lives to be like that?
Me doing all the motherly things while he does
something manly like chop wood. To my mind, the
basket of the title says everything there is to say
about being a wife and mother. It contains wool and
a pair of shears of some kind, which Mary has been
using to make the jacket she is putting on Jesus. Put
it this way, it's clear enough that the work never
ends! I'm sure I don't need to remind you of that.
Still, despite all that it is really a lovely painting. It's
not too flashy or grand. If I say that I would be
perfectly happy to hang it on my wall if the
National Gallery ever wants to loan it out I think
you'll understand what I mean.*

*I must end this letter now. My hand's tired out
from writing and I'm going out to dinner with
Richard, to some canteen that calls itself a restaurant.
Richard is exactly what you would expect from an
artist – flat broke. I don't mind giving up the Ritz,
though. It's the company that counts. Nothing's
happened between us, just the painting – but it will,
I'm sure of it. I've always told you everything
important so I want you to know. Now do try not
to disapprove. After all, we're all grown up and
there's a war on. Things are different now.*

All my love,
Daisy

Claire went to see the Correggio painting on a beautiful weekend, when the sun was shining like white gold in perfect, clear blue skies, and London looked at its best. Rob, yet again, had gone home to see his parents. A picture of him came into her head, sitting at the long, wooden kitchen table with Priscilla fussing over him, being treated like he was still fourteen and not minding a bit, because she, his wife, the one who had stolen him away from that life, wasn't there to disapprove.

'But you've only just seen them,' she said when he told her.

'It doesn't mean that I don't want to go down there again. There's a fundraiser for the church steeple repairs and my mother's running the cake stall. I said I'd help. It's important to her.'

'What's everyone going to say when they see I'm not there?'

'Why shouldn't you be there? You can come. You should be with me. But it's up to you. I know I can't make you.'

She hesitated, remembering Christmas so clearly she could hardly believe it was already four months ago, and imagining a day spent behind a trestle table selling fairy cakes at three for a pound alongside Priscilla. Then she thought of Dominic and was filled with a frantic, awful need for him, for someone who would hold her tight and say nothing that she did not want to hear. 'No,' she said. 'I'm sorry. I'd rather stay here. You can make up an excuse for me.'

'I could just tell them that you couldn't be bothered to come. At least that'd be true.'

'Don't, Rob. Really. Don't embarrass me that way.'

'Why the hell not? It's more embarrassing for me than you, isn't it, if you aren't with me? Anyway, you've got better things to do, I can see that. You must be due to see Dominic about now, mustn't you?'

Not due to see Daisy's next painting, or due to visit the National Gallery. No, he mentioned neither of those. He was disappointed, angry. She could see it in his eyes. She would have to make it up to him later. She could cook for him. She could let him make love to her, if that was what he wanted, which probably it was not. It was not so difficult now. He knew that she and Dominic had visited the del Sarto painting together because she had told him, but only as much as that. He had not asked much about it, just retreated back into silence. But he started whenever her mobile phone beeped, almost as much as she did herself, and looked away or left the room whenever she sent a message herself.

It had changed things between them, of course it had, that kiss with a stranger. It didn't matter that Rob knew nothing about it. He was perfectly capable of imagining it, or assuming something far beyond, well into territory where Claire still did not dare go.

For all those months, Claire had been the one ignoring Rob, hating Rob, wanting to drive Rob away with all his too-obvious efforts to be good to her. Now at last she had given him his reason to hate her. Now he no longer reached out for her in bed, any more than she reached out for him. Now they both had something to weigh in the scales of guilt. But it had not restored the balance. It had just made everything worse, driving them further apart and making the prospect of Dominic more appealing than ever. She had not realised how it would be until it was too late and now, if there was a way back to where they had been once, she could not see it.

'You're right,' she said at last. 'Maybe it is about time. It's been three weeks since I saw the last painting.'

'So, are you going to ask Dominic to come with you?' The tone of Rob's voice made the name sound pathetic – but made Rob sound pathetic too, as if they were all back in the school playground, squabbling over best friends.

'I don't know. I could go on my own, I suppose, or with one of my other friends.'

Now Rob put anger aside and said, more calmly, 'You know I'd prefer that.'

'I'll see if anyone's around.'

Claire did try to contact one or two of her friends just like Rob wanted. Yes, perhaps the effort was half-hearted, but the fault did not lie wholly on her side. People planned too far ahead these days, that was what it was. People without children took mini-breaks, or booked tickets to plays and exhibitions. People with children wanted to spend the weekends with them, going swimming and having lunch at some place with a kids' menu. Still, too, there was that awkwardness that made Claire baulk at seeing many of them, even those who had tried their best to understand and say the right thing, when there was absolutely no right thing that could be said about Oliver. In the rawness of first grief, she had revealed herself to them in a way that neither she nor they would easily forget, and she had given up something of herself in the process that she regretted now, although she could not have held back at the time.

She phoned Dominic from the landline in the flat, just as though he was a friend, but, because he was not, only once Rob was not there and she didn't have to worry about being overheard.

'Hi, beautiful.' That was what he said when he picked up, sounding surprised, yet pleased. God, how good it was to have someone call her that. Rob called her darling, he always had, but nowadays when he used the word it came out so often laced with frustration that it had ceased to be an endearment.

'Hello. How have you been?' A good way to start. Not too personal, not clinging.

'Fine. I wasn't sure whether you'd be in touch. I've been thinking about the last time I saw you.'

There was a pause. The coldness of their held hands. The river's crawl. The press of his lips. The smell of his hair. Still there in her head, just not quite solid enough to grab at.

'So have I,' she said at last. 'I'm planning my next gallery trip. I wanted to know if you could come.'

'Next stop on the Daisy Project, am I right? I'd love to.'

'When?' she asked, too quickly.

'Let's make it Sunday, late afternoon. Then I can take you for a proper drink afterwards.'

'Not before?' She knew that she had given away too easily the knowledge that she had to see him.

'I'm sorry. I can't.' He gave no further explanation.

'OK then. I'll see you there. By the Correggio. *Madonna of the Basket.*'

'No problem. And what are you going to let me do to you afterwards?'

She didn't reply, other than to laugh, a coarse, excited laugh that didn't sound like her own. Maybe it was the laugh of someone having an affair, someone who could be brazen and needn't worry about being loving and marriageable. The boldness of it lingered afterwards, long enough for her to tell herself that these things happened, they had always happened. Look at Daisy. She might not be married but she was certainly engaged and it was clear enough that her letters were soon no longer going to mention

Charles' name or the cottage in the country at all. *Yes*, she thought, as she put the phone down, *just look at Daisy. Not at yourself.*

She hardly noticed the painting at first. It was tiny, just like Daisy had said. It seemed insignificant alongside the larger, more imposing paintings that surrounded it. Initially, she saw only the bold frame, which was made of wood painted gold and carved with flowers that might have been primroses. Only when she got very close did she begin to like the intimacy of this portrayal of a mother and her child. It was not meant to be a grand scene, she could see that. It was meant to be natural and private. To Claire, it felt almost like a snapshot, the kind where the subject never even guessed the photographer was there, because her focus, Mary's focus, was entirely on her blond, curly-haired baby, naked but for the blue jacket that she was trying to pull on to her baby's arms and a white shirt rucked up around his waist. Jesus was not meant to be newly born. He must have been around nine months old, able to sit up but not yet walking. Mary herself looked young, pretty and everyday, nothing like the traditional image of the mother of Christ. She was in rose pink, just as Daisy had said, and there was a shawl drawn up around her shoulders and over her head which rested on carefully braided hair. One hand was laid gently on her son's arm, while with the other hand she held his, three of her fingers lightly touching the baby's palm. Joseph's attitude was one of utter lack of interest in a scene that he must have seen many times before, yet Mary was absorbed. Nothing else was important except this shared moment between the two of them, except perhaps the next shared moment and the one after that and the one after that. There was no backward glance towards Joseph, no attempt to include him.

It seemed to Claire that this was the prophesy of Botticelli's *Nativity* fulfilled. Joseph was firmly side-lined, as Claire had known he would be, to take his place in the ranks of all those other men relegated to no more than background detail. For Mary, the task of dressing Jesus held its charm because this was her child, hers alone, and this was how mothers were with their children. Here they were. This was their life. The hard-working husband, the tender mother and the wriggling child, a child that seemed almost normal – almost, because one of his hands was, Claire now saw, held out in blessing. It was a picture of a distant, imagined past, but it showed what should have been Claire's future.

Daisy had liked this painting. That surprised Claire. She wondered whether she might have liked it less if she had come to see it alone, because it seemed in every way so far from the life Daisy seemed to want. But she hadn't come alone. She had been waiting for Richard to arrive. It meant that the painting would have mattered less. She would have been standing there nervously, only pretending to concentrate, because she did not want to be caught turning around and looking for him. She would have wanted to feel his hand on her shoulder and act as if she had been caught unaware of his approach. Claire could picture it because that was exactly what she was doing herself, or trying to, because suddenly, looking at that painting, the blond curls of Mary's child were all she could see and there was a smell in her nostrils that was not the wood and polish smell of the gallery, but the smell of disinfectant and disposable gloves and blood that would not stop.

Yet she was not alone in such despair, she thought now, in front of the painting. All those families ripped apart by war, all those mothers and children torn asunder — and none of it even occurred to Daisy. Claire had seen an interview once, which had stayed with her ever after. It featured a woman whose child had been evacuated and ended up being happier during the years spent with the new family than she ever would be again with her own parents. 'I still wonder,' this mother had said to the camera, decades later, 'I still wonder whether I should have left her where she was, whether I should never have gone to collect her at all.' The horror of it weighed upon her, but Claire did not let herself cry and then she did not need to, because just at the moment she might have had to begin, that hand was on her shoulder, not Richard's of course, but Dominic's, and she was burying her face in the crisply laundered folds of his shirt.

He did not seem to notice the painting at all, perhaps allowed his glance to flicker over it for a second. But it did not matter, because the reason was that he had eyes only for her.

'Come on, beautiful,' he said. 'Haven't you had enough of art?' He led her out of the National Gallery and on to the street.

'Someone might see' was what she should have said, pulling her hand away – but she didn't. She let it happen. She didn't even ask where he was taking her, which turned out not to be one of the endless bars in the streets nearby, but the restaurant in the crypt beneath the church of St Martin-in-the-Fields, which was right on Trafalgar Square. Claire had been there on several awkward occasions with her father and the new, seven-days-a-week family that had replaced his old one, then, in more recent times, with her sister Laura and her children. She associated the place with jacket potatoes and soup of the day. It was odd, verging on ridiculous, to be in such a place with Dominic, the kind of man who she would have thought would always order champagne given half the chance and would prefer to linger in the American Bar of the Savoy than here. They sat close to each other, squashed into a small, damp alcove, with two half-bottles of white wine and a ham and mustard sandwich on the small table in front of them. Light came from a feeble candle stuck in the bottom of a cheap glass.

'Why aren't we in a smart wine bar paying twelve pounds for a cocktail?' she asked. Yet as she said the words she saw suddenly through new eyes that the whole place was full of gloom and dark corners where people who wanted to be discreet could draw together into the shadows.

'Because then I wouldn't be able to do this.' With an electrifying shock, she felt his hand running up and down her bare thigh, just once, beneath the short patterned skirt that she had put on before leaving the house because Rob had told her once that it made her look sexy. She pulled away, but only for a second, and then his hand was there again, more confident now, stroking her legs slowly, starting all the way down at her calves and moving slowly further up towards her knickers. She could feel that they were already damp.

'Someone might see,' she said, even though the place was mostly deserted, still waiting for the evening rush to begin.

'Who cares?' he said. He flicked the tip of his finger under the elastic trim of the knickers and she felt him caressing her gently, in round, even movements. She leant towards him, across the table, and kissed him long and deep, her tongue immediately flickering against his and tasting the sourness of the wine. He moved his hand to her breasts now, slipping it neatly beneath her shirt. His fingers were feeling their way around her nipples, first one, then the other, pushing at the tightness of her bra. She could hear that his breathing was becoming as ragged as hers. He had one hand still on the stem of his wine glass, gripping it tightly. She moved her own hand now towards the zip of his jeans and touched the denim lightly, enough to feel that he was hard underneath. How long had it been since she had done anything remotely like this? Not since she got married, that was for sure.

And then – 'Christ,' he said, looking suddenly at his watch and pulling away. 'How did it get so late? I've got to run.' He was on his feet immediately, Claire's hand falling away from where it had been. 'I'm really sorry, Claire. It's Ruby. I've got to pick her up. She's been at a matinee just round the corner. It slipped my mind. That's your fault, I'm afraid, all that distraction.' Already she could see that his attention was utterly gone from her, focussed now entirely on the next thing.

'It's OK,' she said. 'I understand.'

She was not even sure that he had heard. 'I'll be in touch,' he said and was gone.

She forced herself not to look around in confusion, to pretend this was normal, not that there was anyone around who cared. She was sure that she should be angry. Briefly she thought about marching out with her head high in the air, but could think of nowhere she could go. So instead she adjusted her skirt and stayed where she was, sipping with would-be non-chalance on white wine that was no longer chilled. Above her, nailed to the wall, was a wooden crucifix. On it, the body of Jesus lolled, bloody and torn, demoted to the basement by the church authorities. No doubt this sort of thing was too wretched for what few church-goers there were left, and they thought that down in the café no one would notice it. Claire averted her glance and from then on kept her eyes firmly down on the table, watching the edges of the sandwich dry and begin to curl.

As the minutes ticked by, the image of the cruci-fied Jesus was replaced by another one, of Correggio's mother and child, with Joseph nearby. These were parents who would always be loyal, always constant. They were bringing up their baby just as a baby should be brought up, with the kind of love that she had once never doubted that she and Rob had plenty of, more than enough to share with a child. Mary was the very image of purity and faith, and Joseph hardly a man to stray. A rush of guilt came upon her, guilt that she was certain Dominic would not feel, as attraction and allure blew by and left her behind, alone in its wake. Yet despite the guilt she wanted more. There was some fierce need inside her, driving her on. Resolutely, she gathered up her things and put that place behind her.

★　　★　　★

When Rob came in the front door that evening, she put her arms around him and held him close, standing on tiptoes so she could rest her warm cheek against his cold one. The knowledge of what she was doing imprinted itself in his face and she could hardly bear it, because she knew that he needed protecting and he didn't even realise it. Rob was taken aback. He offered to make dinner, and she told him to go ahead, and tried not to interfere.

'I've been talking to my dad about Grandma's bequest,' he said to her, as he chopped carrots and an onion for spaghetti Bolognese.

Claire was sitting at the kitchen table, a glass of wine in her hand. She looked up straightaway. 'And? Has he found out something about Daisy?'

'No, not yet. He's trying but there's no one of the right generation still alive to ask. He'll be going out to Canada in a few months, though, to sort out the rest of Grandma's things. He's hoping he might find something useful amongst them. It's something else – the photograph. I told him about it.'

The photograph. It was still sitting in its silver frame in the living room. Whenever Claire sat down on the sofa, she could see it out of the corner of her eye.

'What about it?' Eagerness put a snap in her voice.

'Well, we know it's a wartime photo because of all the barbed wire on the beach, right?' She nodded. 'That means it can't be a picture of my grandparents, because they were never here together during the war. That's what Dad told me. Grandpa Bill met my grandmother in 1937 when he was in England. He took her back home with him at the start of 1939, before war was even declared. They were both in Canada by then. My grandfather came back over as a soldier at the start of 1942, but Grandma stayed in Toronto.'

'But the lawyer said in his letter that it was Elizabeth.'

'He must have got it wrong. He assumed it was her and her husband, just like we did.'

'Daisy,' she said. 'It must be Daisy.'

'I suppose it might be.'

'Of course it is.' She could feel the inexplicable rising of a sob in her throat. Why on earth hadn't she realised it before? The laughing girl on the beach-front, that was Daisy. How could it not be? Claire didn't need to try to picture her now, she could see her clear as day. But was the man next to her Richard or Charles? She pushed back her chair and ran into the living room to get the photograph. In her hands, the frame felt almost warm beneath her touch, not metal cold.

Back in the kitchen Rob was tipping chopped tomatoes into a pan, trying to look as though he did not care, but she could see the edges of a smile on his face, the tiny pleasure he still got out of making her happy.

'Why don't you open it up?' he said. 'There might

be something written on the back, or hidden by the frame.'

'I don't see why,' she said dismissively, her mind more than a lifetime away.

'For God's sake, Claire. Stop being so impossible and give it here.'

She handed him the frame and, with the tip of the same knife that he had been using on the carrots, he flicked up the catches that held the back of it in place. He slid out the support, and passed the rest to Claire without looking at it first.

He was right. There was writing on the front, in some sort of thick white ink against the black background. It was writing that Claire now knew as well as her own. It was Daisy's. *Richard and me, July 1943, Weymouth.*

'Richard and me, July 1943, Weymouth.' She spoke slowly, feeling the words roll off her tongue. Richard and Daisy.

'Who's this Richard?' asked Rob, looking straight at her. 'I thought you told me Daisy was engaged to someone called Charles.'

'She was,' replied Claire, quietly. 'Things changed.'

'And what on earth was she doing in Weymouth?'

This time she did not reply, even though she already knew the answer, or something close to it. Now, even without reading the rest of the letters, she was quite sure how it had all turned out.

7

The Hay Wain – Constable

This was it then, to know not just the shape of Daisy's writing and the words she liked to use, but even what she looked like. The imagined idea had been vivid enough, but now it had become as real as the curl of ink upon the page. She knew what it would be like to reach out and touch Daisy's hair, loosened by the sea breeze, and how her full lips would feel against her own cheek as they kissed each other in greeting. She could see how easy it would be to make her laugh. The rough-edged form that Daisy had taken at first had fled away, ghost-like, to be replaced by someone who had once known everything about being in love. Claire shut out the knowledge that, if Daisy were still alive, she would look nothing like she did in the photograph. She would be old and wrinkled and smaller, even if she was, underneath it all, still the same person. She didn't want to think about her that way. She wanted only to see her as the photographer on the seafront had, all that time ago.

She counted the days down until it was May and she could open the next envelope, more eager now than ever. Once she had done that, she told herself, she would see Dominic again, but not before. Until then messages were enough, phone calls maybe, moments made all the more intense because they were snatched, and given meaning far beyond the words that passed between them. It was the rule she had set, to do it this way, as arbitrary as her rules for the letters. But Dominic was a part of that now. He hardly existed in her mind separately from the paintings and Daisy. As for Rob, he was barely even on the edges of it at all. On the day that she was finally able to flip the calendar into the next month, she waited until he had left the house before opening the drawer that contained the lawyer's box, and in it Elizabeth's neat bundle.

The next letter, she said to herself again and again, thank God for the next letter.

June, 1943
Dear Elizabeth,

Thank you more than I can say for your letter – and also for the chocolates! They reached me almost intact. All of it helps, as does having someone to write to. I don't mean to burden you with everything that is going on here, so don't let me.

There was something wrong. But what? Claire tried to work out what it was. She started the letter again.

Dear Elizabeth. Nothing. Then again. *Dear Elizabeth.*

There it was, she had it.

June, 1943.

But it shouldn't be June. It should be May. She checked frantically back to the last letter, the one about *Madonna of the Basket.* The date was at the top, written in Daisy's rounded hand, and it said April. She went through the rest of the envelopes, scanning the postmarks and scattering them on the floor in her hurry. But no, there was definitely nothing for May. Had the lawyers lost it? Had Elizabeth thrown it away by mistake? Even worse, was she herself responsible? Could she have left it somewhere, in a bag, or stuffed inside a book? No, it wasn't possible, of course it wasn't. She had taken far too much care. She felt hot with panic. Then she took several deep breaths and told herself that it didn't matter, that there was nothing to worry about, there was something else she could do instead. She would read the June letter now, and if the May one had been lost somewhere across the years, so be it. It was fine to get out of the pattern a little. It was fine. She tricked herself into the fringes of calm and began to read once again.

June, 1943
Dear Elizabeth,

Thank you more than I can say for your letter – and also for the chocolates! They reached me almost intact. All of it helps, as does having someone to write to. I don't mean to burden you with everything that is going on here, so don't let me. I know what I'm doing, and I know I could stop this whole thing if I wanted. But I don't want to, it's as simple as that. I am safe and well, and that is all that really matters in the middle of this madness.

This month's painting says it all. I laughed out loud when I found out what it was going to be, feeling the way about Richard that I'm beginning to. It's quite famous and I'm rather surprised they dared put it on display at all. I expect you know it already. The National Gallery is calling it The Toilet of Venus, *which makes it sound somewhat unappealing, don't you think? I much prefer its other name, which is* The Rokeby Venus. *They call it that because it used to hang in a place called Rokeby Hall in Yorkshire. I expect the owners had to sell it off to cover the death duties. They are saying in the newspapers that it is bringing in more visitors than any of the other paintings so far. They're quite right. The room was so crowded when I went on my visit that it was verging on unpleasant. There were masses of men there, far more than usual, jaws dropping, because in case you didn't know, the* Rokeby Venus

216

is the most delicious nude — Velasquez' only
surviving nude, so they say. His other paintings were
tamer stuff. That explains its popularity, of course.
Whoever would have thought a man could derive so
much pleasure from a picture that is three hundred
years old? I suppose the paper shortage has hit the
pornography market just as much as everything else.
Am I shocking you? I hope so. It's good fun to
imagine you reading this and blushing! The painting
is not at all obscene, of course, and there's more than
enough to please a woman, because Venus is actually
rather wonderful. She has been painted lying down,
facing away from us voyeurs, propped up on one arm.
The curve of her body, all the way from her head
down over the smooth round of her buttocks and
along her thighs, is absolutely lovely, just crying out
to be stroked.

The clever thing is that you can still see her face,
because Cupid is in the picture too and he is holding
up a mirror for his dear mama to admire herself in.
What a mother! And what a change from all those
Madonnas I've seen. Venus' face is beautiful, and not
at all haughty, which is rather unexpected in a
goddess, I would have thought. It's the kind of face
men fall for because it's close enough to the girl next
door so as not to be threatening, but there's still that
something special about it. She is very natural, aside
from just the slightest touch of rouge reddening her
cheeks (unless that's actually natural too; it could be,

I suppose). So tell me why we waste our time dolling up for the boys when we could just be ourselves? I expect it's because the fashion papers tell us to. They are full of tosh. I honestly do not believe any girl is going to be more attractive to a man simply because she's got a bit of beetroot juice smeared on her lips to give her some colour. That's not to say this Venus isn't vain. She can't take her eyes off the mirror for one thing. She looks like a woman who enjoys being in the centre of things.

I met Richard in front of the painting. Another assignation and no one at work knows a thing about it! He is still working on his endless sketches. Surely they're finished? I think he only keeps showing up at the office for the fun of it, and all the cups of tea. He doesn't get annoyed now when I don't keep still, so I can be pretty sure that he isn't doing anything important – just looking.

'Do you think I would make such a good nude?', I whispered to him in front of that painting. Goodness, I am getting bold, aren't I! 'I don't know', he said. 'You'll have to take your clothes off for me and we'll see.' He was so blunt about it I felt rather idiotic. I pretended I didn't, of course, but I am sure he noticed anyway, because then he said he wasn't sure that the war artists' committee would approve of a nude. Apparently, they prefer their women looking smart, hard-working, and above all fully clothed. I can't think why. Look how much the Rokeby Venus

is cheering everyone up. I am sure that a painting of a WAAF officer lying on her bed, wearing just her cap and the rest of her uniform hung up on a hook behind the door, would be excellent for morale.

Once we were past everyone, he pulled me back, leant close and whispered in my ear. 'When are you going to let me make love to you? I don't want to wait.' That's honestly and truly what he said, word for word, and at first all I could think of to say was 'I don't know.' Pretty feeble, I'm sure you'll agree. Then I asked him if he talked to all his female models like this, which I thought was quite clever, especially as you can imagine that inside I was in a complete spin. He said 'Not all of them', and I said, 'Good'. There was a bit more of that sort of thing and, well, if I'm actually going to send this letter, I think I had better stop right there and let you imagine the rest if you really want to. I'm not having the censors cutting bits out on the grounds of public decency. After he had left, I had to go and sit down at the lunchtime concert just to calm myself.

I hardly know what to do, of course. There's a superstition about life these days, you see, that just wasn't there before. I don't mind so much about Charles finding out, which he'll have to, I know, if anything's going to come of this. Although it's not an appealing prospect, I can put up with it. No, it's more this silly feeling that if anything happens between me and Richard, it will kill Charles. I don't mean that he'll be upset, which he would be, one would hope. I mean that it will really kill him, as if in some extraordinary way we are all connected. To think I promised myself that I wasn't going to be one of those waiting women constantly worrying over fate and the future. Now just look what's happening to me. I think you'll understand. I feel literally tied to Charles in an odd way. I can't just push him out overnight, either, him or his cottage with the honeysuckle round the door and the vegetable patch – and there's a part of me still that wants what I've grown used to anyway, what I've always expected. A man next to me, telling me what we're going to do next, with no complications or emotional ups and downs. A Charles, not a Richard. It's a lot to give up. How I wish there was someone here I could talk to properly – but there isn't. You're too far away, dearest Elizabeth. There's only Richard and I won't get any sympathy there!

I went to his studio yesterday for the first time. He says it won't be the last. I'll need to come often to sit for him now he's at the painting stage at long last. The place is high up and reeks of turpentine, and is cold even now it's June because of all the windows. Richard needs them for the light – but they also let in the draughts, not that it seems to bother him. All his canvases are stacked against the walls. They're good, at least I think so. There is one that shows a little boy drowned in a bomb crater. Richard saw him being pulled out when it was too late to do anything, and went directly back to the studio to start work on the painting. The boy is floating face down in the water, in a patched shirt and bare feet, because he'd taken his shoes off to go in, you see, trying to swim, they think. Richard painted the sky clear blue, as if it were just a normal, good day. The little boy's shoes, there on the edge of the pit, would be warm from the sun. That's the point. He explained it to me. It was just a normal day, and these things happen every day. He showed it to the war artists' committee and he says they nodded in an understanding sort of way, but they wouldn't buy it. They said it was too depressing. It wasn't what people wanted to see. I can understand that. Richard can't.

I was flicking through one of his weighty art books and I found out something about the Rokeby Venus that I think you'll like. Apparently, before the last war, the one we used to call the Great War when we didn't know any better, a suffragette attacked it with a meat cleaver, of all things, and slashed it to pieces. She was locked up for six months on a charge of destruction of artwork. I will say they've mended it very well. One would never know anything like that had happened. There I was admiring poor Venus and it made someone else want to snatch up a knife! How different the same thing can look to two different people!

I told Richard about the suffragette, but he wasn't interested in that bit, just in the painting, and not even that so much, not when he's got his own work on his mind. He said that he pictured me as Venus before we even saw the painting together. He imagined me up in the studio and lying on his bed, turning around as he came into the room. Him coming closer, all the while trying to work out how best to mix his paints to get my skin tone just right. He said it was like a dream, and now it was almost coming true because there I was, just like he'd imagined – except I wasn't naked, of course (guide's honour, Elizabeth!), I was wearing my favourite summer dress with the flowers on it. When I pointed that out to him he said even so, he was wondering how any man could ever be so lucky. You can see now why he is so important, can't you? I hope you can see it. Happiness is fleeting these days. We need to grab it if we possibly can.

There are flowers growing in the bomb craters now. I thought you might like to know that. You always did love being out in the garden. There are all sorts – clover and cow parsley and willow herb and other ones I don't know the names of. They've brought bees and butterflies out with them, and I watch them sometimes, dipping in and out of the rubble. It's almost grotesque that nature has made something beautiful out of all our tragedies, and so quickly too. But, then, the scent is lovely, and so is the sound of

*the bees buzzing around, and it takes me right back
to being at Edenside with you, walking through the
flower meadow and laughing over some boy or other.
They're men now, the boys we used to talk about so
much. We're all of us grown up and getting older,
and sooner or later we'll be dead and gone too, and
there'll be nothing to remember us by except the
flowers feeding off us. It's just a matter of time. Still,
there will always be butterflies and the sound of the
wind in the trees, won't there? Tell me there will be.
At least there will always be that.*

    All love,

    Daisy

*PS I feel dreadful that I didn't write last month. I
hope you will forgive me, but I was simply too busy
with everything. Work. The painting. Richard.
Charles. I was exhausted from all that thinking. I
couldn't even bear to go to the National Gallery. It
was Constable's* Hay Wain *that was on display, in
case you are interested. You'll know it already,
everyone does, so I thought you wouldn't need me to
describe it to you anyway.*

Claire actually threw the flimsy pages on the carpet
once she had read to the end. What must Elizabeth
have thought, waiting every day for a letter to come
and receiving nothing, with no way of finding out
if anything was wrong? Daisy might have been
injured, dead even. There was a war on, after all. She

might have been transferred away from London, to somewhere even more dangerous, North Africa, maybe. They did that sometimes, even to women, and especially the ones with no attachments. Claire knew that. Daisy had said as much in one of her letters. Elizabeth would surely have been worried. Claire had never thought of Daisy as selfish, but she thought it now, as she saw how casually she dismissed her failure to write in a last-minute, scrawled postscript.

Poor Elizabeth, she told herself. Then, no, not poor Elizabeth. Poor Claire. It was she who felt let down, that was what it was. Elizabeth probably never gave a damn, she would have had enough to do looking after Nicky and worrying about Bill to even notice. Then a dizzy anger swept over her. *Haven't you thought for one second about the effort I'm going to with these paintings? Don't you think I might be busy too? Don't you care about me?* She threw the questions out but no answering voice came back. The letters were just paper, and the girl in the photograph continued to laugh. She wondered if this was what it felt like to be losing your mind. Then, still raging, she strode into the kitchen to clear up from breakfast, clattering the plates and glasses into the dishwasher, wanting one of them to smash so she could blame it on Daisy. At the end of it, suddenly tired, she sat down and made a cup of coffee, black and strong, and forced herself to drink.

The anger was abating, but not enough. OK, she thought, if Daisy could break the rules so lightly, so could she. Why should she have to wait another month before reading the next letter? What was the point of waiting, anyway? There was no reason at all why she shouldn't just get on with it. She left the empty mug in the sink and then, tossing an offhand look at the photograph to show how little she cared, she picked up the envelope postmarked July.

July, 1943

Dear Elizabeth,

Forgive the shaky handwriting. I'm writing this on the train. At least I managed to get myself a seat, which makes me one of the lucky ones. You won't know what it's like these days trying to get anywhere. Unpleasant. Crowded. Either too hot or too cold. There are simply too many people on the move, although we're none of us meant to go anywhere at all unless we absolutely cannot help it. Richard is out in the corridor, and I expect that is where he'll have to stay all the way back to London. Still, he has his sketchbook to keep him occupied, and I've got my writing paper.

Are you wondering where I've been, or rather where we've been? I do hope so. I must tell someone and there's no one else. We went to Weymouth for the weekend. Weymouth, of all places! I can safely say I had never even thought about going there before, and I am sure you never did either. There was a jolly good reason for it, of course, and it's not the one you're thinking, let's be clear about that. Or not just that, anyhow. It was because July's painting was another Constable — this time his Weymouth Bay, *which he painted on his honeymoon. I adored it. I think it might be my favourite so far. It's a natural, flowing picture. Richard says it was never finished. One can tell because bits of the canvas are showing through. But I wouldn't have noticed if he hadn't said. It all looked real enough to me.*

It's a landscape, and most of it is taken up with sand, sea and sky. Then, at the far end of the bay, there is green farmland rising up from the cliff edge into a hillside. The only figure in the picture is tiny and doesn't intrude one bit. There is a lovely feeling of space about it, partly I think because the sky is so huge, crowded with gathering clouds, piling up in white and grey, with enough of a hint of rain to make one wish one had one's mackintosh. Seeing it made me long to be out of London and by the water, clambering down across the rocks with my toes wet and the wind ripping through my hair. London is dry and dusty at the moment. There's so much grit. It blows off the bomb sites and gets in my eyes and throat. The bay in the painting looked like everything I couldn't have. I told Richard all this, and he immediately kissed me and said, 'If that's how you feel, we should go. Leave it to me.' He made it sound quite simple, despite the question of permits, trains, Miss Johnson and my important memos — and that's quite apart from the what thens and whys. Well, it made me want to fall into his arms there and then. I'm out of the habit of having someone else do things for me these days, but I think I might like it.

The next thing was that he turned up at the office with some bits of paper that meant Miss J had to give me leave (to sit in his studio, or so he said), and he got hold of the travel permits on the grounds that they were for 'artistic purposes'. He's very clever about these things. He told the authorities that he wanted to have a go at painting the sea defences and all they said was, make bloody sure you don't paint anything top secret, if you do we'll burn the canvas. They take all that kind of thing very seriously, as you can imagine.

So that was that. A day or two later off we went, crammed into a carriage with a whole lot of soldiers and rattling for hours through the countryside and along the coast. A shocking journey, but Richard brought flasks of water with him and strawberries, which was something close to a miracle. Goodness knows what they cost him or even where he found them. He gave me a bunch of flowers, too, that he'd picked himself from some ruin or other. They wilted long before we arrived.

It was splendid to get away from London, even for

a night. Just feeling the train pulling away from the platform made me laugh, and the joy of seeing the city finally fall away behind us was truly indescribable. It has been an eternity since I saw fields, and now I know that they're still out there. There is still a countryside. It's not all been turned into munitions factories and landing strips. London has lost a lot of its green, of course, burnt away or turned into muddy allotments. All those cabbages where there used to be marigolds – even the moat of the Tower of London has been filled with earth and planted thick with sprouts. It makes us look so desperate somehow.

Weymouth was the final stop (the final one of dozens!), and Richard and I piled out with everyone else and followed our noses towards the sea, which was only just around the corner from the railway station. We struggled dreadfully to find somewhere to stay. Every single building that faces the sea (and plenty that don't) is a guest house or a slightly dingy hotel, but the fact is that the ones that aren't closed for the duration are packed full of sailors and Americans. I thought we would have to give it up as a bad job and go back to London, but Richard wouldn't hear of it and kept knocking on door after door – every door looking just the same! – until, in the end, we found a little hotel that was still half open. Either they took pity on us or they badly needed the money.

Richard filled in the guest-book, and he put Mr and Mrs What do you think of that, Elizabeth? Mr and Mrs Richard Dacre. I think it has a good sound to it. The owner never batted an eyelid even though I wasn't wearing a wedding ring, but it happens all the time these days. People don't want to hang around. I felt – I'm not sure. Guilty, a little, because what I was *wearing was the engagement ring Charles gave me. And of course I can't help feeling I have let my father down, or he would think that anyway. He would never understand any of this.*

The room wasn't too bad. It even had a sea view and when we opened the window we could hear the sound of the tide coming in. The room was clean at least, with cream sheets worn thin. One bed, with an iron bedstead. You're married. You don't need me to tell you what happened next. It made it feel like the beginning of something new and important. Richard was good to me, gentle enough. There was something between us before that made us afraid to say what we really felt. Now it's gone and I'm glad. I hope you can see it my way. Even if you don't, there it is. It's my affair. Well, that's one way of putting it.

Afterwards, we ambled arm in arm along the esplanade. The only other people were in uniform, trading cigarettes and trying to keep cheerful, as cheerful as anyone can be knowing that next stop after Weymouth is almost certain to be the front. We couldn't go down to the beach – it's been laid with

229

mines — but it didn't matter. It was better from the esplanade anyway. There was a way of looking out to sea from there that meant one didn't have to see the barbed wire and the concrete blocks. Water is so very powerful, isn't it? Watching it slapping against the beach reminded me that there is a whole world out there, different people in different countries, all connected by the tides and the currents but forever pulling each other apart. I was thinking of you, all those miles away. Maybe you were thinking of me, too.

There was no reason at all to rush. It felt as if there was nothing wrong with just watching and waiting for the sky to change colour and the sea to creep closer. Like all beautiful moments it couldn't last forever, of course — in the end it got too cold to stand around and we turned back. Near the guest house there was an old man in a tiny booth with a camera. He told us he'd been taking photographs of holiday-makers his whole life. We asked him to take one of us together. He was pleased to do it. He says it's mainly photos of soldiers and sailors that he takes these days, for them to send home to their mothers. There were some of them pinned up on the walls of his hut, the ones they didn't have time to pick up before they were moved on. Christ, Elizabeth, it cut me up. All those boys! They looked so serious in their uniforms. The man said he tries hard to make them smile, because one never knows, it might be the

*last picture they ever have taken. He didn't have to
try hard to make us smile. It's a good photo. It looks
just like I feel.*

*Early next day we set out to find the exact view
that Constable painted. That's why we went to
Weymouth in the first place. Richard had brought
along a picture of it, torn out of a book. It was a
little way out of the town. We had to follow the
esplanade until it ran out, and then trudged along a
track up a hill, then along the edge of some quite
low cliffs until we were more or less in the country.
We walked for at least an hour, I should think. I
couldn't hear a thing except birds singing and insects
buzzing about in the clover. It was almost like a
holiday. Richard held my hand all the way. I didn't
want to let him go either. The place we wanted was
called Bowleaze Cove. We couldn't go right down
into the cove because of the usual barbed wire, and
more mines too, I daresay. Instead we skirted around
the edge and then Richard told me to turn back
towards Weymouth — and there it was, Constable's
view. Ruined by all that rubbish on the beach, but
still in other ways the same even after all this time.
The only difference was that there are one or two
more houses dotted around now, so it doesn't feel as
remote as the painting — then again, it never was
that remote, even in Constable's day. Weymouth was
always hidden just behind the hillside in the
painting.*

*Constable liked painting in the open air. Richard
says it was important to him. I can see why. It was
rather fun to think that we might have been standing
exactly where he did with his easel and brushes,
looking out along the beach. Richard did a couple of
sketches too. I just watched. The absolute best thing
about it was the quiet, and knowing we were on our
own. Molly tells me that before the war people used
to camp all along this bit of coast, but there's none of
that now. It's not allowed, for one thing. So it was
just us. The things he said to me, Elizabeth, while
we were sitting there on the edge of the rocks,
listening to the gulls scream and watching the clouds
and not quite daring even to look at each other. I'm
afraid if I write it down, it will ruin it somehow,
seeing it on the page. But if I don't, I might forget
and you might never know how much someone cared
for me.*

*There'll only be you. I'd die without you. I was
meant for you. You need me. I need you.*

*'What about Charles?' I said, and he said,
'You're not married. He'll find someone else.' He's
right, of course. He will. That started me laughing,
but there were tears in my eyes all the same. It was
the wind, it beat them out on to my face. He held
me so close that I could honestly believe that he
would be with me always. There was truly nothing in
the world right then except us, the crashing of the
water and the smell of turpentine in his hair. I think*

I'm in love. But I expect you guessed that already. It sounds simple, doesn't it? But that's Richard. He makes everything seem simple.

Daisy

PS I am enclosing a copy of the snap of us with this letter, so you can see that I am smiling and the world is not always grey.

A photograph that had gone all the way to Canada, and now come almost back to where it had started from. The cheap picture from the seaside booth turned into history and heirloom by its silver frame but meaning just the same as it had in July 1943. *I am in love, we are in love.*

Claire put this letter down more carefully, imagining it so clearly, this trip of Daisy's where she left Charles behind once and for all and let Richard take his place and more. How was she going to break it to him? Was she even going to tell him? She reached out to pick up the next letter, the one for August 1943, hungry to find out what was going to happen next, hopelessly caught up in it all. August – it would have been hot by then, not cold like it was now, where they still had the heating come on in the flat for two hours in the morning. The grass would have been yellowing in August, if there hadn't been much rain. It wouldn't have been bright, fresh green like the grass in the park opposite, which now in early May was still studded with tulips that were slowly dying. Everything would have changed between May and August.

Claire's hand hovered over the pile of letters, not quite touching them, desperately wanting to but knowing that she was getting too far ahead. There were not many left, she could see that. She wanted to make them last. She had to stop. Now. She was the only one who would feel cheated if the journey came to an end like this, dashed off thoughtlessly on a wet Saturday morning with a void stretching out beyond it. Finally, slowly, she pulled her hand back, and leant over to pick up the pages she had scattered on the floor, ashamed now to see the impressions of her own fingers left along the margins where anger and disappointment had made her press too tight. She would pass over this lapse of reading two of the letters straight after each other, save the next one till the right time. She would go and see *The Hay Wain* too, not just because she felt she should, but because she wanted to. So what if Daisy had missed seeing a picture? It didn't mean that she must do the same.

She sent a text to Dominic, asking him to meet her the next day. It was as natural as seeing the paintings now, to expect him to be there, or somewhere near, circling round her, coming closer.

'Hi, gorgeous,' that was what he said when he called her not even a minute after he must have received her message. 'Listen, I can't be there at the

gallery, not this time, but how about I see you afterwards? Where shall we meet?'

Her mind went blank and before she was able to
reply, he spoke again. 'Why don't I come over to
your flat? Or will Rob be around?'

'No,' she replied. 'He's going out, with some
friends. I'll be on my own.'

'Well then, let's make it your place.'

Direct, that was how Claire would describe
Dominic. Would Daisy just have called him confident? He was probably used to sweeping women off
their feet, but Claire couldn't help her feet being
too firmly on the ground. Her head was suddenly
crowded with the implications of him in her flat,
with Rob away. The only thing to come out of the
maelstrom of emotions was one word, hesitant but
still clear enough. 'No.'

'Another time,' he said, and the tone in his voice
made her regret what she had said immediately, and
want to just get on with it, to be opening the front
door to him right now with two glasses of wine
already poured and placed on the kitchen table
behind her. But she had made her decision, just like
Pollaiuolo's wretched Daphne, and Dominic had
already hung up. Now she found that she wanted to
see him all the more. It was to take her mind off it
all that she decided instead to make her next visit
to the National Gallery that same day, and alone.

★　　★　　★

The Hay Wain was in a different part of the National
Gallery to all the other paintings. Claire had grown
used to going up the main stairs and turning left
into the early Italian and Dutch sections. This time,
though, she turned right instead, towards the more
modern, British painters, although only compara-
tively modern, of course, because Claire had looked
up Constable's dates on the internet before she set
out and found out that he had died in 1837. She
had read, too, that his wife Maria had contracted
tuberculosis young and lived only until she was forty.
It meant just twelve years of married life, although
there had been more of being in love. She and the
painter had been childhood friends first, then sweet-
hearts, but the wedding itself had come late for them.
Constable was said never to have recovered from the
grief of Maria's death, in fact had ever after only
worn black. Love again, she thought, and then grief
and despair. Perhaps none of it was so extraordinary
after all. The thought drove Dominic into her mind
and she could not stop herself looking around the
room for him, even though she was flirting with
disappointment. There was no possibility of him
being there; nor was he.

The rooms on this side of the gallery seemed
bigger somehow, and instead of wooden benches
there were button-studded leather seats of the type
you might find in a gentlemen's club, the kind that
a woman could still only go into for lunch if invited

by a member. She spotted *The Hay Wain* immediately, because of the tour group ranged in front of it. It meant she could see only parts of it, around a fret-work of heads and rucksacks, just enough to give her a sense of leaves and sky, and to allow her to overhear the tour group's guide explaining that the pastoral idyll hidden from her was, whilst accurate in location, really no more than a fantasy, because the sort of life it portrayed was long gone by the time Constable painted it. The keener members of the group nodded in understanding, Claire seeing only the backs of their heads and conscious that the next groups were already gathering, vulture-like, outside the door.

She went straight up to the picture as soon as the first group moved on, taking the chance while she had it and standing there, right in front of it, too close really, before anyone else could block her view. Already, she could feel other people coming in from the sides, pressing around her and making disap-proving sounds. It made her uneasy, and perhaps that was what made her dislike the painting at first, which seemed to her to be no more than a picture of a cart being pulled across a river, while a dog barked from the banks. To the side was a little house which had the look of a gingerbread cottage about it, with flowers growing around the windows and a vegetable patch to one side, smoke coming out of the chimney and the leaded windows upstairs kept ajar to let in the fresh air. These days, thought Claire, a wealthy professional couple would pay over the odds to buy a place like this as a weekend retreat, spend even more doing it up exactly in period style if they could get the planning permission, and only then find that they couldn't insure it because of the risk of flooding.

Thinking back to Daisy, she wondered whether this was the setting that Charles would have chosen for his wife, lifted out of the ground-in grime of London's streets, taken away from the papers and newsreels with their endless words of war and waste, and framed within a setting of flickering green leaves and freshly raked hay. It did not seem a bad life to Claire. In fact it looked like the kind of life most people dreamt about and these days seemed to need to move abroad to achieve. Still, millions too many notelets and mouse-pads and mugs showing this very scene had been churned out in factories across the world. She had seen it so many times before that it was as if she couldn't really see it properly now – any more perhaps than Daisy would have been able to, even if she had made her usual visit to the picture of the month. Maybe she was the sensible one for deciding to skip it, and keeping herself in the real world for once instead of allowing herself to retreat into another, imaginary one.

The funny thing was, she had a feeling that Daisy might have rather liked *The Hay Wain*. She talked a lot about the countryside in her letters, fields and meadows and flowers. War would have made people nostalgic for that kind of thing, whether it was real or not, just as in Constable's day, because it was something that would take them away from the place they were in. She could see why, with nothing to look at in London but wrecked houses and empty shop windows. The reality of day-to-day living could be desperately mundane. No wonder so many people wanted to escape it. Maybe too her own difficulty with the painting was not the painting at all but Dominic, whose voice, with its timbre of annoyance and finality combined, still sounded, intrusive, in her head, ruining a pleasure she might otherwise have found.

Claire turned away and then saw, to her surprise, that right next to *The Hay Wain* was the other Constable painting, the one that Daisy *had* seen, her July painting *Weymouth Bay*, with its wide open beach, fringe of galloping sea, its gathering clouds and promise of rain. It made sense to take a proper look at this one too while she was here and save herself another trip, of course it did.

She paused and sat down, feeling the cold air from the air-conditioning gust up around her through elaborately wrought vents in the floor. Now this painting she was sure that she liked, perhaps because it wasn't well known, not like *The Hay Wain*, or not so far as she knew — or perhaps just because Daisy had loved it so much. There was something about the way the sand stretched out as far as one could see, drawing the eye on and on towards the far-off cliffs. It made Claire want to be there, running barefoot, sandals dangling from one hand, feeling the sharpness of every grain beneath her feet. Daisy was right that this part of the painting was unfinished, but it didn't make much difference so far as she could tell. If anything, the roughened clay colour Constable had used for the sand, and the way he had streaked the paint carelessly across the foreground, made it even more real. The thinness of colour over canvas seemed to give the beach a coarse texture that it would not otherwise have had.

There was something about the coast and the sea that had always pulled Claire in, right from when she had first been sent to stay at a great-aunt's house on the South Coast during the too-long summer holidays. The first time she had fallen in love, or so she had thought, it had been to the sound of waves and the crunch of sand. She had been fourteen, and considered herself unattractive beyond belief, even though when she looked back at photos now she realised that she hadn't been; in fact she had been pretty and slimmer than she ever would be again. The boy had been called Andrew and was staying in a nearby cottage with his parents. They had kissed once, more in embarrassment than pleasure, the day before he was due to go home, and then he had turned and run away across the beach towards a crowd of other boys who had heckled and pointed as he came close, then drawn him into their group all the same, hiding him from her sight. The memory of it came to her vividly as she looked at the painting, and made her laugh out loud when what she really wanted to do was cry at the thought of her teenage self, paralysed back then with a pointless, painful fear that had made it difficult even to breathe – yet left with a memory that was still sweet over fifteen years later. Here she was, so much older and wiser, yet her life was more complicated than ever before. There was no stopping at kisses now, she thought, the feel of Dominic's arm around her shoulder and his lips against hers so strong he might have been there beside her after all. It was all still a game of sorts, but the stakes had become much higher.

Looking again at *Weymouth Bay*, she saw the sky now huge and lowering, full of drama, and rolling with clouds that seemed to be clawing their way out of the painting towards her, almost as if they might catch her up in their clammy embrace. This rawness in the painting made Claire feel afraid, the open spaces suddenly closing in on her. She wondered whether, even on his honeymoon, Constable was trying to show that he was not blind to the bitter realities of life, the knowledge that even the most perfect things were not really perfect at all. Perhaps he sensed that his wife was already concealing the beginnings of illness, turning away from him to cough, and responding in clipped tones if he dared ask how she was. He might already have been waiting for the time to come when he would be left behind to paint on in gloom and despair alone. Even if Maria were still quite well, the simple joy of the honeymoon might have been tinged with regret, that they had waited so long before the wedding, feeling heavily upon them the weight of social convention that had said he was too humble to marry her and she was too rich to marry him.

Now when she looked back to *The Hay Wain*, Claire found the crowds had inexplicably cleared, perhaps because it was lunchtime and God knows tour groups needed to eat if only to rally their strength for the next onslaught of information. So she tried again with it, this time making all the effort she could to absorb herself in its unmistakable depiction of the perfect English summer's day, a day in which, even though the sky was not perfectly blue, the clouds were at least small and, whilst not pure white, did not threaten immediate downpour. Below the sky, the equally perfect English countryside was laid out, the flatness of fields edged with hedgerows, the broad span of river that took up the foreground. The hay wain itself was hitched to three black horses with red-trimmed yokes, standing in limpid water that was only fetlock-deep to them. Two men sat astride the cart, one of them flicking out with his whip above the flank of one of the horses. It was a scene she could almost hear, now she was actually looking at it properly. The flow of the river, the creak of wheels and wood, the shouts of the labourers as they urged their horses on, impatient, then resigned, then impatient again, the sharp yapping of the dog.

As for the hay wain, stuck there in the middle, the river running either side, she now saw it for what it was: an allegory for that fork in the road, or the point at which the path of life can wend one way or the other, forward into the unknown, or back to where it came from, with no place for simply standing still, frozen with indecision. It had not taken much for impulsive Daisy to make her choice. Weymouth with Richard, and any lingering sadness about Charles overwhelmed soon enough by the beauty of a summer's sunset shared and the brilliant shine of being in love. Claire's path was more difficult to find. In her heart of hearts she thought she might be happiest staying right there in the middle, and not going anywhere at all. But life wasn't like that, it never had been. From the very beginnings of childhood it was all about moving forward, getting on, making a success of things, never about standing still. The hay wain couldn't stay where it was forever either: it would have to be got out one way or the other; it was only a matter of time. So back to Rob, who had been weakened by her merciless, endless barbs into something different from the man she had wanted, or forward to the unknown and Dominic, arms she was sure would welcome her, arms she would not push away.

It was with these things on her mind that she shook herself into movement and turned to go, not home this time but up from Trafalgar Square to Piccadilly, to Fortnum & Mason, to buy her mother a birthday present of the kind she could not fail to like, of perfumed soaps in a box lined with marbled paper perhaps, or smart tins of tea that would stack neatly on a kitchen shelf, or honey even, made by the bees that were kept on the roof of the department store itself. It was more of a palace than a department store really, Claire had always thought, an elegant, opulent palace of the old style. To step through the glass-panelled wooden doors, which deserved doormen to hold them ajar even though there were in fact none, was to enter a world where every object on display sparkled in the blaze of chandeliers set in a golden sun, and jams were magically turned into jewels, and biscuit tins elevated to treasure chests.

She was slow to make her purchases, reluctant to give up the gold wire shopping basket and exchange the abundance of truffles and Turkish delight, and the thickness of the red carpet beneath her feet, for the discarded cigarette butts and dirt-streaked concrete pavement that awaited her outside. It was into this idle lingering that Dominic stepped, coming out of her thoughts as Daisy sometimes almost did. In that first moment, out of context as it was, she wondered even if it was him, and then, knowing that it was, knew too that the child clinging to his hand, in the scarlet coat with the velvet collar, and silver shoes embroidered with flowers, was his daughter. This was Ruby. She was chattering words that Claire was too far off to hear. He was smiling, the encouraging smile of a parent who is struggling to understand the story that is being told. While she was looking on in confusion and wondering whether she should just turn and walk towards the door, he looked up and, seemingly without any hesitation or surprise at all, just pleasure, called out, 'Claire, over here.'

'Hello, Dominic,' she said. 'What are you doing here?'

'Hi,' he said, and kissed her on both cheeks as friends do, although she read more than that in his eyes, and in the pressure of his hand against her shoulder. She felt instantly forgiven, instantly ridiculous, knowing he wanted her still, just as she wanted him. 'Ruby, this is Claire,' he said. 'Why don't you say hello?'

'Hello, Claire,' she said easily, not at all shy about meeting a stranger, which was as it should be. Claire didn't like those children who were forever hiding behind their parents' legs. She had been like that herself and she had always said no child of hers would

245

do the same. No child of hers. That was what it all came down to, didn't it? No child of her own. She looked away from the girl's eyes, which were exactly the same remarkable, open blue as Dominic's.

'Good girl. We've just been in the café having a slice of cake and breaking all sorts of rules, haven't we, sweetheart? I'm going to get into trouble with her mother.'

Claire raised her eyebrows.

'Mummy said I wasn't to ruin my supper,' Ruby supplied by way of explanation, and Claire noticed some of the smile left Dominic's face and his brow furrowed.

'We've decided not to tell her,' he added, giving her a conspiratorial wink.

'Ah,' Claire said, not understanding what, if anything, she was meant to say. She saw only how Dominic had become transformed utterly, from lover to occasional father, the transition played out before her eyes.

'We're just leaving, I'm afraid. Got to get this one home in time for bed,' he said.

'Me too,' she said.

'Well, in that case, we should go as far as the tube together.'

His suggestion, not hers, and it was what they did, the three of them. Awkwardness and awe, or somewhere in between. Those were Claire's feelings as they walked, slowly because of Ruby, and looking to the world like a normal family unit. Father, mother, child, everything she dreamed about at night. Except of course it was nothing like the dream was meant to be and she was too clearly the odd one out.

'Which way are you headed?' asked Dominic as they entered the underground at Green Park. It was the polite question of an acquaintance encountered by chance, and it reminded her suddenly that that was what they were, even though she could still feel the press of his hand against her shoulder, and his lips against her cheek.

She answered automatically. 'The Victoria line.'

'Us too. Isn't that right, Ruby?'

They trailed along the tiled corridors, swept along with everyone else, not touching because one of Dominic's hands held his daughter's and the other was holding her tiny bag, which was made of pink velvet and decorated with a butterfly made in sequins. She was relieved that, once they reached the platforms, it turned out that she was going north and Dominic and Ruby were going south.

In the distracting fluster of parting, Claire quietly allowed herself to say, 'I'm sorry.'

'I'm sorry too,' he replied, no louder. 'But I'll see you soon, won't I?'

'Come on, Daddy, I can hear the train coming,' said Ruby and was hauling him away before Claire could say what she wanted: 'Of course. Soon.'

There was time only for him to wave before the two of them were jumping on to a train, still hand in hand, and being carried away, leaving her standing there more alone than she had ever been.

When she got back home, she found that Rob had returned early and was cooking supper for them both. She said thank you and smiled, but she wished that she had found the flat empty. Then she would have had the time to scatter the day's confusion of complications, misunderstandings and reconciliation out across the fading light, leaving only the good memories still held in her hand.

8

The Rokeby Venus – Velasquez

Dominic and Daisy. Daisy and Dominic. Richard, too. They now seemed to be with Claire wherever she went, or the idea of them at least. On her way to work, while she was eating her sandwich at lunchtime, when she arrived back home, laden with bags after calling in at the overpriced supermarket next to the underground station. Her mind seemed always to be straying to one or the other. She found herself in conversation with them, sometimes even out loud, laughing coyly in response to an imagined flirtation from Dominic, telling Daisy to describe Richard to her again and again, asking Richard when he meant to finish his painting of Daisy. It was as if they had all become caught up in each other, turning madly in the hemispheres of her brain until there was no escape for any of them.

She was the one who had let it all happen. She had allowed herself to retreat into this different place, where everything felt real, even though nothing actually was, and the problems of her daily life took on a different, less concrete, form. She wanted to explain it to someone, but the only person who needed to know was Rob, and he was also the last one who could be told. Anyway, she couldn't find any words that would come close to being the right ones. They were in her dreams, too, alongside Oliver's sleeping form, and in the mornings she was slow to open her eyes and lose them again. It was a release, and a refuge, and it at least caused her bitterness towards Rob to subside into indifference.

It had gone on long enough with Dominic, this dancing around each other. She knew that, the next time she saw him, it would have to stop, with either a yes or a no, and surely it was going to be a yes. The encounter at Fortnum & Mason had left her with odd, unsettling memories, of Ruby's small hand held firmly by her father, whilst her tiny pink bag swung from his thumb, of that brief moment of non-recognition and unreality. She held back from contacting him until nearly the end of June, when she had decided her next visit to the National Gallery was due. Her loyal side, the side that had promised to love Rob and be faithful to him forever, told her that she did this because she hoped it would make the allure fade and give her one last way out. But the other side of her knew full well that the delay was only making the anticipation of seeing him all the more intense, which was how it was meant to be, because she was having an affair. It was meant to be exciting and a little frightening, wasn't it? That was why the spark between them was magnesium-bright. In the meantime, if she wanted him, her imagination easily brought him forth.

'*The Rokeby Venus?*' he said when she called him. Rob was not even out of the house when she picked up the phone; he was just lying watching television in the living room and she was in the kitchen. That was how little she had come to care. 'That'll give us something to think about.'

'I'll see you in front of it. Sunday?'

'I'll be there.' His voice sounded firm. Good. He had not missed the determination in her own voice, so different to last time.

She told Rob only the next morning that she was going to the National Gallery. They had been sitting up in bed together, eating croissants that he had gone out to buy specially, before she was even properly awake. They were tearing them apart with buttery fingers and trying not to drop strawberry jam on the duvet cover. He had been making her laugh, picking crumbs off the side of her mouth with the tip of his tongue, but the laughter faded when she thought of Dominic.

'Don't be too late back, OK?' he said, when she had said her piece. That was all. He did not ask her if she was going alone. He did not say Dominic's name. Just those words. She promised him that she

would be home by four o'clock, in time to go out
for tea with him at the café down the road. Then
silence fell between them, crushing all the fun that
had been there before. As she threw back the duvet,
she leant over and kissed him lightly on the forehead,
as if he were her little boy. He turned his face away.

She dressed carefully, washing her hair with an
expensive shampoo that the hairdresser had persuaded
her to buy, and spraying perfume that Rob had
bought for her on to her neck and wrists. She put
on a new dress, with buttons up the front and which
she told herself she had bought because she liked it,
when really she was hoping it would impress
Dominic. Underneath she wore matching underwear,
not white but red. Rob had given her that as well.
Was it too much, too obvious? Yes, of course it was.
She knew that in the background her husband must
be listening to the clatter of her preparations and
the sound of her humming and feeling sickness rise
inside him. Still she could not stop herself.

She already knew where *The Rokeby Venus* was,
because she had seen it before, a year or so back
when she had come to the gallery with a friend
from work who was studying for a Masters in Art
History in the evenings and writing a dissertation
on Velasquez. It meant that she didn't have to ask at
the information desk for directions or even pause to
collect a map. Instead, she headed straight for the

room containing pictures from Spain 1600 to 1700, nerves making her steps fall quicker than normal. Her breathing was coming rapidly too, but she couldn't slow it down. This had been an important picture for Daisy. It had meant that there was no going back. So it would be for her. She found herself pushing her hair back, trying to look relaxed even as she felt the strands of it catch against the setting of her engagement ring.

The Rokeby Venus. The painting that said, lie me naked on your bed. The one that had told Daisy, choose Richard, not Charles. Choose Dominic, not Rob.

She approached it wanting Dominic to enter the room and see her in front of it, wanting him to have to come closer and whisper something in her ear, or wrap an arm around her from behind. Yet for once, she saw, he was there before her, sitting on one of the benches right in front of the painting. She thought how easy it would be to turn around, walk out of the grand door and just carry on, away and home, and he would never know how close to him she had been. But in fact it wasn't easy, any more than it would have been easy for Daisy to make love to Richard, not really, not with thoughts of the landlady and Charles and her distant father pulling her down into the undertow of emotion. She was only saying it was easy afterwards, writing her letter on the train back, because by then Richard had said all of those reassuring things, more than enough to dispel doubt or regret.

Claire did not turn back. She could not. Nor did she approach Dominic immediately. Instead, she went only a little closer, enough to see the painting, and from that standpoint she surveyed this woman whose naked body was arrayed so splendidly before her and waited for Dominic to turn around and seek her out.

Venus reclined on a sheet of silk the colour of a storm at sea. The sheet had been thrown over a couch of some sort, and her body curved along its hidden form. A pot-bellied Cupid, wearing only a blue sash, stood to one side, white wings tipped with blue protruding from his back and brown curls loose around his head. Behind him draped the folds of a curtain made of red velvet. In his hands, he held a wooden-framed mirror hung with pale pink ribbons.

Venus' face in the mirror seemed blurred to Claire, impossible to read, the features too soft. She wondered how she was appraising herself, as women always did when they were in front of a mirror, whether they were at home alone, in the changing rooms at the gym or, pretending not to, in the lift at work. Some women seemed only to see their flaws, others only their beauty. Venus was the second type, nothing could be clearer than that. She wore her nakedness lightly, without the slightest self-consciousness, in a way Claire could only dream of doing. She was seemingly careless of the watchful gaze first of Velasquez himself, and now of the endless passers-by, none of whom, man or woman, moved on to the next painting without taking at least a second look at this one, if not a third. This was still a popular painting, still attracting a crowd, just as it had when Daisy saw it.

She wondered what a man would think, what Dominic was thinking, coming across this painting glowing rosily amongst all those sombre, darker pieces, with portraits of stern, moustachioed men hung on both sides, their eyes like everyone else's looking in admiration on this goddess of love. *This is a woman I would take to my bed. This is a woman who would never have me. This woman is beautiful, but there is more to her than that. This is a woman I would be afraid to marry but would never forget.*

Claire could only guess, but knew that when she looked at the painting she thought only, *This is how I would like to be.* What woman would not? She would not be gauche or uncertain with Dominic. With the image of Venus held firmly in her mind she would be experienced and poised, elegant and sensuous, and as ready to seduce as to be seduced. And, with that, Dominic sure enough did turn, and stand up and come close to her. When their hands touched, the effect was electrifying. She almost couldn't bear it when he moved away.

'Come on,' he said, his eyes turned one last time

back to Venus. 'I want to get you home, and quickly. My place, not yours. We're getting a taxi. We'll be there in ten minutes.'

'OK,' she said and knew he had it planned out as much as she had, that when they reached his flat, they would make love to each other. It was what they both wanted, she was certain enough of that, what they had both wanted from the first time they met over a too-small table still damp with someone else's spilt coffee. *Rob*, she thought. *Poor Rob*. Then she thrust the thought far away.

His flat was on the fifth floor, a smooth lift ride away from the grand entrance hall. Inside, it was small and slightly untidy, like bachelor pads were meant to be. It was open plan, with the kitchen divided from the living room by just a counter surface. She hesitated by the door, unsure where to stand, while Dominic kicked aside the heap of junk mail on the floor. She saw from the item on top, a catalogue of some kind, that his surname was Travers – something that she had not known before. An elegant sounding name, the epitome of Englishness, and just right for someone in the high-end auction business. She watched as this Dominic Travers started throwing books and old newspapers into a precarious heap on the coffee table in the living area, then gathering up plates and glasses and depositing them in the kitchen sink. In the corner of the room was a functional, metal-framed camp bed with a green mattress, folded up and leaning against the wall. Dominic saw her looking. 'That's where Ruby sleeps when she stays here,' he said. 'It's not much, I know, but she isn't here very much. I tell her to pretend she's camping out in the Sahara underneath the stars. What she'd really like is a four-poster with pink curtains.'

He disappeared along a short corridor, which must lead to the bedroom. Claire could hear him moving things about hurriedly, probably shoving scattered clothes into the bottom of a wardrobe and pushing dirty mugs out of sight. She did not follow him. Instead, she wandered idly around the room. It was rather elegantly decorated, more so than she had thought at first glance. There were some interesting pieces of glass arranged on a mantelpiece, and one or two small pieces of furniture that were clearly old and expensive. Wooden shelves set between the room's two windows were lined with books about antiques and art, together with an array of detective novels, a few of which she had read, and a handful of well-worn children's books which must have been Ruby's. There were one or two paintings on the walls, but no photographs. It didn't surprise her. Men weren't bothered with that kind of thing, not like women, or some women anyway, who would have put pictures of their wedding or their children on every surface if their husbands would let them.

There was a mirror on the wall, and in it she saw

herself, as difficult to read as Venus. If even she could not follow her face's lines and creases and read the meaning in her eyes, she wondered how she could ever expect Rob to, or Dominic for that matter. The superficialities were clear enough at least. Although the mascara she had applied that morning had not been as long-lasting as it claimed to be on the container, and the shimmering stickiness of her lip gloss had disappeared long ago, she thought she still looked right, like she should, like Dominic would have expected. The right amount of effort made, reflecting the right amount of anticipation. She imagined Dominic standing each morning just where she was now, checking the careful sweep of his hair, and she half-expected him to appear behind her, to join his reflection with hers, but he did not. Not yet. Still a waiting game.

At first, the room seemed dark and full of shadows, penetrated only by the scant daylight forcing its way through London's gloom. It sent a chill down her, and she moved over to stand right by the windows, which looked out over the Thames as it curved down towards the Houses of Parliament. It would not be cheap to live here, not with that view. When she turned back, she saw that Dominic was there and watching her. It was only a matter of time now. This was where it was all going to start. The true beginning of something new, without all the baggage that went with something old. Her heart lurched and her hand went instinctively to her chest, because she was not sure about the feelings now, whether they were excitement or fear.

Dominic must have sensed something of her disquiet. 'It's OK to be nervous,' he said, his own voice utterly composed. 'Let me get you a drink. What'll you have?'

'Just water's fine.'

'Don't be silly. You need something stronger. Calm the nerves. How about a gin and tonic?'

'Fine,' she said, knowing he was right. She watched him take a lemon out of a fruit bowl, get the ice-cube tray out of the freezer and pour fridge-cold tonic on top of the gin, all with expert smoothness. He slid the glass to her across the counter-top between them, and only when she went to pick it up did she realise that her hands were shaking. She began to drink it quickly while he made another for himself. It was strong and cool, and left her fingers wet with condensation. Still her fingers trembled. Looking up at Dominic now, she saw that his did not.

'So, what painting did I miss last time?'

'Constable. *The Hay Wain.*'

'And what did you think of it?'

'It reminded me of chocolate selection boxes. The kind they used to sell in the newsagents when we were growing up, remember? They were kept out of the way and usually had a layer of dust on them and

a picture of a thatched cottage under the cellophane.
I would save up my money for ages to buy one for
my grandmother and she would pretend to be thrilled
even though the only one she liked was the hazelnut
whirl. You don't see them these days, do you? We're
all too sophisticated for that kind of thing.'

Dominic smiled. 'You are so pretty when you're
reminiscing. It's like you've gone off into some other
place and just left a part of yourself here with me.'

'Really?' Claire felt herself smile in return, and
there was real pleasure in it.

'Really. Now come back, because I want all of
you here. It's a long time since I met anyone like
you. You've made me feel alive again. I hope you
don't mind me saying it.' His voice sounded firm,
convinced, and when she looked into his eyes she
knew that he meant what he said, just as Rob would
once have meant it when he told her the same things,
using the same words – words which in the meantime
she had read a hundred times in books and heard a
thousand times on TV, knowing always that they
didn't have to mean a thing. Immediately she didn't
want him to say anything else. It was better that he
stop right there and they could get on with what
they were there to do. She put down her glass on
the counter and said, 'Please. Not another word.'

'OK,' he replied.

He put down his own glass, came round the
kitchen counter that until then had kept them apart,

and reached out to take her hand. Then he pulled her towards him and they were kissing, and the force of his tongue in her mouth took her by surprise. Already, she felt his hand running up against her breast, then against the buttons of her dress, starting to undo them, one by one, slowly does it. There were so few left that she could shrug it off her shoulders, if he didn't pull it off first. He moved away from her now, reaching for his own shirt, pulling it out of his trousers, reaching for the buttons, doing what Claire now realised that she should have done but had not. The flat suddenly felt cold, unexpectedly cold.

It was in that moment of broken contact, that briefest of pauses, that one mistake of his, that the sun suddenly shone for the first time bright through the window, lighting up the room, casting all darkness away. In that light Claire looked straight into Dominic's eyes and thought at long last, and with perfect clarity, *This should be Rob. Why is this not Rob?* Almost as suddenly, the sun retreated behind the clouds, a shadow fell across the two of them and the last faint threads of excitement slipped wraith-like through Claire's hands, even as Dominic was taking her once again by the hand and trying to lead her towards the bedroom. She found herself pulling away and knowing that she had gone as far as she ever would. 'I'm sorry, Dominic. This isn't what I want.'

He turned towards her, framed by the bedroom door. 'What did you say?'

Now it was tumbling out again, more easily than before. 'I don't want this. I want to stop.'

Still he did not move, just watched her. She drew away slowly, without turning around, back into the living room. He followed.

'Say it again,' he said. 'I want to hear you say it again.'

'I'm sorry. I made a mistake. That's all. I made a mistake.' She reached out, thinking to take hold of his hand or rest her own upon his shoulder, but he was too far away and seemed to be retreating ever further all the time.

'My God, Claire, what are you saying? What do you think we've been doing all these months? Just messing around like kids? I thought this was what you wanted. I know it's what I want. I thought I was making you happy. Wasn't I?'

'Yes, of course you were, more than you can know. But I think I was hoping for something easier. I thought this would be easier. It's not. None of it has been. All I've done is got myself more mixed up than I was before. I have another life, Dominic, a whole other life. It's that one I need, not this.'

'But there's a spark between us, isn't there? I know you can feel it. I'm not wrong about that.'

'It's there. Of course it is,' she said. 'But can't we just leave it at that and be glad about it? Can't I just be with my husband and learn how to be happy with him?'

Now he was throwing himself back on the sofa in exhausted resignation. 'Sure. Why not? But it might not work, Claire, however much you try. Trust me, I know what I'm talking about.'

'But I'm not you, Dominic. It could be different for me. And if it isn't, at least let me find out on my own.'

'I'm not going to stop you. Who am I to stop you?'

'Thank you for understanding.'

'I'm not sure I do.'

'I'm not sure I do either,' she replied.

She smiled at him ruefully, regretfully, but there was another smile beneath, that she kept concealed. One that she was keeping for Rob. A wave of calm had descended upon her. Her breathing came steady at last. 'I'd better go,' she said.

'Yes,' he said. 'You should go.'

There was no final touch between them as he saw her out, no lingering glance, no promises – *I'll call, Let's stay friends* – made only to break. Claire was simply out of the flat, and he was closing the door upon her.

As she left the apartment block and breathed in the cold air, she felt an exhilaration arising out of the certainty that she had done the right thing, because her place was with Rob, her life lay aligned with his, her future was to be shared with him. Her decision was made. She could never have shared with Dominic everything she had shared with Rob, she knew that. He was a fantasy, that was all. She might be intelligent, interesting and full of new ideas with a man like Dominic, but she could never have been honest. She could never have laughed completely freely, without archness or expectation, with Dominic as she had once so easily been able to with Rob. She might have shared her dreams with him, but never her fears. He was wrong for all that. She had made him too much a part of her story, but now that chapter was shut.

Home now. Home to her husband and his familiar hands and arms and voice, home at last. Home for good.

She turned to go the only way she knew, back up towards the National Gallery, past a deserted branch of a cheap Italian restaurant and a bookmaker's, skirting round the last of the patches of Saturday night vomit that scattered the pavement, most of which had already been trodden away. The sky was all swelling grey clouds, and a brisk breeze had risen up, blowing crisp packets and chocolate wrappers along the street in rapid bursts. Discarded newspapers slapped rhythmically against the paving stones, too wet for more than just their edges to be lifted off the ground. London had become ugly and dirty in an afternoon, yet she felt something close to happiness, because she was going to say to Rob all that he wanted to hear: *I love you. I need you. I want you.* She would wear the perfume he had given her, and wear it for him, she would light a candle for dinner that night. He would make her breakfast, send her text messages all day. They would go out together again, drink wine at tables for two, and hold hands in the street. It would be just as it had been all that time ago. Nothing had changed, not forever, she was still the same person – not her mother, not Daisy, not Dominic, just herself. It would be a new start, not an easy one, but she could do it.

The thought hastened her step until she could almost have broken into a run. Arriving in Trafalgar Square, she turned straight into the underground station, went through the ticket barriers and started the long walk down to the platforms. As she approached the escalators, she saw a young woman standing hesitant at the top, with a little girl alongside her and a baby in a pushchair. She looked up with relief as Claire approached.

'Will you hold her hand?' she said. 'She doesn't like going down on her own.'

'Of course,' said Claire, and when she looked down at the child, she saw that she was afraid. 'Come on,' she said. 'It's not so far to go. Don't be frightened.'

The girl put her hand straight into Claire's, and she held it carefully. It was warm and clammy, and impossibly soft. She smiled reassuringly down at her and in the eyes that looked back saw a ridiculous, undeserved trust. They stepped together on to the escalator, the girl's mother grappling with the push-chair right behind them, and headed down. She didn't know whether she should try to speak to the child or not, and in the end said nothing, so the only sound was the whirr of machinery, punctuated by distant electronic announcements. The escalator was slower and longer than she remembered, the child more vulnerable than she had seemed at the top, grasping her hand tightly now, with her mouth shaping itself into the beginning of a sob. *Oliver*, she thought, *one day this might have been you, in ironed beige shorts and a fresh blue shirt, clinging on to your mother*. But the thought was gone as quickly as it had come and she was left only with this real child, right there by her side, relying on her.

'Don't cry,' she said. 'It'll be OK. We're nearly there.'

Unbelievably the girl was giggling now, and she was giggling back, and then before she knew it they were at the bottom of the escalators at last, and she was lifting her off the flattening steps and back on to solid ground. The mother thanked her and was gone, walking smartly away, wheeling the pushchair in front of her and telling her little girl to hurry up because Daddy was expecting them home – but at the turn in the corridor they both turned around to wave. Claire found herself waving back.

When she opened the door of the flat, she was still smiling, ready with the words that she would pour out as Rob listened, smiling too, a weight as heavy as their tiny baby had been light lifted from their shoulders.

The note was on the kitchen table: *I'm sorry, I need some space. I'll be in touch.*

Neat, written after consideration, not in a rush but carefully.

Claire knew already what it felt like to have something die inside her. She had hoped never to feel it again.

9

Weymouth Bay – Constable

Never before had time passed more slowly or more quietly, slower than the Thames' muddy flow, quieter than the fall of snow in dead of winter. She carried on with the normal distractions that made up life – going to work, buying a pint of milk (not two) at the shop at the corner – but it was as if Rob's departure had muted the world around her. In the flat, in the evenings, she waited for the phone to ring or for the front door to be pushed open and for her husband to come in. Day after day, neither happened. She was impossibly restless, unable to sit on the sofa for more than a few minutes at a time before moving to stand by the window, curtains pulled aside, looking out into the street below, then to the kitchen to make a cup of tea or pour a glass of wine. Sometimes she even found herself collapsed on the hall floor, the back of her head against the wall, waiting, waiting, waiting. A woman waiting for a man just like the women in the de Hooch painting she had seen so many months ago, waiting while ordinary life carried on for everyone else in the background.

This then was love and loss combined. Before, when Rob took himself away, she had felt relieved, exhilarated even, as if she had triumphed over him. But now she knew what loneliness felt like. It had been too many years since she had truly been alone, because for so long there had been Rob. Dominic was nowhere in all this. She did not want him to text or call, nor did he. She did not want to picture what had almost happened.

She assumed Rob had gone to his parents. It was only to parents that one could truly lay bare such a failure as theirs. She was sure that he would not entrust that knowledge to a friend, however close. Every evening, more than once, her hands would stray to the phone, and sometimes even begin to dial his parents' number, but she never went further than that. His note had said that he would be in touch. All she could do was hope desperately that he would come back, just as Rob must have been hoping all these past months that she might one day return from the exile that she had imposed upon herself, an exile from their joint lives. She thought sometimes about going out, calling a friend or arranging to see a film, just to pass the time – but she didn't want to miss him, and have him think that she did not care when now she cared more than ever before.

Instead she called her sister, and her mother too, more often than she had for many years, and cried and cried down the phone in desperation until none of them knew what to do.

Apart from work (her colleagues wondering at her renewed vigour for long hours and short lunch breaks), the only place she went to was the National Gallery, but to its archives this time, accessed through the staff entrance to the side of the main doors and hidden away from the public. There she read its record of the war because she could not read Daisy's, because the letters had gone from the place in the bedside cabinet where she had left them carefully tied up in their ribbon, and she knew without a doubt that Rob had taken them with him, to toss in a bin or hide away, to teach her a lesson of some sort.

The archives' box files were full of photographs, showing the paintings stored away in underground caverns in Wales, the canteen set up for war workers in the Gallery itself, the daily concerts organised by Myra Hess, and visitors eating sandwiches on the lawn. There were newspaper clippings too, reporting the success of the picture of the month scheme and calling for suggestions as to what should be displayed next, and minutes of meetings of the National Gallery's board. These were as old as Daisy's letters, and recorded in unsensational terms the risks of aerial attack, the damage caused by the latest raids and enemy seizure of British paintings abroad. Finally there were careful, handwritten lists on lined paper of attendance numbers, recording every visitor there had ever been to every picture of the month, counted up morning and afternoon and added together for daily, weekly and monthly totals and averages, recording more than half a million people in total passing through. A comment, once or twice, when numbers were oddly high: 'Weather wet', or 'weather dull'. Somewhere amongst the anonymity of each stroke of those figures strolled Daisy, and Charles and Richard too. So many visitors, Claire thought, leaning back in the wooden chair, Daisy as anonymous as the rest to everyone but her.

When at last she did hear the key in the lock, on a Friday evening after an endless, awful fortnight in which her visit to the archives had been the only bright light, she started up from the chair at the kitchen table and was in the hallway before Rob was even through the door, saying the words that had been trapped inside her since she had come headlong home from Dominic's flat.

'I love you,' she said. 'I need you. Thank God you're back.' She did not leave it to him to hold her in his arms, but took him in her own and stroked his hair, and smelt it, and tried desperately not to mind that she could not feel his response.

'I missed you,' he said, and it was enough.

She cooked for them that night, using a recipe and ingredients bought specially, opening a bottle of wine and pouring out two glasses. All he had to do was watch, which he did, his eyes, she knew, following her around the kitchen as she moved here and there, waiting for him to say something that mattered.

'I've been to see the paintings,' he said at last. 'I read the letters and then I went to see the paintings. I loved every minute of it.'

She paused, stock-still.

He had walked in her path and in Daisy's.

He had stood silently in front of *Noli me tangere* and thought of all she had put him through. He had watched the demon-beasts scurrying around the corners of *The Mystic Nativity* and wondered what it meant.

Had he thought of her when he saw the lonely woman in her courtyard in Delft? Had he, too, faltered in front of *Madonna of the Basket*, seeing in Mary's arms the baby that looked like Oliver might have done?

'I didn't think you cared,' she said, or that was what she thought she said. It was hard to hear herself, because her heart was screaming only, *What have I lost?*

He had been gazing at her intently, but now he looked away. 'You didn't give me the chance to care,' he said. Just hearing him say it made her flush.

'I've let you down,' she said.

He said nothing to that, only, 'I think we should see the rest of the paintings together.'

'I'd like that,' she said. 'I really would like that.'

'But first, I'm taking you away.'

'Where?'

'Wait and see. I'll tell you on the day. It's a surprise.'

Claire smiled uncertainly. She had forgotten what surprises felt like, and he had only ever carried her off like this once, without them sitting down beforehand and discussing where they wanted to go, and then her doing all the booking. It had been for their honeymoon, a fortnight in the Azores where together they had watched flying fish and dolphins from a yacht moored far out to sea and lain on broad, perfect lawns crowded round with hedges of blue hydrangeas.

'When?' she asked.

'Tomorrow. I don't want to wait.'

'OK,' she said. 'Tomorrow.' She never even thought to say no.

They left in the morning, after a night spent in the same bed, Claire sleeping as she rarely did, with her hand against his chest, feeling the pulse of his heart, his hand on hers, no more than that. They had to get up early to set out for the station, which meant that they could also avoid the confusing uncertainty of lingering in the flat together. It was not until they arrived at Waterloo that he told her where they were going.

'Weymouth, of course. Didn't you guess?' She hadn't. She had thought it must be Bath or Brighton, or one of those other places where young, childless professionals in their late twenties and early thirties were always spending the weekend, in boutique hotels with expensive toiletries in the bathroom and spas in the basement.

'Because of the painting?'

'Why else? And because of Daisy's letter. I liked the way she made it sound. I thought it might give it all some context, actually being there, where she was. I thought you'd like it.'

'Oh.' She should have thanked him, but it was too unexpected. The Weymouth letter, she thought, which was so redolent of infidelity and excitement and new beginnings with new people. What on earth could Rob have liked about that? A dread came upon her that the trip was to be about Dominic, and not Daisy at all.

The train journey took three hours, which Claire supposed might not be very much quicker than it had been when Daisy went the same way. She looked out of the window most of the time, rather than read the endless sections of the Saturday newspaper that Rob began by offering her across the laminated table between them – she knew it would be saying just the same thing on just the same topics as it had the year before and the year before that. She was unwilling still to look at Rob, whose face was as pale underneath the artificial lights as her own must be. The air conditioning was set too high and it made Claire cold, the more so because she could see that the sun outside was blazing. There was no way of opening a window. They were all trapped inside the carriages together.

The train never got up enough speed for the view outside the windows to become a blur, and sometimes went so slowly that Claire could pick out every nettle and discarded beer can that lay beside the track. The countryside – where there was still countryside and not the familiar blend of industrial parks, DIY centres or estates of new-build houses in cartoonish colours – was green from recent rain, in some parts neatly cultivated, in others patchworked with wild gorse and open moorland. Here, for a brief time, a group of horses cantered alongside the train, tails flashing and already gone before she could point them out to Rob. Further into the journey, the view became all rivers, inlets and hints of the sea. There were boats moored out in the water, trailing buoys that had long ago faded from red to pink.

A woman came along the narrow corridor wheeling a snack trolley, and Claire followed its path as it got caught up on stray rucksack straps and inconvenient knees. She bought a bar of chocolate for too much money, but sharing it with Rob felt right, even though it was not much of a peace offering and was soon gone, leaving her with an unpleasant stickiness on her fingers, which quickly picked up the train's grime. She wiped her hands impatiently on her jeans, because the water in the lavatory at the end of the carriage had run out within an hour of leaving London, and thought about reading Daisy's letter, the Weymouth letter, which Rob had snatched up at the last minute, just as they were leaving the flat, and slipped into her bag. No, she decided. She wouldn't read it here, amid the racket of mobile phones, computer games and idle chatter. It came too much from another place. A place without neat wheelie suitcases and foil crisp packets, a place where soldiers and kit had been piled up on top of one another, and most of the voices would have been male, rough and tired. A place where a man called Richard had squeezed himself against a rattling window with just enough room to move a pencil in his hand, while a girl called Daisy balanced a pad of writing paper on her knee, sucked at the end of her pen and wondered whether she should use the word 'love'. The power of the thought, which felt so much like a memory, was enough to send a chill draught running along the carriage.

When they finally reached Weymouth, she and Rob tumbled out with everyone else on to the platform. As the other passengers dispersed, they found themselves somehow still standing there.

'So here we are,' she said.

'Here we are,' said Rob.

An odd hesitation seemed to have come upon both of them, a sense of time running out that nonetheless made it difficult to move despite the restlessness in their limbs come from narrow seats and cramped legs. When Claire felt the buzz of her mobile phone in her jacket pocket, instinct made her pull it out. The flash of an envelope showed that a message had come in. A message from Dominic, the first since that awful time: *When can I see you again, beautiful? I'd still like to.* It ended with a bright yellow smiley face as if he had managed to pass over the finality of her last words by deciding she surely could not have meant them.

'Who's it from?' she heard Rob say, and knew that if she looked up now he would see the outlines of a story she did not want to tell in the darkness of her eyes.

She pressed the delete button. 'No one important,' she said and was only then able to smile at him, and know that the smile she was giving him was utterly truthful. 'So, where are we staying? You lead the way.'

Rob produced a map from his pocket that he had printed off the internet and they used it to get themselves away from the station, past a fish and chip café that advertised a pensioner special on Wednesdays, past a set of roadworks that gave off the acrid, addict-ive scent of melting tar, and out on to the esplanade. It couldn't have changed at all, this place. Every house

along the front was still a bed and breakfast, each
with a name like Ocean View, Sunbeam and Daybreak,
just the same as in 1943 and God knows how long
before then, ever since people had travelled out of
cities and to the seaside just to taste the salt upon
the air. One of these places was theirs, and in one
of them, no one would ever know which, Daisy and
Richard had stayed sixty-five years ago. The place
Rob had booked was a small hotel, which could
not have been called boutique, but which did, like
Daisy's, have a room for them with a view out to
sea. There was no mini-bar, and, so far as compli-
mentary toiletries went, only a bar of unopened soap
in the bathroom, but the walls were freshly painted
in blues and whites, and on the side there was a
kettle, two teabags and two packets of shortbread
biscuits. On the wall, there was a wide mirror that
was meant to make the place look bigger than it
was and, hanging alongside, a picture of a lighthouse
with impossibly high waves smashing against it. Rob
kicked off his shoes and fell back on the bed, which
was buried deep beneath a duvet and pillows, and
said, 'What first?'

*We talk about the future. Isn't that what we need to
do? Isn't that why we're here?* But instead she said, 'It's
up to you. The esplanade, or the Constable view.'

'Let's start with the view. It might be raining
tomorrow.'

'I suppose so,' she said, but in her head was the

thought that Daisy and Richard had done it the other way round, and Rob knew that too. It made her feel uncertain, because they weren't doing it right, and then foolish, because none of this was meant to be about Daisy after all, not now. It was meant to be about her and Rob. 'Yes, let's do it that way,' she said more firmly. 'It's not really important, is it?'

'You know what, Claire, it's not important at all. Now come over here and kiss me. I'm getting lonely, lying here on my own.'

She did kiss him, lightly on the lips. His response was more urgent and he pulled her down on top of him, putting both of his arms around her. She gave in to the feeling and kissed him again, her ears full of the sound of water being dragged back and forth across the beach, her head thinking of Daisy, for whom it had been the first time. A light breeze came through the open window and played against her legs, which were bare underneath a summer dress.

'That's better, isn't it?' he said.

Yes, Claire thought, remembering that moment of understanding in Dominic's flat, that feeling that she must stop. *Yes, it is.* 'Don't stop,' she said, and he didn't.

The heat of the day was beginning to fall away when they left the hotel and set out along the front. Rob surprised her by producing a copy of the painting and a scrap of paper on which he had written the caption that hung alongside the real thing in the National Gallery: 'The view is towards the west across Bowleaze Cove, part of Weymouth Bay in Dorset.' She was not used to him being so organised. Usually he left all of that to her. The cove was away from the town, just as Daisy had described, way past the beach huts with their handmade gingham curtains, the municipal displays of gaudy begonias and dahlias, the lonely stalls selling tea and soft drinks, and the drips of ice cream fallen on concrete. Slowly, the amusement arcades and shops stocking fudge and rock fell behind them, and soon the only people that she and Rob passed as they walked along the weed-edged concrete slabs that made up the path looked like locals.

They paused in front of a war memorial, which listed the dead of Weymouth from the First World War and then, lower down and somehow more reluctantly because there was little space left for them, yet more dead from the Second. Claire read off some of the names silently, just in case they still, somewhere, cared whether anyone ever thought about them. Next to the memorial was a flower bed which had been labelled Garden of Remembrance and planted with crosses made out of wind-whitened wood and adorned with red paper poppies. Here, too, they hesitated wordlessly, before continuing on, somehow hand in hand now, leaving the path and striking out across the shingle, out to the point where the sand was hard from the lick of sea water and the seaweed was a bright cabbage-green. From the top of the low cliff that now rose up from the beach they were watched all the time by haughty, strutting crows.

Looking ahead, Claire saw at last what they were aiming for, a short pier that jutted out into what must be Bowleaze Cove. Behind it was something that looked like the biggest hotel she had ever seen, a vast fortress stretching endlessly out across the bay. She had not allowed herself to think that the place could be so different. That had been a mistake. Rob's gaze followed her own.

'Well, there's something that certainly wasn't built in Constable's time.'

'Nor in Daisy's,' she said. 'She would have mentioned it. You can't miss it.'

That was only the first disappointment. The second revealed itself slowly as they edged around the cove, taking the shape of a permanent funfair complete with a helter-skelter in bright pink and yellow, a go-karting track, the edges of a caravan park and a café, squat and braced against the possibility of winter gales. There were houses too, which she thought, but didn't know for sure, might have been built in the fifties.

She turned to Rob. 'It's changed, hasn't it? It's not like it was when Daisy was here.'

'Of course it's changed. But it's not surprising, is

it? It's been a while, you know. What hasn't changed in the past few decades?'

'I wanted it to be the same.'

'Well, if you stop worrying about the dodgems and the bouncy castle and turn around, maybe you'll see it isn't so different after all.'

She turned and saw, immediately, that he was right again. When on earth had it happened, him being right, not her? Because there it was, the view that Constable had painted, not so different from how it had once been after all. There were more houses scattered on the hills, and the edge of the cliff-face had become blunter where the rock had crumbled away, but the sea and the beach were still the same, and as for the sky, it had surely looked different every single day since Constable had been there. The sky was something that would always have been changing, even between every brushstroke he laid down on the canvas.

'See,' said Rob. 'It's not too bad, is it?'

'No. It's not.'

'Good.'

He bought them both polystyrene cups of tea at the café. They took them away and sat on a bench which had been put up in memory of someone who had, according to the plaque screwed into the back of it, always loved the view from that place. The silence between them was a waiting one, waiting to see who spoke first. In the end it was Rob.

'I didn't understand at first why you were so caught up in all this stuff about Daisy. I couldn't understand why you were talking about her all the time. Now I've read the letters, I can see why it means so much to you.'

'I think I've let it mean too much, Rob. I'm sorry. I've thought of nothing else for months. It's just that she was there for me, when I needed someone.' It felt almost embarrassing, saying these things, admitting to what she felt for someone who had never really been there, whom she had never even met, who had not even written the letters to her.

'It's OK,' he said. 'I'm saying I understand. But I want us to think about the future now, not the past. Our future. The letters are just a bit of family history. They weren't meant to become your life. If it was all that important, don't you think Grandma would have talked to us about Daisy? She didn't. Daisy's not a part of you, you're not the same. I've read the letters and I'm telling you, you're completely different. Read the letters and see the paintings. I still think it's a wonderful idea. But don't feel you have to impress Daisy. Don't think that because she does something or thinks something it makes it right.'

'I can't help liking her.'

'It's not *her* you like, it's what she chose to write down in her letters. Look at this view. Someone could paint it today and it would look almost the same as when Constable painted it. But it still wouldn't show you that there's a whole town just round the corner. You'd never know that there was a coachload of kids pulling up at the amusement park behind us. It would only tell part of the story. That's what the letters are like, you see, just a part of her life.'

'She was lonely, like me.'

'Maybe, at first. But the way I see it, she didn't stay lonely for long. And you don't have to either, because you've got me just like she had Richard. You've still got your friends, you've still got your family, just like she had. They're right there if you want them.'

He had not mentioned Dominic's name and now, she realised, he did not mean to. Dominic had become so tied up with Daisy she had allowed him to be a part of it all. It was yet another thing that she had never given Rob credit for, that he could simply be so kind. The only sounds now were the sea and the distant hum of traffic on the busy coast road, and the screeching of gulls overhead. Claire knew that it was her turn to speak, and at last she did, looking out to sea and that still grey sky, scuffing at the loose sand beneath her feet and the torn plastic wrapper from a lolly, thrown down long ago by a tired child on the way back to a car. 'I know,' she said slowly, thinking it out for herself as she spoke the words. 'I just forgot for a while, because I only had room in my head for Oliver. Did I ever tell you how it was? Did I ever really tell you?'

'Yes. A hundred times. If you want to, tell me again. Only this time, don't cry. Tell it all the way through.'

It began at the police station. They took me there in a police car, to make a statement while I could still remember what those boys looked like. I didn't mind going; I wanted to get it over with. I didn't want to be on my own. I didn't think there was anything wrong, not really wrong. I was winded from that punch in my stomach, but that was it. It was mostly just shock. But I should have gone to the hospital straightaway, of course. Would it have made a difference? The doctor told me no, it wouldn't, but he could hardly say yes, could he, not then, when it was all too late? They made me a cup of tea in a polystyrene cup. No one asked how I took it. A woman brought it over to me. Milk and two sugars, I still remember her saying that. I just sat there, waiting for them to come and talk to me, feeling like I was wasting their time.

I knew there was something wrong even before I saw the blood. I could already feel the warmth of it in my knickers. I put the tea down so fast I knocked it over. I can see the tea now, trickling down the table legs and pooling on the floor and everyone around just watching, blank-faced. I rushed into the police station toilet, pushing past all these strangers, and locked myself in a cubicle. Then, the blood. It was thick, with dark clots in it. There wasn't much of it right then. Christ, there was so little of it. Who would have thought there was so little to my child?

Yet I felt like there was blood all over me, on my hands, on the floor, dripping on to the stained tiles, running into the cracks. I didn't know what to do. I screamed, I think, and someone must have gone to get help, and they called a first aid officer and he phoned for an ambulance. His name was Rob, too, I remember that. He didn't know what to do. He took me into a side room and held my hand while we waited for the ambulance to arrive. There was a woman there too. Maybe they thought it would help. 'Is there anyone we should be calling?' she kept saying. 'How can we get hold of your husband?' They tried your mobile and your work number and the line at home. I wanted you so much right then. I've never been so scared as I was then. I didn't know where I was going. I needed you, Rob, and you weren't there. You had somewhere more important to be.

At the hospital, they put me in a wheelchair and took me into a cubicle. I didn't have to wait. Then the doctor came in and he asked questions. He asked how pregnant I was, and I told him twenty weeks. Can you imagine having to say that? God, I was so proud of telling people twenty weeks, halfway already, for God's sake. He got me to spread my legs and he felt inside me. There was someone with him, a student, and he looked at him and said, 'I'm checking the cervix, to see if it's dilating.' Then he didn't say anything. I could still feel his hand pressing inside me, and then he looked up and said he was afraid that it was what they called an inevitable miscarriage, a late miscarriage. 'I'm sorry,' he said. 'It's happening already. Do you understand what that means? It means that there's nothing we can do. We'll give you an ultrasound, to be sure. Are you on your own? You'll need someone with you.'

They wheeled me off into another room, and someone else came in to do the ultrasound, a tired woman who looked like she'd been on duty for days. She did a scan, just like the other ones. Do you remember them? How happy we were? Do you remember we couldn't believe how fast the baby's heartbeat was? How we got to take photographs home with us? She put the gel on my stomach and pushed down with the probe, moving it quickly, clinically, and then she was looking at the screen, and I was trying to look, too, craning my neck because she had moved the screen away. It wasn't like the first time, not then. There was nothing there, no movement, nothing, just the ragged outline of what should have been my baby, clinging to me but already gone. 'I'm sorry,' she said. 'Is there someone you can call?' That's what they all said. 'I'm sorry. Is there someone you can call.' The times before they had said, 'Congratulations, well done, do you want a boy or a girl?'

Those were the words that she could have used, but
instead she said, 'You're right. I've made you hear it
enough times already. We don't need to go over it
again.'

At last they were both looking at each other, right
into each other's eyes, and seeing nothing but regret
and pain. Claire almost reached out across the cold,
empty space between them, to take his hand again.
Then instead she leant down and took off her sandals,
turned to him, made herself smile and said, 'Race
you.'

Before he had time to act she was away and
running, running desperately across salt-damp sand,
allowing the abandonment of it to creep through
her and make her run all the faster. Then she could
hear Rob's steps behind her, coming up closer and
closer. She knew he was going to catch up with
her and she was going to let him take her in his
arms there beneath what had suddenly become the
bluest and clearest of skies. Then they were back
in the hotel and in their room. There they cast
aside the last of grief and sadness with each other's
clothes and made love to each other once more,
with conviction and hope and what she remembered as love. The windows were wide open and
all the time the curtains tugged in and out, but
she heard not even the whisper of Dominic's name
in the breeze.

★ ★ ★

The next day was bright and fresh, exactly like a seaside day should be. A new day, with yesterday's footprints washed away by the tide – but the rest of it still there, including the memory of the tears they had both cried the night before after he had withdrawn from her, and how they had fallen asleep in each other's arms, as they used to once before.

Rob stirred first, and shook her gently awake. 'It's the esplanade this morning,' he said, 'if that's still what you want to do.'

'Only if it's what you want too,' she replied.

'Of course it is. It's like I said. We'll see this through, but we'll do it together.'

They set off after a breakfast that was much better than Claire had imagined it would be from the hotel's façade and made her wonder why they paid so much more for less in London. They turned right out of the front door this time, towards the town centre and away from Bowleaze Cove, walking briskly along the front, lungs full of sea air. Claire felt a tight sense of excitement stuck lumpily in her throat, thinking how easy it would be to run into them now, Daisy and Richard with their arms wrapped tight around each other, blind to everyone else. Yet it was Rob who was the one to say, 'To think that they must have walked right where we are now.'

'They had their photograph taken, too,' she said. 'That was here. We should have brought the picture with us. Then we could have worked out the exact spot.'

'So let's at least have our photo taken too. I've got the camera.'

All the time that they had been walking, the wind had been rising, and now she felt it cold and strong against her, nudging her away, turning her back the way they had come. It was starting to rain, too, big, heavy drops that splashed and darkened the concrete beneath their feet. There was suddenly almost no one to ask, but then an elderly dog walker strode past, a little way off, and Rob caught up with him, brandished the camera and said, 'Would you mind?'

They stood together, leaning against the railings, and Claire felt Rob's arm around her. 'Smile, then,' said the stranger, and she did, and hoped Rob did too, because the rain was pelting down now, the man was already impatient and she could tell they were only going to get one chance. Then it was over and she and Rob were bending over the tiny screen and she was seeing them both looking every bit as happy as they had in their wedding photographs.

'See,' she said, looking at Rob and smiling again but with tears in her eyes. 'We are happy, aren't we?' She could not keep the catch out of her voice.

'Yes,' he said, still smiling too. 'I think we are.'

The train back to London left in the late afternoon, and they had been ready for it for at least two cold, gloomy hours of the worst of British weather, but it was two hours at least spent together, keeping each other warm and close in a fish and chip shop. They had sat next to each other, touching, not opposite, as if they were in a Parisian street café, watching the world go by, what little there was of it in the rain.

It was on the train that Rob asked Claire if he could have another look at Daisy's letter, to read what she'd said about the view again.

'You've got it,' she said. 'I saw you with the envelope before we left the hotel.'

'No, I haven't. I thought I gave it to you. You said you wanted to keep it in your bag.'

'But you didn't give it to me, Rob. I'm sure of it.' Claire was already rummaging through the bag, knowing that it was not there, that somehow they had left it behind. The train was moving, the doors were locked. The outskirts of Weymouth were beginning to fall away.

'I put it on the bedside table. I remember that much. It was right next to your bag. You couldn't have missed it.'

Claire looked up from her search, which had been made useless by panic. 'It's not here,' she said. 'We've left it behind. How could I have been so careless? We should never have brought it with us. Maybe it's in the suitcase. Could it be in there?' Her glance had shifted now up to the luggage rack at the end of the carriage, where their own case was hidden by a mountain of others.

'It's not going to be there,' said Rob, and she could see that he was watching keenly for her reaction. 'We both know that. If you really want me to look, I will, but first I want you to tell me what's the very worst that could happen if we have lost it, and lost it forever. And take a deep breath first. Think about what really matters.'

'We'll have lost part of the story. We'll have lost a piece of history. It's valuable.'

'Yes, but it's also just a piece of paper. That's all. You know the story already, you've read it enough times. Whether we have the letter or not, it doesn't change what happened, does it? There was still Daisy, doing what she did, getting through life just like the rest of us. You can see that, can't you? You don't really need any of the letters, not now.'

'No.' She shook her head slowly, then more firmly, almost meaning it.

'Good. Now I'm going to call the hotel and see if they've found it. I bet it's still there.'

He was right. The letter was still there, just where he had remembered leaving it and she had not picked it up. The receptionist said she would post it on next morning. Claire heard the tail end of the conversation as Rob came back from the corridor into the carriage. He was telling them to send it registered mail, because it was important. Then she was thanking him, for accepting how much it mattered, kissing him and tasting the sea water still on his lips. Leaning back against him, she turned to look out on to the endless, shifting views beyond the confines of the train, dreaming of being out there and part of it, running through the grass with nowhere to go but with Rob always there beside her.

10

Self-portrait — Rembrandt

When Rob's father Nick telephoned one evening, a week or so later, only Claire was at home to pick it up. Normally she passed the phone straight to Rob, if he was there, or, if he was not, said just a hasty 'I'll tell him you called' before hanging up. This time, he cut her off before she had a chance to come out with the usual line. He wanted to speak to her just as much as Rob, he said. He'd spent the past week in Canada — hadn't Rob told her he was off there, arranging for his mother's house to be sold? His voice rang with excitement, even as he dragged over the unimportant things, the price of parking the car at the airport, the delayed flight and the poor food on board the plane, taking her with him all the way through immigration at the other end and into a taxi that crawled through the traffic to his mother's house. She could have interrupted, or told him to hurry up, but she knew the story was rising up inside him and wanted to follow its every turn. They moved slowly on together with his words up the front steps on to the porch, through the door that had jammed on its hinges and needed to be kicked open, and into the house which was being emptied by a clearance company he had employed.

Here his voice started moving more quickly, as he described how he had wandered around echoing rooms, which he barely knew himself because his mother had moved there only in recent years, into this new easy house, right for a woman who no longer wanted to put up with unreliable plumbing and vast spreads of carpet.

The house clearance people had stacked cardboard boxes up in the middle of each room, and pushed what little furniture there was there too, so that he could easily point at each item and say (as he mostly did) throw it out, or else sell it or ship it to England. He had gone last of all into her bedroom, fearful even now that he was invading his mother's privacy. Here, amongst everything else, he had come across her antique mahogany writing desk, a box really, no more than that, which opened out on a hinge to reveal a sloped writing surface edged with leather and tooled around the edges in gold. It was the kind of object on which one could imagine women from another age having written elegant letters on expensive paper, although in fact, he said, most boxes of this kind had been owned by military men, not ladies sitting in drawing rooms, and in their day had been carried across the world to all its many battle-fronts.

Opening it up, he had seen, lying at the very top, a photograph of his mother and an unknown woman, both still girls, at Edenside, and it had called to mind an old story, that his mother had brought the writing desk over to Canada with her when she married, just the desk and a trunk of clothes with which to begin her new life. He knew then that he was going to shut the lid of it now, and take it home, not leave it to be shipped. He had taken it back to the functional motel where he was staying, taped it up carefully and brought it back to England with him as checked baggage, handle with care. The flight had been delayed again, the food just as bad and now, finally, he was home and the writing desk had not even been lost in transit.

'So what do you think of all that?' he said at the end.

She thought only that she might find something of Daisy here, as alive as her letters, more alive than ever.

'When can we come and visit?' she asked.

There was surprise and pleasure in his voice when he replied, 'Whenever you want, of course. You should know that by now. How about this weekend?'

'I hope so. I'd like that. I'll check with Rob.' She had heard those words often from Rob. *I'll check with*

Claire. It made a change to hear them switched around.

They took Daisy's letters with them to Hertfordshire, all of them, from the very first until this month's, the one for August, which she had not even read herself yet. She no longer felt the need to hold them so close, not like she had once, not now they were no longer the only thing in her life, because she had Rob back in it too. They arrived on the Friday night, in time for a late supper. The writing desk was in the hallway, still wrapped up. Claire saw it as soon as they stepped inside. Good. Nick really had waited for them. Rob followed her glance and said, 'It's too late now. We'll start on it tomorrow.'

'I was thinking that we could read out the letters tonight,' she said 'We could take it in turns, to catch your parents up with what's happened.'

Nick, approaching with two glasses of cool, crisp white wine, overheard them. 'Good idea, Claire. We should start at once. I'll tell Priscilla.'

So that was what they did, late into the night, later than she had ever stayed up before when she was with Rob's parents. She felt no need to use any of the excuses she traditionally kept for making an escape. They passed the letters around and took turns to read them aloud in order, Claire letting the words flow through her even when the others, less familiar with them, stumbled. Nick sat back in an armchair with his eyes closed, and Claire knew that he was trying to imagine his mother young again, a mother long ago replaced in older, frailer form. He liked the parts where Daisy mentioned him or Elizabeth, Claire could tell from the way he sat up straighter against the worn, flowered chintz of the sofa and paid closer attention.

It was Priscilla who was the first to comment when Claire reached the part where Richard met Daisy for the first time.

'What did you say the man's name was? Richard something?'

'Dacre.'

'Richard Dacre. Nick, don't you remember the fuss there was when Robert was born? Your mother wanted to call him Richard, but I wouldn't have it. She really got quite agitated about it, and we never got to the bottom of what the problem was. She wasn't the type to make much of a fuss normally, was she? Come on, surely you can't have forgotten.'

Nick opened his eyes. Claire and Rob both looked at him expectantly. 'Yes, now I think about it, I do remember something about that,' he said. 'We stuck to our guns and in the end, what was it she said? Hang on, I'll get it. That's it. She said she supposed it didn't really matter, because the initials would still be right. Robert Dawson. R.D.'

'Richard Dacre,' said Claire triumphantly. 'She

wanted to call him Richard after Daisy's lover. It must have been her way of remembering it all.'

'Daisy's lover?' said Priscilla, shock showing in the way the edges of her mouth, where the day's lipstick had begun to run, had tightened.

'Wait and see, Priscilla,' Claire laughed. 'Wait and see. Rob, it's your turn to read one now.'

When they got to the end, it was nearly midnight, but to Claire it felt later, her emotions had been pulled so taut as the story built. It felt odd to hear it through the others' voices. She had grown used to hearing it only through Daisy's voice, for all that it was really her own.

'How about reading the next one now, Claire? The one for August?' said Nick.

'OK,' she said, and then, with great effort, 'Priscilla, why don't you read this one?'

'I would love to,' she said and Claire knew that she meant it. They had moved on to coffee by now. Priscilla drained the rest of her cup, cleared her throat loudly and began.

August, 1943
Dear Elizabeth,

My most important news is that the painting is finished at long last. I was right there when Richard laid down the brush, and just dying to see it of course, but simply terrified too. It has been pretty nerve-wracking, waiting for him to show it to me. I hadn't taken even a peep before. He made me swear not to and I kept my word. It was the perfect time, a beautiful summer evening and the sun just beginning to set. The studio was full of a warm, orange light and it lit up his face just so. One has time to notice these things, when one is sitting for an artist (and how grand that sounds!); the only thing to do is watch and think.

He took me by the hand, and we walked together behind the easel. It was like stepping into his private space, because that's where he always is. You can see his footprints there, and no one else's. They are ground in chalk and paint into the floorboards. Then, with great flair, he swept off a sheet he had flung over the canvas and showed me — myself, or a version of myself at least. It was a shock at first. No one knows what they really look like, after all. I didn't know what to think at first, but I made myself stay there and told myself to keep looking. It was frightening, yet wonderful at the same time. To think that there is now a record of how I am, today, on the 4th of August 1943! In years to come, I will be able to tell my children and grandchildren that, for a time, I was just like this. No wrinkles. Soft hair, gently waved. Smart. Important, at least so far as Richard is concerned. It is awfully hard to describe it to you, because although I can see that it's me, the colours aren't exactly right, nor is the shape. But when it's all put together, and one steps back, it forms itself

into me. Richard is thrilled with it. He says it
captures exactly how I am. I'm wearing the patterned
scarf you gave me for my eighteenth birthday. Do
you remember it? The one with the flowers. You
moaned endlessly about having to save up for it.
Now you'll be pleased you did.

There I am hard at work in the office, and looking
far more proud of the work than I actually thought I
was. That's nice of him — for me, of course, but also for
Miss Johnson who is longing to see it and never lets a
day go past without asking, 'Is it finished yet?'! There
is a row of sharpened pencils beside me, and a
withered plant on the window sill behind. Those things
are there in real life, although he has painted them
brighter than they really are. I do wish he had at least
painted the plant more alive, because now everyone
will know that I never water it. He could have done,
after all. Artists can do what they want, more or less.
But he says he liked it the way it was, green in the
living parts, but then a lot of wrinkled brown around
the edges. It's symbolic, it seems, of the way things are
good and bad these days, and how life somehow keeps
going endlessly on even though it's become rather rough
around the edges. Once he'd explained that to me, I
could see what he meant, but will anyone else?

In the picture, the window behind me is criss-
crossed all over with brown paper, in case a bomb
goes off and the glass blows in, and even that looks
better on the canvas than it really does — almost like

*stained glass. Outside you can see the wreck of the
building opposite the office, where there used to be
more offices. That's still ugly, he can't make that
beautiful, even now they're starting to build it up
again. He hasn't painted flowers growing around it,
even though there are some. Symbolic again, he says.*

*The first thing Richard is going to do is take it
in to the office, to show Miss J and the girls. After
that, it's off to the war artists' committee, and keep
your fingers crossed that they like it. He'll be frantic
with joy if it goes on display. It's a funny thing. I
used to want that too, more than anything, but now
I'm none too sure. For ages it's been something
private, just between me and him, and I don't much
want to share it. But I know that Richard never
meant it just for us.*

*I didn't skip seeing this month's National Gallery
painting you'll be pleased to hear, even though there
was my picture to finish. I'm too used now to going
along and marking off another month. It's a self-
portrait by Rembrandt. He painted a lot of them,
apparently, in all sorts of different poses and wearing
different clothes each time. What I would dearly love
is to see them all together, lined up in order of age,
so one can see how changed over the years (or how
he thought he had at any rate, because no one can be
sure he really looked like his self-portrait, can they?).
That isn't how the gallery works these days, of
course. The one they are showing is the last one ever,*

because he is sixty-three years old and that's when he died. Not too bad an innings, I suppose. I thought everyone was meant to be dead by forty in those days. He has arranged himself against a dark, earthy background, and he is emerging from it into yet more brown. He's wearing a coat, buttoned up and edged with something that may well be fur, but it's hard to tell because of the way all the browns run into each other. To my mind, the effect is not very cheerful, however skilled Rembrandt might be. In fact it's jolly gloomy. According to Richard, colours like brown aren't as expensive as yellows and blues, and Rembrandt was desperately short of cash by the end of his life so had to stick to the cheap stuff. Rather depressing, isn't it, the way lives — even famous ones — so often end up dark and dingy? I'd prefer to end my life full of colour.

I've decided that Rembrandt painted this self-portrait purely for his own pleasure. It's certainly hard to imagine who would have bought it. Who wants a painting of an artist when they could have one of themselves? His mistress and son were dead by this time, so the only person left to appreciate it would have been Rembrandt himself. It's rather sad to think of him rattling around in an empty house, with only pictures of himself for company. It's a sad painting all round in my opinion. Rembrandt's face has all the problems of life drawn into it. It's age, that's what it is, and it shows in the bags under his eyes and lines across his forehead, and all these clouds of white, receding hair. He has a grey moustache too, which I expect is nothing like as splendid as it once was, and a scrawny sort of beard. Well, it comes to all of us in the end. I can't hope to get away without any wrinkles at all, I suppose. His features are rather vague, as if he were already fading away and knew it – but perhaps I'm imagining that.

It started me wondering what Richard will look like when he's sixty-three. White hair like Rembrandt, or nothing there at all? He'll still be tall, unless he's started to stoop. He'll probably be wearing the exact same tweed jacket he has now, only with more paint around the cuffs. What about me? I asked Richard just that, and he said he'd paint me again then, so we can see how much I have – or haven't – changed. It's a nice thing to say, isn't it? It means something, maybe everything.

I haven't said a word to Charles about Richard. Of course I haven't. I haven't heard from him either, not for weeks. You don't think he's guessed, do you? I don't want to let him down, not when he's in the thick of things, not unless I really have to. He doesn't need to know, not yet. It can wait.

All my love,
Daisy

The next day was glorious, at least that was how they described it on the radio, a glorious August day.

The sun shone, even the cold stones of the house seemed to grow warm, and for once Claire saw the beauty of the place as soon as she pushed open the window in the morning and breathed in the garden's nectar-sweet air. Was this what Constable had been trying to capture in *The Hay Wain*? She could understand now why it might have mattered so much to him to get it right. The roses that clambered up the wall were in full flower, rioting in brash pinks and reds, their scent stronger than ever before. Below in the flower beds were late poppies, flagging already in the heat, their petals bruised by the exertions of just trying to survive.

They sat outside in the garden for breakfast, which was croissants, baguettes and strawberry jam, as if they were on holiday in France. It should have been delicious but it reminded Claire too much of the last time she had eaten croissants, in bed with Rob before leaving him to go to Dominic – then coming home to find Rob's note, the crumbs still scattered on the kitchen surfaces. She could not bring herself to drink any of the coffee made fresh in the cafetiere. It smelt too strong. She wondered how much Rob's parents knew. 'Nothing,' Rob had assured her. 'Nothing at all. I didn't come here when . . .' He didn't like to say it any more than Claire. *When I left. When I left you. When I thought I might not come back.*

'So where . . . ?' she asked.

'A hotel,' he said. 'It was lonely, just me and the TV. Room service. Warm white wine from the minibar.'

Might these absurdities one day become something they could laugh about, Claire wondered. No, she thought. Probably not. Probably none of it would ever bear laughing about, nor a second of it be forgotten, but perhaps that was how it should be. Perhaps it would remind them that what they still had left had been worth the struggle.

At breakfast, they talked about Daisy, because now that the four of them had something in common for the first time, no one wanted to let the bond go. They speculated about what might happen next until the coffee was cold and only the faintest trace of its aroma still hung in the air. Whether Daisy was going to stay with Richard. If so, what would happen to Charles. What the painting of Daisy was really like. Where it had gone. What Elizabeth had thought of it all. No one asked the question that Claire now asked herself whenever she took another envelope from the pile, which was why had the letters stopped. 'Can't we read the next letter?' Nick asked plaintively, and it was Rob who told him no, he would have to wait until September for that. At last, the speculations ground to a halt, and into the expectant silence Nick brought out the cardboard box, and Priscilla produced a pair of kitchen scissors to cut the tape away. Together they lifted out the writing desk, which had been at Edenside, at which Daisy herself might have sat once or twice, penning a thank you card or an invitation to a dinner, resting her delicate hands against its leather surface. Nick swung it open on its hinge, lifted up the writing slope and revealed all that was concealed beneath. Claire had not realised until then how easy it was to lay open a person's whole life.

Right at the top was the photograph of the two girls, both of them young, ready to be grown-up, with the same smile and sure eyes. Their hair was pinned carelessly up around their heads, and they were sitting outside at a wrought-iron table, with a couple of bikes lying in the background. They wore short-sleeved V-neck jumpers over cotton shirts, and their knee-length skirts looked too heavy and hot. They could almost have been twins, the same clothes, the same hair, but one of them was Daisy and one of them was Elizabeth, and Claire recognised Daisy by her ready smile and the way she looked straight and fearlessly into the camera. Behind them were the walls of a stone-built house, with ivy clawing its way up towards the roof, and Claire would have known, even if Nick had not recognised it, that the house was Edenside. Had Elizabeth been the one to write their names on the back, and then 'Edenside, 1937'? Had it been Charles, she wondered, who stood behind the camera and told them to smile as he pressed the shutter release, following through the view-finder their figures turned tiny and distant?

Next came a tightly folded piece of paper. Nick unfolded it and spread it out on the wooden outdoors table with its rough coat of lichen. Claire saw at once that it was a family tree, the kind that looked like it had been written hastily in the course of an afternoon, not carefully, in calligraphy on parchment paper and with the idea of it being passed down through the generations. Claire saw how Nick's finger was pulled naturally to his mother's name, with her date of birth, in 1920, written underneath, then his own name beneath it, his own date of birth in 1942, and next to him his brother Brian. There was a hyphen leading from the birth-dates of all three into a blank space that meant in Nick and Brian's case they were still alive, and in Elizabeth's that there had been no one to record her death. She caught Nick's eye when she saw that, and knew that he was thinking, like her, *We should fill that in later.* There was nothing either about Nick's marriage to Priscilla, still less any reference to Rob. That meant it must be decades since Elizabeth last took it up.

'Where's Daisy, Nick?' she asked. 'I can't see her name.' And then she followed the line of his finger as he moved it slowly, hesitantly, across the page. There she was, Daisy, although 'Marguerite Milton' was what she read, written in a clear hand. It hadn't occurred to Claire until then that Daisy was not her real name – stupid really, because it was short for Marguerite, of course, Daisy was often short for

Marguerite back then. The name made her sound more grown-up somehow.

Like Elizabeth, her dates too began in 1920.

Then ended, awfully, in the blackest, thickest of ink, in 1943: 8th November 1943.

Seeing it, even before she took it in, Claire's hand went instinctively to her mouth and she thought she might vomit. Rob had seen her move, and brought his hand just as instinctively to rest on her arm. She looked up at him gratefully.

'That's why the letters stop. Oh, God, that's why.' Claire spoke only what she had always known.

Rob kept his hand where it was. 'We always assumed, didn't we, that she couldn't still be alive?'

'But just twenty-three, Rob. I never expected to find her dead at twenty-three.'

Priscilla and Nick were looking at them oddly. But they didn't care about Daisy, not like she did. They couldn't be expected to. She was no more important to them than any other name on the family tree, in fact less important than some of them, like Elizabeth and Bill, whom Nick had loved, who were not just names or curiosities but his parents.

Now she herself found her finger drawn to Daisy's name, then to Elizabeth's, and then up through the sharp, firm lines on the page that meant marriages and children, more marriages, more children, towards their only family link, a shared great-grandparent.

She paused along the way only at Daisy's – Marguerite's – parents: Edmund and Alicia, old-fashioned names for people born in an age different even to the one their own children would live through. Alicia had died in 1935, when Daisy would have been just fifteen. Poor Daisy, thought Claire, another reason for poor Daisy, though she had known already, from the letters, that by 1942 it had been just her and her father.

'So what does it mean, Dad?' asked Rob. 'How were Daisy and Elizabeth related?'

'Well, looking at this I think it means they were second cousins, or is it first cousins once removed? I always get confused. Daisy's grandmother seems to have been the sister of Elizabeth's grandmother.'

'And how am I related to Daisy?'

'I've got absolutely no idea. I don't have a clue how to work it out. Cousins removed in some way, perhaps? What do you think, Priscilla? You're much better at working out that sort of thing than me.'

'I think it might be second cousin twice removed. The connection's rather distant. We can all see that.'

'Well, maybe not so distant as all that,' said Nick, with a careful look at Claire.

She took a deep breath and spoke a truth she had repressed from the very beginning. 'Don't worry, Nick. She isn't even related to me, not really, not even distantly. Related by marriage doesn't count, does it?'

'It makes me feel ashamed,' he said suddenly. 'It's seeing it all written down like that. To think of all these people in my own family. I never even knew their names, and now they're dead and gone.'

He was right. Claire could see it too, as she traced those same names now with her own finger. It wasn't just Daisy. There was everyone that came before her, and alongside, Elizabeth too, and all no more than dust. Daisy only meant more than the rest of them because of the letters. The letters had brought her back, but that was all that there was. There was no branch of the family tree stemming from Daisy, no children or grandchildren filling up the empty space. Just letters, just pages and writing and a life that ended too soon.

'My mother would have been pleased that you'd done all this, read the letters and seen the paintings. I know she would have liked to hear about it,' Nick said now.

I'm not so sure, thought Claire. *If it hadn't been for the letters, I would never have met . . .* She refused to let herself complete the sentence. She shook her head fiercely. Over now, though. It was all over now. At that very moment, Priscilla leant over and reached out her hand to Nick, saying, 'You did what you could. She didn't expect any more.'

He turned to her and said, 'I know. But I miss her.'

'Of course you miss her. You always will,' she replied. 'Now go on, and make some more coffee.'

There's no need to cry in front of the children, that was what she meant, and Claire saw at once that that was what he was about to do. He picked up the cafetiere and went inside and it was the first time in all those years of knowing them that Claire realised that there was still some love between them. She checked herself. Not just some love, but more than enough to get by on. That made them luckier than most; she understood that now.

As if they had all been caught out, they turned their attention back to the box. Rob took charge now, and started pulling out papers of all sorts, old receipts, faded cards and tickets, all of it meaningless to them. It was mostly the rubbish of decades, quietly building up for no better reason surely than that Elizabeth had not bothered to throw any of it away at the time. Over the years the things had slowly acquired a patina of significance that meant they must be kept. Amongst it all was a magazine, something called the *Burlington*, curling up at the corners and dulled by age. They set it aside, to be read properly when they had the time. Most interesting were the rest of the photographs, just a handful of them, which had never been pasted into albums or stuck into frames, but meant too much to discard. There were one or two poor, blurred snaps of Elizabeth and her little baby Nicky, and they all studied them dutifully. Then came ones of the whole family restored, Bill returned from the war and standing proudly upright with his arm around his wife, the baby in the picture now Brian, with Nick to one side holding on to his father's trouser leg.

As Rob and Nick pored over it all, Claire picked up that first photograph once more, and it was like holding a memory that was not her own. They had been friends, Daisy and Elizabeth, good friends. She could see it. All those holidays spent together, the shared fun, the long letters. They were the ones who had really had something in common, who had built up a history together. She and Daisy had none of that. Daisy had written her letters without the tiniest thought for Claire because Claire had simply not existed. It was Elizabeth who was real, and Richard, and Charles, and Molly and the other girls in the office. How would Daisy have reacted if someone had told her back then that one day someone would be reading her letters and seeing the same paintings she had seen and almost falling into bed with a beguiling stranger she had met somewhere along the way? Claire did not know. That was the point. She could not know. But she thought that Daisy might just have laughed.

Then there was only one piece of paper left in the mahogany writing box, which had survived so many more wars than just this one of Daisy and Richard.

'It's from Edmund. Who's he?'

'Daisy's father,' said Claire. 'Remember? Look, he's

there right above her on the family tree.' Would Elizabeth have guessed what had happened before she had even read it through, before she got beyond *My dear*? Rob was the one who read it aloud.

12th November 1943
My dear Elizabeth,

I have thought for a long time how best to begin this letter to you, because you are the hardest person to tell. I know you were very close to Daisy, and there is no easy way to say this. She is dead. My daughter is gone. Who would have thought it took so few words to say so much?

I want you to know what happened, so far as I know it myself. I think it will make it easier for you in the end, if not now, to have a sense of it. It makes it easier for me too. The more times I have to explain, the more practised I become. It will be difficult for you to believe, being so far away, but I have seen her body and felt her hand, and all the life in it was gone. It was a raid. Can you believe such a thing, after all these months without one? I think we had all begun to think the sirens would never sound again. How wrong we were. She was too far from a shelter. A bomb exploded and brought down a brick wall. It fell, not just on her, but others too. They were all trapped together. They say she died immediately. Perhaps they say that to all grieving parents. It is the worst of it, imagining her helpless, and her body giving way beneath the weight of all those bricks, knowing that she could not get out.

They identified her from her ration card. I still hoped there was a mistake and she might be alive, but all of the way to London it was only a dream that kept me moving. I was sent to a mortuary, to identify her body. I expected her to look just like she did when she was a little girl asleep in bed. I had forgotten she had grown up.

They cleaned her up because they knew I was coming. It was kind of them. There were others there, dead, not even covered up. Their faces were blank from plaster dust. Every one of them looked ancient. It was that dust that did it, drying them out like those wretches who died in Pompeii. She amongst all of them, my only daughter, my beautiful child, looked at peace, or so I told myself. There was no blood on her. She died from internal injuries, that was what they told me. She was wearing the scarf you gave her all those years ago, the one with the flowers on it. She always loved it.

I would have buried her next to her mother if it could have been arranged, but bodies cannot simply be moved around these days. There are too many regulations in the way. There isn't the time. The funeral is tomorrow, at the cemetery in Highgate. I do not expect many mourners. I hardly know who to tell. I have received kind notes from a girl called Molly at the office and the supervisor, Miss Johnson.

I do so hope they will come. The girl Molly asked if I had told Richard, as he was someone who should know. Do you know who she meant? She gave no surname and Daisy never mentioned a Richard to me. I have sent word to Charles. He will feel her loss, of course. I am sorry that circumstances mean you will not hear about any of this until it is long over. It does not matter for Daisy's sake. I know it, because I saw her body. She had gone. But visit her grave one day, if you can, and try to think over the old times.

We have become used to death these last years, more than is natural, but I did not think I would have to bury the only two women I ever loved, my Alicia and now my Daisy too. I should not have let her go to London. I should have kept her with me. These are the thoughts I have every day. But you know well enough what she was like. She could never be stopped once she was set on something. So perhaps all I mean is that it should not have happened this way. My poor, crushed young Daisy. I still reckoned myself almost young until the past week. Now I creak through each day, brought low by this awful grief. I got through my war twenty-five years ago. Dear God, why could my beloved Daisy not have got through hers?

But please Elizabeth, forgive these ramblings. I know you will have grief of your own to bear, without being burdened with mine. She did not leave

much behind her, poor child, some clothes and papers,
nothing more. I am packing anything that looks as if
it might matter to you into a parcel and hoping for
its safe arrival with this letter. It doesn't seem right
for me to read my child's secrets. I would be too old
to understand.

    Affectionately,
    Edmund

'Why didn't he send a telegram?' asked Claire, when
Rob finally got to the end of the letter. 'Elizabeth
should have been told straightaway.'

'He might not have wanted to spend the money,'
said Priscilla.

'Or perhaps he thought it didn't matter,' said Rob.
'Dead is dead after all. There's no changing it.'

Claire didn't respond. She was thinking about how
the slowness of a letter had given Daisy a few extra
weeks of life, just as the finding of the letters had
somehow given her these few extra months.

On the train back to London, they hardly spoke,
both of them exhausted by it all. Claire fell back
against the carpeted seat, feeling its roughness through
her hair, thinking how many flaking, balding heads
had rested there. Then Rob took her hand in his
and she leant her head against his shoulder as the
train rattled on.

'You'll come and see the Rembrandt painting

317

with me, won't you?' she said at last, looking up at him.

'Of course I will. You don't need to ask,' he replied.

She let herself lean against him once more and then was asleep. No dreams. No nightmares. Just sleep.

They saw the Rembrandt self-portrait the very next day, in the early evening when the gallery was virtually deserted. At first the visit felt awkward, like an early date, full of rushed talking followed by sudden silence. Side by side they passed through the gallery, their work shoes sounding sharp against the floors, knowing they did not have long before the place was shut for the night. But the Rembrandt self-portrait was easy to find in the Paintings 1600–1700 section.

Rembrandt did not seem to Claire to have been a handsome man, not at sixty-three in any event, with his bulbous nose and puffy features that had perhaps lost their sharpness with the years. The small triangle of beard on his chin seemed pathetic, the hands clasped before him too large and, just as Daisy had said in her letter, the whole painting was somehow mired in gloom. It seemed unkind for it to have been hung between two other, more beautiful Rembrandts, in Claire's eyes at least, one of a woman bathing in a stream, her undergarments held up around the tops of her thighs, and one of a woman weighed down with jewels and gold – both women beautiful and young, and, according to the captions, modelled on his mistress. Poor Daisy, she thought, who had hoped to sit for Richard over and over, but never got the chance.

Rob stood beside her, relaying information from the audio guide he had picked up at the entrance, which told her mostly what she already knew from Daisy's letter, but also that, quite apart from the loss of his mistress and son, Rembrandt had never recovered from being made bankrupt. As the years rolled by he had lost his home, his collection of prints and paintings, and his own artworks, along with his reputation. The few commissions he had still been given, no doubt only with misgivings, were received poorly and he had passed from acclaimed public figure to old man hidden in the shadows of a poor world, a world of bread and cheese, not meat and wine, and burnt umber sparingly spread. She wondered what all of that would have made him think of life. Was he thinking what little he had left, as he stared at himself hour after hour in the mirror, paintbrush in hand? Was he thinking of his dead son? Or was he still praying to cling on forever, with or without the money for paint, because however disappointing life might be, it was still at least an existence of sorts?

She was amazed that Rembrandt's eyes could still be so self-assured. No doubt he had wanted to live, because that was what almost everyone wanted really, to live forever. She wondered how she would feel, when she came to be that age, looking in a mirror at deepening lines and dry lips, clasping age-spotted hands in front of her. Would she still be searching for the shape of Oliver somewhere in the distance, knowing that it was not so long now as it once had been before she might feel his fingers tighten around her own? It would be better if Rob was there to join her reflection, to stroke her thinning hair and feel in it the memory of how it had once been and believe even that it was still the same. The thought made her see loneliness behind the defiance in Rembrandt's eyes.

Yet at least Rembrandt had managed to live on through his paintings, just as Daisy had hoped to live on through hers. At least people still knew who he was, not like the families trapped in those black-and-white family portraits that got passed down through the generations until no one could name even one of the solemn faces looking straight out into the camera. Faces in a photograph, dates on a family tree. She had seen it in all of their eyes when they shuffled through the contents of Elizabeth's life. It did not amount to much. Fame had held Rembrandt in people's minds and their galleries and bookshops. But might he have traded all of it for one more joyous family gathering, with no expense spared, one more happy memory of his own before he laid down his paintbrush and shut his eyes on the world? Daisy would have, surely. Daisy would have traded all of Claire's love, all of Claire's efforts, all of her own letters for a life with Richard. Claire did not blame her for a second.

Looking at the painting again, she realised that Rembrandt needn't have painted himself so wearied and wrinkled at all. It was in his own hands to make himself look strong and still ready to grapple with the world. But he had not bothered. It was an honest painting, she decided, showing the truth that everyone knew and never more than as they approached death, that it was nearly over and there was nowhere left to hide. Riches, jewels, none of it was going to make the slightest difference. Here was Rembrandt, revealed to himself alone, because no one else cared to look, and choosing to show himself as almost a broken man.

11

The Arnolfini Portrait –
Jan van Eyck

It was Rob who found Richard's painting, announcing it with so little fanfare that Claire didn't understand what he meant at first.

'Richard's painting of Daisy,' he said, reading the blankness in her face. 'It's in the Imperial War Museum. Not on display, but somewhere in their archives. That's what happened to the war art, that's what I found out. It mostly ended up there. They'll show it to us, Claire. I've made an appointment for us to see it on Saturday.'

Her heart was thumping. It was not over yet, all this with Daisy. There was still more to do, other reasons to keep going. 'How did you find it?' she said.

'I did some research. I called some places. It wasn't too difficult.' Hearing the excitement in his voice she realised that he, too, was now caught up in it all, this thing that was helping to hold them together, and she was grateful to him.

An excitement that felt too close to dread kept her awake long into the night, long enough in the end for her to give up the hopeless effort of sleep and slip quietly from the bedroom, to sit alone with empty hands in the living room – until she saw in the corner Rob's rucksack, thrown down on the floor after their return from Hertfordshire at the weekend. Neither of them had had the energy to do anything about it, so wearied was Claire, at least, with the emotion of it all. Inside, she knew, was the magazine that Nick had pressed on them as they left the house, and something told her that now, without interruption and in a night as silent as Daisy would have prayed every night could be, was the time to read it.

She flicked through the pages idly, as Elizabeth or Daisy herself might have done once, although then those same pages would not have been quite so yellow, nor would they have left the musty smell of old newspapers behind on the reader's fingers. Her eyes scanned advertisements for uniforms and gas-mask covers alongside ones for toothpaste and lemonade; and classifieds placed by women in the country wanting staff, alongside calls from vicars for donations of clothes for the bombed-out needy. A full half page was dedicated to berating housewives who encouraged a mysterious creature called the squanderbug, which would attack at the first sign of throwing out a skirt rather than mending it. It was a mixed up world they lived in then, she thought, yawning; an awfully wearisome world.

It was the advert halfway through, for artists' supplies, that caught her eye first, with its sketch of a palette and paintbrush, evidence that there were some supplies of that sort left, even four years into war. Only then did she see the article beside it. It was called 'Love and Life in Times of War: Observations from the Rooms of the National Gallery', and it was written by one Richard Dacre. She sat up straight, scarcely able to believe it, then understanding that this, of course, was why Elizabeth had kept the magazine so carefully, surely after it was sent to her by Edmund with the rest of Daisy's papers.

She read it slowly, this study of the very paintings that she and Daisy had seen, Dominic and Rob too, formal sentences that she imagined would not have come easily to a man more used to holding a brush in his hands than beating out words on a typewriter. He wrote of techniques and styles, painting media and pigments, but he wrote also of the artists and their subjects. In these words, Claire read something more, that he understood that these pictures were telling a story, one bigger even than themselves, which was that all of art was about life, and much of it about love. It was a lesson they had all learnt, her and Rob, and Daisy too.

Suddenly she did not want to be alone, and she

crept back to the bedroom, holding the magazine, listening at the door to the rise and fall of her husband's breathing and knowing she would wake him.

'What is it, Claire? What time is it?'

'Late,' she said. 'But you'll want to see this.'

The postcard fell out as she thrust the magazine into his hands, landing on the duvet between them, picture side up to reveal a painting that she recognised at once despite its faded colours. It was Jan van Eyck's *Arnolfini Portrait*, and it showed a man and his wife standing before the artist, the woman's hand resting open-palmed across the man's. The man held his other hand up in greeting, the woman rested hers atop her stomach. Both were dressed richly in fur-trimmed robes, the woman in bright colours, green and blue, that showed up her beauty peacock-like against her husband's drab cape and dark hat. They were set against a backdrop that said wealth in every elaborate detail. There was blown glass in the windows, imported oranges scattered around the window sill as if it did not matter if one rolled away. There was a burnished chandelier and a scrubby, hairy lapdog that was clearly intended only as a pet, not a guard. To one side was a four-poster bed, made with red coverlets and draped with red curtains. It was a painting of a wedding, Claire remembered learning that much in school, of a merchant and his already pregnant wife, held still by van Eyck together in stiff gesture and uncertain love. A mirror on the far wall reflected it all, and it was as if that reflection was carrying this distant, long-gone couple even further away.

The postcard lay there between them, neither of them moving at first. It was Rob who picked it up and turned it over, with Claire by now held in his arms and only the dull gleam of the lamp on the bedside table to read it by.

My darling Daisy Milton,

    I've written to Sir Kenneth Clark to ask if the National Gallery will display the Arnolfini Marriage. It's one of theirs. If he says yes, I'll take you there and kiss you right in front of it.

    While we're waiting for that, will you marry me? 8th November at the Chelsea registry office. That's this Monday. It's all arranged. You just need to be there. Wear flowers in your hair.

    With all my love for ever more

    Richard

The 8th November 1943. The same day that had been written so firmly on Elizabeth's family tree. The last day of all for their irrepressible yet fragile Daisy. There seemed so very little left to say, yet they both began to speak.

'Do you think . . .'

'I wonder if . . .'

'Before?'

'After?'

Utterly unable to complete any sentence worth saying, because there were no answers and Claire feared only what she did not want to hear. That Daisy never made it to the registry office. That she died alone. That she was on the way to buy her flowers or waiting for the bus to get to Chelsea. That she never got to hear Richard's voice say *I, Richard, take thee Marguerite, to be my wedded wife,* or whatever the words would have been then. Yet still she would have had proof, if she needed it, that he had loved her, that he had meant all the things he had ever told her, and that he wanted them to be together for all of time. *With all my love for ever more.* There was a future in those words, a whole lifetime laid out, without fear, with honesty. Did anything matter but that?

On Saturday, Claire put the photographs of Daisy, the one of her with Richard, and the one of her younger self with Elizabeth, in a bag to take with them. 'So we can see how good a likeness it was,' she explained. Rob took his camera, to take a picture that they could frame.

They took the underground to Lambeth North, a part of London they would not normally go to, and followed the unpromising span of Kennington Road from the tube station. It was crawling with traffic and, like so many London streets, lined with a mix of discount food and wine stores and betting shops interspersed with the occasional freshly painted shop struggling to make the place up and coming, not down and out. Claire was tired, and knew Rob must have been, too, as if the dust of the street was being whipped into her eyes, even though there was no breeze at all. She could still picture the form of Richard's article, printed and published in narrow, long columns, in bold font, words broken across the end of lines, and there for anyone to see; and his postcard, simply worded, meant to be read by Daisy alone.

They walked quickly, eager to get to the museum, overtaking families trailing children who were already crying and couples wanting to fill time before lunch at some gastro-pub or other. Rounding the corner into Lambeth Road, the Imperial War Museum lay in front of them, set in a park named after someone who Claire had never heard of and must have been forgotten long ago. At the main entrance was a pair of vast guns, with a smattering of visitors posing in front of them. Claire veered away, but Rob went up close, drawn towards them with all the other men. She waited for him inside, sitting on a grey metal seat that creaked when she leant back, her feet flat against a tile floor that reminded her of hospitals. She didn't bother looking at any of the other exhibits. She only wanted to see the painting. She was more than happy to leave the rest of it behind. She knew what there would be without even having to look. Ration books, gas masks, propaganda posters, long lists of the dead, letters written by children struggling to hold pencils to fathers who did not write back, then never came home. All those endless stories. Just one was enough for her. Daisy and Richard's.

A curator came down to meet them at the information desk. 'We've been expecting you,' she said. 'Was the subject a relative of yours?'

The question was addressed to Claire. She hesitated, then knew she had to say, *No, she isn't. She's nothing to do with me.* 'No,' she said. 'She's not from my side of the family. She was actually a distant cousin of my husband's.' Husband. When was it that she had last said that word out loud? A word that said, *I do. I do still have some right to him. We have a right to each other.* She smiled, and when she looked at Rob she saw that he was smiling too.

'That's right,' said Rob. 'I think we worked out that she was my second cousin twice removed.'

'Right, well, come this way. She's down in our oil painting section.'

They followed the woman through the hidden maze of the museum, behind the public areas, along grey carpet through grey corridors past grey cabinets, then into the print room where watercolours and charcoals were kept in drawers that gave off the rich scent of wood and polish. Then even further into the depths of the place, emerging into a vast storage area so bright with swinging ceiling lights that at first Claire did not see the paintings retreating into the shadows. Then, when she did see them, she realised that they were hundreds in number, thousands maybe, mounted alongside each other in gold frames hung upon heavy metal grids that could be pulled out on runners.

'Right,' said the curator. 'Now, it was Dacre, wasn't it? They're stored alphabetically. Here it is. D for Dacre.'

She stepped into the gloom and pulled out one of the metal grids, which screamed out on its rollers into the sharp light.

Suddenly there was Daisy, more suddenly than Claire had expected, revealed as she had been once before by the throwing aside of a white dust sheet. Her laughing smile was instantly recognisable, and painted even bolder than it appeared in the photographs. Claire did not even have to get them out of her bag to see how like her the painting was. It was the first time that she had seen Daisy in colour, not simply imagined her that way, and as if to make the effect all the more striking Richard had painted everything about her, not just her smile, more brightly than could possibly have been real. Her eyes sparkled blue, and the same colour was picked up in the scarf around her neck, the scarf that Elizabeth had given her. Her cheeks were rouge-red, and that colour too was picked up, in a red note-book lying on the desk in front of her. The type-writer itself took up much of the foreground. It looked heavy and unwieldy. It would have been hard work, beating against its keys all day, but Richard had painted Daisy's hands delicately, as if they were better suited for passing round teacups and plates of sandwiches. Well, that was the life Daisy had expected would be hers, wasn't it, at least before the war, before the job, before London, before her life had really begun? Richard had always liked her hands, Daisy had said so. It was the very first thing that he had noticed about her, as he passed her the glove that she had dropped.

Here we are, Daisy, she said to herself, *here at last. Is that love in your eyes? What have you got to tell us, with your sharpened pencils and withered pot plant?* And then, looking again, she saw that the plant was not withered. It was green and vibrant, heavy with buds, not dying at all. And the bomb site outside the window wasn't barren and grey. Richard had painted the flowers that grew there after all, rampaging across the fallen bricks.

'Look, Rob,' she said. 'He changed the painting. Why did he do that? It's not how Daisy described it.'

'I've no idea,' he said, and, turning to the curator,

'Do you? The description we have of the painting is different.'

'It's probably just one of those things. It does happen, with artists. Often they aren't quite happy with the end result and can't stop themselves making little adjustments. Perhaps that was the reason why he changed it. It's quite common.'

Claire, whilst knowing she was right, was unsatisfied and asked too brusquely, 'Was the painting ever exhibited?'

The curator turned to her. 'As a matter of fact, I looked that up for you and it was. There was a rolling exhibition of war art at the National Gallery, and it was selected for that. I can't find any record of it being put on display again, though. Some of these sorts of paintings were exhibited around the country or shipped over to America to publicise the war effort, but there was nothing to suggest this particular painting did the rounds.'

'Why on earth not?' asked Claire, feeling the stab of affront at the same time as Rob's warning arm around her.

The curator replied nervously. 'Well, I suppose they didn't think it was quite up to the standard of some of the rest. It was a competitive business. Only the very best paintings went on tour. The Henry Moores, the Stanley Spencers, that sort of thing. You see, there were an awful lot of these artists and this particular one, this Richard . . .'

'Dacre,' said Claire shortly.

'Yes, that's it. Dacre. He wasn't particularly well known at the time, I'm afraid. He wasn't one of those artists that people were already talking about as the next big thing.' She must have seen the look on Claire's face because now she was trying to recover the situation. 'Of course, he was very young when he painted this. He hadn't had a lot of time to establish a reputation. He might have ended up quite famous, but who knows?'

'What do you mean, who knows?'

'Well, he died in 1943.'

'*What?*' Now Claire's voice rang only with shock.

'Oh, I'm sorry. I thought you knew. Perhaps I should have said before. I did some research about him when I knew you were coming, and yes, he died during the war, in a raid, I think. Rather sad, of course, because one of the reasons for the war artists' scheme was actually to keep painters safe, out of the firing line as it were, not that anyone could admit it, of course. Naturally, though, some of them didn't make it.' She sighed. 'So dreadful, isn't it, thinking of all that waste? They saw a lot more of death then than we do now, of course, not that it makes it any better.'

Richard dead too, that was all Claire really heard. Like Daisy, in 1943, and surely not just like Daisy, but with Daisy? She felt a sickness well up inside her and turned to Rob. She didn't need to say a thing.

'My wife,' he said to the curator. 'Can we have a chair for my wife?'

But there was no chair, only rolls of polythene sheeting and bubble wrap and a stepladder propped against the wall. In the end, the curator and Rob helped her over to a wooden trolley that must normally have been used to move the paintings around, and she felt an impossible sense of relief as she slumped down on to it. While Rob took photographs from every angle, she looked again at the painting. Not good enough to put on display outside London during the war, and not good enough for the Imperial War Museum to put on display now. It had been dismissed, packaged up and put away with countless others, marked out only by an entry in an index, with no one to want it or even to look at it until now. Poor Daisy, who had hoped for so much from it and thought it would survive forever – and it had, so far at least, but only in the dark and the dust.

It was not Richard's fault, she did not think he was entirely to blame. Part of the problem was the subject matter, she could see that when she really took it in. It showed no more than a typist at work. It was not the stuff of great art, not like some of the other paintings she had seen of the time that showed men and women at work in shipyards and hospitals, fighting against a backdrop of sparks or oil or blood, or fighter planes trailing smoke through the air in their hunt for prey. No, this was simply a record of the routine and boredom of war. It showed none of its drama. She realised now that Richard had not chosen to paint a masterpiece. He had chosen to paint Daisy. This was where his love could be seen. So there was no poor Daisy, after all. She had been lucky with Richard.

They were home early enough for Claire to go out again, to the library, determined to establish that Richard was mentioned in some volume, that someone had thought it worth writing down his name; she was not foolish enough to think that the art encyclopaedia that Rob had given her would contain a Dacre, R. sandwiched in between Cranach and Degas. Rob went with her. She sat him down amongst the old men and their newspapers while she visited the Art and Design section. A book about British artists, that was what she needed. She pulled one out and scanned the index. There was nothing. No mention at all. She ran her finger along the shelves, slowly, not wanting to miss it, the book she did not know existed but needed to find. Surely there must be a line or two somewhere. Surely he and Daisy deserved that much. Then she found it, a book on British artists of the Second World War.

Yes, he was listed in the index.

Page 186. Only the one reference, but a reference

all the same. She turned back through the pages slowly, wondering how often this book had been opened – rarely, no doubt, and how often anyone had then reached page 186 – possibly never.

There he was.

Dacre, Richard.
Born 1915. An artist employed by the War
Artists' Advisory Committee, Dacre's work was
exhibited alongside that of other artists at the
National Gallery. He was part of the small
Chelsea Group about which little is now
known. Much of his body of work is thought
to have been lost during the Second World War.

No photograph. No print. None of his paintings named.

A footnote. Nothing important was ever in a footnote.

Footnote 32, at the bottom of the page, squashed in tiny print amongst all the others, telling only the most conscientious of readers that a handful of war artists had died in the course of the Second World War, and Richard Dacre was among them.

True, it was all true, as true as she had always known it must be. Richard and Daisy, fallen in love, married or not, and both gone, their lives turned into history long before Claire had even been born. Library regulations were not enough to prevent

Claire from crying out Rob's name, nor to stop him running to find her amongst the shelves, the book fallen from her hands.

12

The Painter's Daughters Chasing a Butterfly – Gainsborough

Claire kept the knowledge of her baby a secret from everyone and almost – not quite – from herself for weeks. The headaches and the exhaustion could be explained away easily enough at first. Daisy was dead, her life cut short before the happy ever after of her and Richard had begun. It was as hard to accept for Claire, looking back through the years, as Elizabeth must have found it, discovering the news only too late and from a distance. Then there was Rob, and the joy mingled with the effort of what felt like the beginning of a new relationship altogether. She had more reason than most to be tired. But the period that began as late was, she now knew, missed, and so was the next. She found herself ranging through the shelves of the local chemist's, cash in one hand, the newspaper in the other, hoping that no one she knew would come in between her picking up the cellophane-wrapped white-and-blue box of the pregnancy test, taking it to the till, paying for it and pushing it deep down inside her bag.

She did the test at home, on her own, knowing what she wanted to see, knowing too that there was no real need to do a test at all. The faint blue cross became bright and sharp as the seconds ticked by and then stayed there, fixed, sending a thrill surging through her like the one she had felt before, the first time, when they had both been imagining her pregnant for weeks. That time, Rob had been there, waiting for her. This time, he was not, and she had no idea what he would say when she told him the news.

She decided to start the telling with Daisy, to take her secret with her to the National Gallery and whisper it through the dust motes and into the silence. It was time for the next letter anyway. She picked it up from the top of the heap. There could only be one more after this one, her October letter, before Daisy's pen fell from her hand. The act of going through the remaining letters now felt like counting down to the end, even though it didn't really make sense, because Daisy had always been dead, from the very beginning. Claire just hadn't known it. It shouldn't make a difference. She was determined it wouldn't.

September, 1943

Dear Elizabeth,

Let me take a deep breath and begin.

I'll start with the painting. You'll soon know the rest. It is by Gainsborough and shows his own daughters, his two little girls, Mary and Margaret. It's a wonderful thing, don't you think, for an artist to paint his children? It seems more meaningful than just painting a wife or mistress, which is what all artists do. I like to think that this picture has a father's love in every brushstroke. It's a special thing, I'm sure, the love between a parent and a child. You must know. You've got Nicky. I don't understand it, not yet, but I expect it's the sort of thing anyhow that one can't understand until it happens — until there's a baby right there, warm and wriggling, that only wants to be held and kept safe. Mother was always wanting to paint me when I was tiny. I'm not sure I ever let her. I thought it was all a game. I remember running off once and hiding behind the curtains in the drawing room, and turning round to see her brandishing her paintbrush at me and laughing. I didn't realise then what it would have meant to her, to paint pictures of her baby growing up. And I lost something, too — the chance to hold one of her paintings in my hands and know it was created out of love.

Richard told me that Gainsborough painted several portraits of his girls, and they always show both of them together. In this particular one, they are running along a garden path, hand in hand. Margaret is the younger one and she is stretching out to grasp a white butterfly with black-spotted wing tips that has settled on the top of a thistle. Mary is holding her back – how nice of her to look after her little sister like that! It seems most improbable, given the way siblings usually treat one another. I expect in real life Margaret would have been seething inside at all those 'Don'ts' and 'I'll tell Mummy' that older sisters seem to go in for. I don't believe Margaret would ever have caught that butterfly anyway. It would have flown off before she got any closer, like most things one wants – always just out of grasp, leaving her with nothing more than a pricked finger and tears for her father to wipe away with a paint-stained handkerchief.

Shall I just write the words now, Elizabeth, so there's no need for you to guess?

I'm having a baby.

There is no easy way of saying it, is there, particularly when one is unmarried? All I've got is Charles' engagement ring, which is worse than nothing at all. Besides, I stopped wearing it after Weymouth. I wouldn't have felt right with it always there on my finger, sparkling in the sunlight. You are the only one who knows for now. Do not say a word to anyone, swear to me, not while I'm waiting to see whether my life is going to crumble apart.

*I haven't told Richard yet, because I'm scared stiff
of what he might say, or, more to the point, what he
might not. What if he doesn't at least say that it's a
surprise, but we'll make the best of it, we'll get
married and we'll be happy? What if there is just
silence and sadness and both of us walking away from
each other? What if he forgets that he told me he
loved me? Don't think I'm going to get rid of it,
either. The girls at work talk about that kind of thing,
how it can all be sorted out and no one need ever
know. Well, that way is not for me. I'm in love with
Richard. How could I ever harm his child? How could
I ever harm my child? It's growing inside me. It's
already a baby. It needs me.*

*Do you know what I thought to myself when I
found out? If Richard doesn't want me, I suppose
there's still Charles. There'll always be Charles. I can
marry him when he's next home, he'll agree to call the
child his own and no one will be any the wiser. It's
not unknown, after all. Well, I was a fool to think
such a thing. Yesterday a letter came through from him
at long last. He's met someone else, a girl working out
there just behind the front line – a girl who really is
helping win the war and who really wants to be
Charles' wife. He was very nice about it. He always
was very nice. He said that he was very sorry to upset
me, but he was certain I would understand that it was
what he wanted – and besides, we both knew that I
wasn't ready for marriage yet. He ended by saying*

that he'd always remember the good times, and I must try and do the same. No hard feelings.

So that explains why he never did send me the stockings he promised he would, or anything else come to that. I wish I could laugh about it, but I simply can't. They are to be married as soon as he can arrange the permits, that's what he says. It'll all be over bar the honeymoon by the time you get this letter. What is there for me to do but write back and wish him all the best? The more I read his letter, the more it hurts. It wasn't even a page long, and he must have known exactly what he was going to say before he began. There were no crossings out, just very firm words, line after line of them, adding up to a curious mixture of apology, regret and (quite the worst bit of all, but I suppose he couldn't help it) excitement. It could only be worse if I were still in love with him, or thinking I was. Well, those feelings I had for him before, whatever they were, went away a long time ago and just look at how I've been behaving myself. I can't exactly blame him for any of it.

So it is going to be me and Richard, or me alone, and just think of the fuss if it's just me. I don't expect Daddy would ever speak to me again. He simply would not understand. He still thinks I'm his little girl, chasing after hopeless dreams when all he wants is for me to settle down. Poor Papa. I won't tell him a thing, not until I absolutely have to. If only I still had Mother. She would know what to do. She always knew what to do. Forgive me, Elizabeth. Just thinking about her is making me cry, or maybe the baby's to blame for that, too. I cry over everything these days, every hopeless tragedy of our miserable existence, every boy knocked down in the blackout or unwanted baby left in a wooden box outside a hospital without even a note to say what it's called. Well, I want my baby and that's the only thing I'm sure of. I am going to hold her in my arms and love her forever. Do you remember when I told you about The Mystic Nativity? *All that rubbish I spouted about the unfairness of Jesus being the centre of attention and where did that leave Mary and Joseph? You must have laughed and laughed. But I know better now. I can see that I was wrong about all that, and do you know why? Because my baby will deserve nothing less than total adoration from me and everyone else. My baby will be beautiful and clever and perfect in every way – just like your Nicky! Look at Botticelli – even he understood how it was. It's just taken me a little longer than you to work it all through. It's like a secret that no one told me – or if they did tell me I was utterly deaf to it. But no more. I'm changing, my mind as well as my body.*

If you saw me, you wouldn't know there was anything there. It's only been two months – since Weymouth, of course. I might be starting to lose my waist, but not enough for anyone to notice but me. Miss Johnson keeps telling me off, though, because I'm so distracted, and feeling awfully sick as well. She might just be an old spinster, but she's nobody's fool. She knows there's something wrong, and with us girls she can be sure it's going to be man trouble of one kind or another.

I can't help picturing the baby inside me, what little there is to her yet. I imagine taking her to Weymouth with Richard, wheeling the perambulator along a seafront that is just sand, not barbed wire, and turning to him and saying, 'To think that this is where . . .' I am praying hard that the war is over before she arrives. I don't want my child born to the sound of an air raid siren. I want Richard to paint her, not straightaway when she is still wrinkled up like a dried apple, but once she has begun to walk and he can call her into his arms. That would be a good time.

What do you mean, it might be a boy, why do I keep saying 'she'? Well, the fact of the matter is that I've got girls on the mind after seeing the painting of Gainsborough's daughters. A girl is what it will be. I know it.

I'm more glad than you will ever know that I saw this month's painting, Elizabeth. It's made me think about what this means, about the tiny thing that is starting to grow inside me and is going to become a little child running along a woodland path

*after a butterfly – then who knows what after that.
It has made the whole thing seem more real, for
what that's worth. When I think about that picture, I
can almost believe that there may be a future for the
two of us at least, even if not for us three. What do
you think? Well, what can you know being so far
away? Just say whatever I want you to say. You'll
know what that is. That's all I ask.*

*By the time I write next, I'll have told Richard,
if I can find the courage.*

All love,

Daisy

The shock of it meant that at first Claire hardly saw
the painting she had come to see, even though it
was right there in front of her. She held Daisy's letter
tightly in her hand. Daisy, too, having a baby. Daisy,
too, thinking of that new life to come. Daisy, too,
feeling something, not quite joy, and already caught
up in the difficulties and uncertainties of it all. Then
came the realisation, catching in her throat, that it
wasn't just Daisy who had died. Her baby had died
with her, its barely formed heart slowing together
with Daisy's beneath the weight of that falling wall.
Claire had been imagining that Daisy's last thoughts
would be for Richard or the father she was leaving
behind, or the mother she might soon see again.
Now she was sure that they would have been for
her unborn child. When the assistant in the mortuary

wiped her face clear of dust, what would he have seen on her face? Acceptance, panic or simple grief? Would he have guessed what lay behind it, what secret she had concealed? No. Her father had said in his letter that there had been no blood. There would have been no post mortem because there was no point. It was clear enough how she had died.

As for Richard, had she been able to tell him? If so, what had he said? She would not have had long to break the news. She could imagine Daisy, curled up on her bed, writing paper in hand, crying or close to it, not knowing what to do, while all the time Richard was somewhere else, putting the last touches to a painting that would be named after her, or maybe buying a postcard and thinking of just the right words to write down on it. If only she had known, how much anguish she would have saved herself. If only she could simply have ended things happy, without the slightest anxiety traced out across her brow. That was all Claire wanted for Daisy now. Perhaps it had been that way. This was the September letter after all. The article and the proposal had come after. But that had been November, right before the end of it all. What if, in the meantime, there had been nothing for Daisy but uncertainty and tears?

The thought of it made her want to tell Rob her own news straightaway, so someone would know, and know now, that she was being given another chance at motherhood.

First though, there was the painting, now that she was there. She put Daisy's letter in her bag and made an effort to concentrate. A group of school-children, no older than seven or eight, were clattering through the room, filling it with their shrill noise and unceasing movement. Once she might have been annoyed. Now, all she thought was, *One day my child will be here, following after a teacher and hoping it's nearly time for lunch and wondering what I put in her sandwiches. It will be a girl, of course, just like Daisy's would have been, and prettier even than Gainsborough's daughters.* There they were, chasing their butterfly just as Daisy had described, full of hope and optimism, reminding Claire of how she and Laura had once been, when their father had still been there to push them on their bikes and buy them ice creams in the park. How quickly it had all passed. Gainsborough's Margaret was surely no more than four, dressed in pale blue, her apron blown to one side by her haste. Mary looked around seven or eight years old, and was in yellow with the lap of the apron tied around her waist tossed over her shoulder. Both dresses were of the kind that only flower girls at a wedding would wear now. Both girls had brown hair, tied up around their heads, and pink flushed cheeks in pale faces. That would have been enough to show them as sisters, even if their eyes had not been the same. The edges of the background were unfinished, as if Gainsborough had realised that the only thing that mattered in the painting was his girls. They held hands as if they really loved each other, as perhaps they had. *One day*, she thought, *soon enough I will have children just like that, not one but two, maybe even more.* Her heart soared butterfly-high at the thought.

'I'm having a baby,' she said quickly, as soon as Rob opened the front door and came in from work. Last time, she had said we, not I. She had lingered over the words, not pushed them out. She had known how he would respond.

Silence. His face inscrutable.

'It's what I want,' she said, and just forming the words made her realise how true that was, and the longing was urgent inside her.

Silence.

But then, slowly, something that she knew was going to be a smile appeared and she did not risk it fading. Instead, she threw herself into Rob's arms and said, 'Thank you. Thank you for being pleased.'

He wrapped his own arms around her and said, 'Of course I'm pleased. Why on earth would you think I might not have been?'

Because of what happened to Oliver.

Because of what happened to me.

Because of the way I treated you.

Because of Dominic.

Because I don't deserve any of this.

She said none of these things, because Rob was preventing her with a kiss.

Later, much later, he told her to go and take a look at the kitchen table. She thought there might be flowers but instead there was just a brown envelope bearing Rob's name. 'What is it?' she called out to him. She heard him come to stand in the door frame.

'It's some records I sent off for. I got in touch with the General Record Office and they ran a search for Daisy's name. They said they would be sending something through. I thought you might be curious.'

She remembered how desperately she had wanted to lay bare the contents of Elizabeth's writing desk. Now she hesitated, thinking about Daisy and the darkness, the weight, the thick dust slowly clogging her lungs. How easy it was for people to die, to be alive one minute and to be utterly gone the next. And not just people – but Daisy, who Richard had somehow painted more alive than life itself.

'Shall we open it now?' she said.

She knew what she wanted him to say, and he did. 'No, let's wait. Just until we've read the last letter.' A little more time, then, before she would have to say goodbye. Some time, but not much, not enough. There would never be enough time with Daisy, there never could have been. Hers was a life that was gone. The thought saddened Claire, desperately, but it didn't hurt her as much as it would have before, this new before – before she knew that another life was just beginning, not only her baby's but also, somehow, her own.

13

The Entombment – Bouts

October, 1943
Dear Elizabeth,

  *I was awfully glad to hear from you. Your letter
reached me so quickly I can almost believe it when
the papers say that the war is really going our way.
It is good of you to say that I can come to you but
we both know that wouldn't work, even if I could
get a crossing. You have Bill and Nicky to think
about first and foremost, and it wouldn't be easy to
explain me away.*

  *This month's painting is a wretched one, I'm
afraid, but that's how it should be, because I feel
pretty wretched myself. I didn't think anything could
make me as dog-tired as I am at the moment. It's
an uphill struggle from the moment I get out of bed
in the morning until I drag myself home at the end
of the day. I expect it's good preparation for
motherhood. And the sickness! Well, you know all
about that. Molly says it will pass. I told her, just*

her. Not that there was much to tell, because she'd
already guessed from the way I'd been acting. She
asked me straight out and I didn't want to lie.

I must admit I did rather put off seeing the
painting, but in the end I told myself firmly that I
had to keep my chin up and get on with it. There'll
be time enough for sitting at home moping when the
baby comes. So, here we go. It is called The
Entombment, and the artist is Dieric Bouts. Have
you heard of him? I hadn't, though he sounds
Dutch. It shows the body of Jesus being lowered into
a stone tomb by two men, who they think are Joseph
of Arimathea and Nicodemus, basically a couple of
Jesus' hangers-on, helped by the Virgin Mary and
Mary Magdalene – who incidentally is looking a lot
more wretched than she was in Noli me tangere.
There are various other people in the background, all
looking stricken. It's hardly the best painting to
herald our entry into yet another year of war, is it?
But it almost doesn't seem to matter. You see, I've
come to believe that my life has always been the way
it is now, and all the memories, good and bad, that I
have from before are dreams and not real at all – the
memories where we were never afraid or alone, and
no one ever died except the person who mattered to
me most of all. Still, I am hardly the only one to
have grieved these past few years. Who hasn't?

If it weren't all bad enough, the picture itself is in
dreadful condition. Even I can see that. It was

painted on linen, you see, not wood, so it is terribly delicate. Also this Bouts didn't use oil paints. I'm not sure what he did use, but whatever it was, it hasn't lasted. Over the centuries (five of them altogether) the colours have either faded or picked up the dirt. Mary Magdalene's robe looks as though it is stained right through and it can't always have been like that.

Right at the top there is a tiny strip of sky which has kept its original colour – more or less – because it was protected by a frame for a time, but the rest of it has a pale, green-brown tinge that makes Jesus look even more dead than he actually is, if that's humanly possible. I'm quite sure that his face didn't look so awfully grey when it was new.

When I told Richard what I thought about it, he said that of course the colours would have been better once, and the cloth backing cleaner. It's age that's done it. It was a masterpiece once, he says, so why not still? None of his explanations made me feel any better about it, though. What I see is what I see. It doesn't matter to me that someone five hundred years ago saw it looking completely different. It's now that matters. So far as I'm concerned, it's a poor choice for the painting of the month. It's not that the figures aren't perfectly executed, and the background, too. But who could possibly think much of a picture like that, living as we all do these days? I gave it a good hard stare, and all I saw was a dying painting of a dead man.

There have been enough dead in this war without having a corpse on public display.

For me, looking at this awful Jesus, all I could think about were those thousands of men and women being lowered into their graves, utterly cold, utterly dead, never knowing who was there to send them on their way with that final human touch. And the children, too, dear God, the children, just tiny babies, some of them, gone before they even learnt to smile but their graves dug as deep as their parents'. Not just here but in Germany too, and France, and Poland, Italy, Burma, Japan and all those other countless places. It seems quite endless. Perhaps that makes it not such a bad choice of painting after all. It's certainly honest. At least dead is dead. That's the end of it so far as I'm concerned. The ones who really suffer are those who are left behind, when the last they see of their loved one is the body where the person used to be. Better never to see them again, that's what I believe. Better to receive the telegram and imagine a wooden cross than to be confronted by blood or mangled limbs or the simple truth of death.

I used to keep a list of everyone I was acquainted with, however slightly, who had been injured or killed. Not for long, though. There was something dreadfully macabre about it — and anyway the list was getting too long. There was no one I really knew, it was all just friends of friends, the brother of someone I was at school with, the

fiancé of someone at the office, that sort of thing.
Some might say that makes me lucky, but that
didn't make me like that damned list any better. It
gave me the feeling that Death was circling around
the peripheries of my life and just desperate to start
creeping steadily closer if I gave it the chance. I
chucked the piece of paper in a fire in the end, and
watched all those names being burnt to nothingness
and forgotten all over again.

I'm afraid there have been raids over London this
last week or so, which means more names than usual
on the casualty lists. We're all fed up about it. The
shelters are packed every night and the Anderson in
the garden is flooded out, so this time around I have
decided to stick it out in my own bed, dreaming of
the sirens even when I'm not listening to them. A
bomb went off down the road from the office last
night, a heavy one. I had to walk through the rubble
on my way to work. Picture me, Elizabeth,
tap-tapping neatly along in my nice clean clothes,
trying not to trip over the firemen's hoses, with the
men still trying to pull people out and telling me to
move on, everyone absolutely filthy and choking from
a night of smoke and plaster dust. The best thing is
not to breathe in too much, and ignore the smell of
burning, I learnt that the last time round. And don't
think about what might be underneath all those
smouldering bricks. That's the absolute most important
thing.

*Can you imagine being buried alive? There can't
be much worse than that. I hate the very thought of
it. In fact I try desperately not to have thoughts like
that at all, but they edge their way in, trying to take
me by surprise. It's yet another reason not to like*
The Entombment, *I'm afraid. Seeing that body
being lowered into its rough, grey tomb was enough
to make me shudder. Think how dark and airless it
would be once the stone lid was slammed down into
place. Not that any of it would have bothered Jesus.
He was getting out in a few days, after all. But it
certainly does bother me.*

*Now don't go worrying. You'll be wasting your
time. We're used to this sort of thing. I know how to
look after myself, and anyway I have Richard and
the baby, too. As long as he is with me, which is
most of the time, I'm not afraid — and even when
we're apart, there's still that part of him always there
to keep me company. Richard and I sit up together
in the small hours and watch the spinning white of
the searchlights through the window, and listen out
for the thud of the next bomb falling. We tell each
other stories about how things used to be; only
enough to start us laughing. We stop if either of us
looks like crying. When he falls asleep, I like to tell
him about the baby. I whisper it in his ear, in case
he might still be able to hear.*

*I want him to sleep as much as possible. He needs
to rest while he can, because he has just heard he is*

being sent abroad, to catch up with the front and send drawings back of our boys advancing. He doesn't have a choice, but even if he did, I know he would go. He wants to feel part of it, and I don't blame him. They all do, the men. Richard is no different from Charles in that way. I don't want him in danger, of course I don't, with me left here on my own, growing steadily larger and larger, always waiting to hear something, good or bad. We have a week or so left together. That's it. Just enough to get together everything he needs, but with little left over for goodbyes. Is he more or less likely to die if he knows that there is something he really needs to live for — my littlest of little babies? Will knowing make him more or less careful? Would I ruin these last hours and minutes by breaking the news? Or is it better to spend the time we have left in the here and now, not thinking about the future, just telling each other how much we care? Christ, I am so afraid for him. When he has a pencil in his hand it's as if he can't see a thing except his notebook and what's straight in front of him.

Now, let me pull myself together. I've had enough of gloom for the time being. I can cast it off more easily these days than I used to. It's because of this life inside me, growing bit by bit by bit. My baby is still so small, I can't understand how she can possibly be strong enough to push away all the death there is in the world — but she somehow does, and I know

*absolutely that Richard will be safe. Together she and
I will keep him safe.*

*There's some good news too. The war artists'
committee has decided to exhibit Richard's painting
of me. He cannot stop smiling. Nothing is better than
seeing him that way. His smile takes my breath
away. It always has. He has to write a caption to go
with it. I wonder what he'll say. Do you think he'll
mention me by name? Miss Daisy Milton. I hope
so. Do you think they'll hang it in a gallery, or just
up in some works canteen somewhere? Keep your
fingers crossed for the National Gallery. It's like a
second home to me these days. I can go and visit it,
even if Richard can't.*

*Next month it's a painting by Renoir. It's called
Les Parapluies. Richard says I must be sure to see
it, even though he won't be here, because it is utterly
different to the awful Entombment and he knows I
will like it. He wants to give me something to do,
in case I fall apart without him. I will go, of course.
Then I'll be able to write to him about it, as well as
you.*

*Goodbye and good luck. That's what we all started
saying to each other when the first bombs came, even
strangers. We're saying it again now. So think of me,
here in London, and wish us all good luck.*

All love,

Daisy

That was the letter, but it wasn't the end of it after all. Claire had known the moment Rob passed her the envelope that there was more in it than just this letter. It was too thick, too heavy. Claire knew exactly the usual weight and the feel of Daisy's letters. This was different altogether. More pages, more words. They were letters from Daisy to Richard, that was what they were, never stamped, never sent, just thought about over and over, picked up and put down, folded and refolded, then left to be passed on to a far-off cousin by a grieving father who had not dared read them before they were parcelled up for fear of what his little girl might have written. She took a deep breath and began to read, first one and then the next.

October, 1943
My darling Richard,

How do I begin? You are going away and there is so much I want you to know before you leave. I don't want you to go, but go you must, like everyone else, and be grateful it did not happen until now. Ever since you told me, I have been daydreaming about going with you, just part of the way, but that's as impossible as everything else. Instead I'll just be here, the same as always, alone in all the places we used to go together and thinking of you every minute.

Once upon a time there was another life mapped

out for me. This life had dancing in it, in sparkling ballrooms, and dinners with crystal glasses, even house parties from time to time. It was full of the friends I had at school, growing up and getting married, or married already and wondering when the babies would start coming along. I would still have been living with my father, playing at running the household while the maid laughed at me. Soon enough, in that other life, I suppose I would have been married too. I very nearly was! A smart young girl in a white satin dress embroidered with pearls marrying a smart young man in a fine new suit. I would have worn my mother's veil, if ever Daddy kept it, and orange blossom in my hair. Daddy would have walked me down the aisle, his face turned away so I couldn't see the tears in his eyes and know how much he cared. My cousin Elizabeth would have been the maid of honour, holding my powder compact and lipstick in her bag, and making sure my hair looked just right for the photographs. I would have told my smart young man how much I wished my mother could have been there, and he would have pressed my hand in his and said he understood. At the wedding breakfast we would have eaten and eaten and eaten, without a thought for powdered eggs or saving up the sugar or all the things we could do with the leftovers. There might even have been grapes, shipped in from somewhere hot and far away, the smallest of them dropping on the floor and rolling off into the corners without anyone even noticing or caring. My God, Richard, imagine such a scene. The voices, the laughter, the sheer ease of it all!

I might have been happy with that life. I might have been bored. I might have simply known no better. But if someone had told me when I left school how differently it was all going to turn out, I wouldn't have believed them for a second. And I would never have guessed that I would grasp that difference with both hands and refuse to let go.

This war has given me a gift of a different life, and not just me, you and everyone else, too. It's a life of sleeping wherever you can, next to stranger after snoring stranger. It's a life where Harrods sell more uniforms than evening dresses. It's a life where one day you can have a home and possessions and the next day the only word for it all is rubble – but still you tell yourself it could have been worse. Most important of all, it's a life that smells of oil paint and turpentine and a summer's breeze drawn in through an open window far above the sunlit street.

I have learnt what love is, Richard. You have taught me that, and everything else. But love has brought fear with it. In four years of war, across all the awfulness and death and ruin, I never was as afraid as I am now, every night that you are not with me. You tell me I don't have to be afraid, not if I have you, but can't you see how scared I am to *lose you? I used to think the war was about England and liberty, and waiting for the whole damn show to be over and done with. But there's more to it than that. It's about love and you and me and a whole new world laid open before us.*

I am fighting for my life, Richard, day in, day out, struggling on, hoping beyond hope just to stay safe. Like everyone else in this place! You must promise that you'll do the same. You're going away from me and I need you to be careful and come back to me.

I'm rambling now, rather than saying what I set out to, which is that whatever happens I am grateful to have met you and filled these past months with you and thoughts of you. I am grateful for your love. I want you to know that you have all of mine in return. I am having your baby and whatever might happen I have no regrets about any of it.

With love to my Richard, from his Daisy

October, 1943
Darling Richard,

I am going to put this letter in amongst your kit and hope you find it soon so that you know I am thinking of you and wishing you well. Maybe in one of your socks? Or in your pencil box? I know then you'll find it soon enough.

I don't know where you are going, but it will be far away, of course. That is one thing we can be

*assured of. We must both just try hard to get through
the rest of the danger and all of the unhappiness
apart, and hold on to the belief that it is almost over.
I will be praying that you are safe, and all those
others with you. Write when you can. I won't mind
one bit if the news is dull. If you get a hint of some
nylons for sale, snaffle them up and send them to
me. I will save a pair for the express purpose of
meeting you at the station when you get back home.
It won't be long now, that's what everyone's saying.
In the meantime, I will keep up with my little trips
to the National Gallery and try not to mind too
dreadfully that you are not there alongside me.*

*I love you and I know you love me and I don't
think there can be anything that matters more than
that.*

*With kisses and love and looking forward to your
safe return,*

Goodbye, just for now, and good luck,

Daisy

Two letters, two ways of saying goodbye, and Daisy
not even knowing which Richard would prefer. The
outpouring of love and the burden of wife and child
that went with the first, or the short cheerio that
would leave him without a concern in the world.
She had not realised there could be such uncertainty
in Daisy. She had always seemed so assured before.
Yet here she was, when it came to it, with no idea

which way to go, acknowledging that she had not learnt to know Richard well enough across the months to be sure of what he would most want to read, or perhaps not knowing what she herself most wanted to say. By the time Claire finished reading it all, Rob had come to sit beside her so he could read the last lines over her shoulder for himself.

'Do you think he knew, Rob?' she said at last. 'Do you think she told him that he was going to be a father?'

'Probably. At least once she read his proposal. I don't think she would have been afraid to tell him after that.' A man's view, making it all seem straightforward.

'She never sent him either of these letters.'

'But that doesn't mean to say she never said something. Think how much more to her there must have been than she bothered to write down. The letters are only a tiny bit of her.'

'I'd like to be certain, that's all. It was important. He should have been told. Wouldn't anyone want to know, just in case something happened?'

His hand had strayed towards hers and she knew he had understood exactly what she meant, just like he used to long ago. 'Nothing's going to happen, not this time. There's no reason for you to be scared. It's a world apart from this thing with Daisy. Anyway, of course he knew. He was an artist. He knew every last inch of her. He would have seen her changing.

And what about all that whispering in his ear, and hoping but not hoping he was asleep? He probably heard every word.'

She found herself beginning to cry again. It was the pregnancy, of course. All the hormones making everything seem worse than it was.

'Are you sure?' she said.

'Yes, I am. Take a look at the photos we took of his painting, if you don't believe me. Why do you think he made the changes to the plant and added all those flowers? It can only be because he knew, and just didn't want to say it out loud any more than she did.'

'So he put it in the painting instead.' She was standing now in front of the photograph that Rob had taken of Daisy and her typewriter, and that she had had framed and placed next to the picture of Daisy and Richard at Weymouth. Tracing out the form of the flowers, and the burgeoning buds on that pathetic office pot plant, she knew that Rob was right, yet still more tears welled out. Rob wiped them away with his fingertips, and it made her feel suddenly safe. 'Enough of this now,' he said. 'It's a lovely day, the sun is shining. Enough of this, OK?'

'I still wanted it to end happily, I can't help it. I wanted the last letter to be full of love and light and it isn't. It's gloomy and miserable, just like the painting. I hate to imagine Daisy spending the last of her time sitting in her room, all on her own, wondering what was the right thing to do.'

'That's what people are like, Claire. They don't always know what to do. They need to work it out in their heads.'

'I know,' she said, and could not help but look away. 'But there's no sense of it being the end of something. The strands aren't all drawn together. They're just dangling.'

'It's because it's not a story. Daisy didn't just make it up. It's real life. Daisy and Richard didn't know what was going to happen to them. They probably thought they had a whole lifetime ahead of them, more than enough to say everything they ever could to each other.'

Like us, she thought, and said the words, making it sound like a question.

'Yes,' he said. 'Like us.' If she had had tears left, she would have cried again. 'Now, how about getting the whole thing over with and looking at those certificates the General Record Office sent through?'

He went to the kitchen to fetch them, came back, and sat down beside her. Then he made to tear open the envelope. At the very last second, Claire stopped him.

'I'll do it. I need to do this.'

'You sure?'

'Definitely,' she replied, and without giving herself any time in which to hesitate, she ripped open the envelope and pulled out the thin slips of paper that were inside, three of them in all. She laid them out on the coffee table, one on top of another, and it was as if death had seeped through all of them.

Certified copy of an entry of death.

When and where died.

Cause of death.

The words leapt out at Claire, while Rob was poring over the details and saying, 'Right, this is definitely our Daisy. Look. Marguerite Milton. Twenty-three years old, and her occupation is given as typist.'

'Those aren't the bits that matter.'

'Yes, they are. We don't want to make a mistake. We need to be sure.'

But they both knew it was definitely her, because they could both see the cause of death, which was given as 'Due to war operations', and the date, which was 8th November, 1943. Geoffrey Smith, ARP warden, had informed the authorities of the event. It seemed so blunt, put that way, in black letters on white paper.

'What about where she died? There's still that.'

'Here we go. Elm Park Gardens, Chelsea.'

'Chelsea? That's where Richard's studio was. He must have been with her. Thank God. Thank God she didn't die alone.'

'Let's check,' said Rob, picking up the second slip of paper and comparing the details. But Claire didn't need to check to know that she was right, and already she was imagining the scene, the two of them dying, not immediately as the bricks crashed around them, nor too slowly, but dragging out their final breaths without realising that they were nearly their last. Their arms wrapped around each other. Daisy whispering with the last of her strength, 'Richard, I'm having a baby.' Richard saying, 'I know, I'm glad,' and using the last of his strength to smile. Then the two of them slipping calmly away. Of course it could never actually have happened that way. She knew that really. Probably they were terrified and in dreadful pain, caught in awkward positions and unable to move, let alone say anything or hold each other. But as she could not know for sure, she picked the scene she liked best, the ending that Daisy deserved.

'Am I right?' she said.

'Yes,' said Rob. 'You're right. They were together.'

Then the third slip, and thank God for that. A marriage certificate, pulled from the records of the Chelsea registry office, and looking no different to their own dated just two years before, and solemnising the marriage of twenty-three-year-old Marguerite Milton to her artist Richard Dacre. It was signed by each of them. Richard's signature was the same as that on his painting of Daisy; Daisy's, too, was recognisable despite that formal, upright 'Marguerite'. Dated 8th November 1943, it was all the proof she would ever have needed that Daisy had been happy before she died, and Richard too. There had been a brief moment, at least, when all the fears of separation and war, and a future filled with cradle and cot as well as paint and easel, had been cast aside for the pure joy that Claire had seen already in their faces, in the photograph of Weymouth, in the painting in the Imperial War Museum, written even in the few words on the back of Richard's postcard.

Claire had, earlier in the week, called the archivist at the National Gallery. She had learnt that these days the art historians no longer thought that Jan van Eyck's painting showed a wedding. They called it *The Arnolfini Portrait* now. Nor did they think that the merchant's wife was pregnant; rather the bulge of material over her stomach simply reflected the curious fashions of the day. As for the bed that took up so much space in the scene, that wasn't meant to be in any way suggestive of marital pleasures. No, the voice at the end of the telephone had said, it was nothing like that. The painting actually showed the merchant's living room and it was quite normal to have a bed in the living room back then. It hadn't even been displayed as a painting of the month during the war, although plenty of people had requested it, no doubt because it was considered too expensive and important to take the risk. Yet none of that was important, not to Claire, for whom the merchant and his wife were nothing more than stiff subjects held tight by a centuries-old frame, nor to Richard

and Daisy, who wouldn't have cared. All that mattered
was that these two had married, in a simple service
quickly over but enough to prove to each other, and
everyone else, that now they were bound together.

'I want to see where she and Richard died,' she
said.

'Are you sure? Are you really sure?'

'Yes,' she said firmly, the scene she had written for
them still in her head. 'It will be like completing the
story. It will be beautiful. That is how it will be.'

Elm Park Gardens was still listed in the *A to Z* that
Rob pulled off the shelf, its name unchanged in the
intervening years, and then there in reality, a street
no different to any of the other streets they had
walked along in order to get there. Now she was
here, Claire realised how rarely she ever bothered to
look around her. She had never before, in all these
London years, glanced down a road and wondered
why there were new buildings amongst the old, and
thought what she did now, as she turned with Rob
into Elm Park Gardens, which was that this was
where bombs had fallen, sending some people
running, trapping others. Killing others. So many of
those concrete and metal offices and tower blocks
were there because that was what had been built
afterwards, on flattened, wasted spaces which had
once been homes and were now not even
memories.

The death certificate had not said exactly where Daisy had been found, but, scanning the length of the street, Claire saw at once that there was only one place where it could have been. Most of the houses still looked exactly as they must have then, Georgian terraces, she thought, or even if they were not, certainly old, built long before the war. Only one of the buildings was newer than the rest and immediately unsightly, its façade streaked with grey from the city's dreary rain. She broke into a run as soon as she saw it, unable to stop herself. The effort and speed drove an eerie whine into her ears that she knew was the sound of the air-raid siren warning Daisy to seek shelter now, now, before it was too late. When she reached the building, she fell against its ugliness, panting desperately from the effort, feeling the concrete grazing her cheek. God, not more tears, please. Rob had come up behind her; she had heard his worried steps following her as she ran.

'It was here, wasn't it? She died here, didn't she?' she said, looking to him for reassurance, as she had done long ago.

'I think so. I think it must have been.'

'There's nothing left of it.'

'They couldn't leave it the way it was. Imagine what London would have looked like if they had. They started rebuilding straightaway, even before the war was over. I remember my dad telling me that.'

She pushed herself away from the wall, still leaning against it with one hand. 'I would have liked there to be something to mark the spot.'

'That's what her grave is for, Claire. That's all normal people would have got. You couldn't have a plaque or a bench for everyone who died, could you? There were thousands of them.' Now he pulled her gently away. 'There are some seats over there. Let's go and sit down a while. You can recover your breath and we can decide what to do next.'

She let him lead her across the road and through a wrought-iron gate into a park. It was the kind of place that might have been taken care of once, but wasn't any more. There was a basketball court in the corner, meant to give teenagers something to do but unused, of course, its surface crawling with moss, grass forcing its way in around the plastic-coated wire netting. Some of the black metal railings were cracked and jagged. Rust spilled out of their cores like marrow. There were few good places to die, thought Claire, remembering again that dirty floor, the blood, the smell of the hospital, the smell of her fear. Above her head, the autumn leaves shook their dry snake-rattle. She shuddered involuntarily, and felt Rob's arm fall around her and draw her body closer to his.

'Can you feel anything, Rob? Can you feel her?'

'No,' said Rob. 'She was here a long time ago. She only ever passed through.'

'I can't either,' she said sadly, then they walked away, leaving the place where Daisy had lain, crushed and afraid, maybe with Richard beside her, but maybe too far away. For Claire it had become ghoulish, wandering around the uneasy haunts of the dead with night beginning to fall, thinking how many bomb sites, how many ghosts she must walk past every single day. All that was important was that Daisy and Richard were dead and gone.

They went next to the National Gallery. There was nothing about *The Entombment* to lift her spirits. Just as Daisy had said, the colours had all faded and browned. There was no sense of individual brush-strokes in it, of this Dieric Bouts, whom the Gallery now called Dirk, standing back, surveying what he had painted, and then carrying on. Instead, the group of figures around Jesus' body looked flat, as did the landscape in the background for all that it was meant to show trees, fields and rolling hills ever further in the distance.

Mary Magdalene was indeed there again, kneeling in the foreground, dressed in red, but a red faded away to leave nothing striking still there. A cloak lined with green was pulled around her, and her off-white face was shrouded in an off-white headscarf that looked like a nun's wimple. She seemed a very different figure to the graceful beauty that Claire had seen in *Noli me tangere* so long ago. Here, strik-ingly, Mary was allowed to touch Jesus, albeit only the dead and empty form of him, one of her hands supporting his thigh as he was lowered gently downwards into an unadorned, sharply rectangular tomb. The Virgin Mary too was allowed one final moment of contact, and she had her hands clasped loosely around her son's wrist, holding up his hand to show the mark of a crucifixion nail struck through it. She looked nothing like the fresh, natural figure painted by Correggio in his *Madonna of the Basket*. No, it was hard to imagine this stark figure ever laughing as she struggled to dress her child – but that was because her son was dead and perhaps she would never laugh again.

The figure of Jesus himself was thin and vulnerable, wrapped around with a winding sheet that age had dirtied with dust. A crown of thorns was twisted roughly around his head, caught up in lank, dark hair, and beneath his ribs was a gaping wound, the blood that trailed out of it surely dried by now but not washed away. There were other figures too, nondescript and unidentified, there only to add their grief to the scene as they wiped away their tears with robes and headscarves. It was the two women who made an impression on Claire – the mother and the prostitute – no companions more unlikely yet united in grief for a man struck down in youth, who had left them behind to struggle through the rituals of death and then on through lives now become empty and cold as the tomb's stone.

It struck her how women so often framed every human life, sobbing for joy at a baby's first breath, crying out in despair at a man's final one, rocking back and forth, dressed in black, rending their clothes and tearing at their own faces with frightening power. It occurred to her too that, of all the paintings she had seen, and every one of them painted by a man, most had included a woman, and a woman at every point in life and in every role. Even del Sarto probably had a woman in the background as he worked, standing behind him, bringing him food or trying to sweep the floor around his feet. As for Rembrandt, focused only on himself, he would most likely have wanted one there.

All that suffering and loyalty, that strength and weakness inexorably intertwined. There was the mingled terror and joy of motherhood in Botticelli's *Mystic Nativity* and Correggio's *Madonna of the Basket*, every woman wanting nothing more than that her child always be happy, but knowing he could never be, not always, however much she tried. The tentative first steps taken into life by Gainsborough's pretty daughters, still not sure where even to tread. Then there was the pain and pleasure of love of every kind from Apollo's unrequited passion for Daphne to the *Rokeby Venus'* ready sensuality. And behind it all, the women who simply carried on, day after day, with the never-ending tasks of life, like de Hooch's court-yard maid or Constable's woman, hidden at the fringes of *The Hay Wain*, who would most likely pump water, prepare meals and wash dishes every day of their lives, and at the very end of it all still be there to hold a hand as white as marble and shed a tear for a dead man. Suddenly she wished more than anything that there had been women at Daisy's funeral, as her father had hoped women like Miss Johnson and Molly, who had at least understood her even if they did not love her, who had known what clothes she might like to be buried in, and who had prayed as they threw earth down on the wooden coffin lid that her mother would meet her, and Richard, and perhaps even her baby too.

Poor Daisy, she thought, buried and hidden away. There was no joy to be found in this painting. She turned away, wanting only to be home with the lights turned on, the kettle boiling for tea and thoughts of her child and its beating heart in her head.

14

Les Parapluies – Renoir

It was the kind of gravestone that strangers might throw a glance at once in a while when on their way somewhere else, and say to each other, *A pity that she died so young*, or, *It must have been the war*, or, *That poor man, having to bury his child*. Then they would shake their heads, walk on and never think about it again. Claire thought those things too as she stood there, reading the words easily in the firm stone, which was not much weathered yet, still untouched by ivy and lichen, because it was not so old, not compared to many of the others.

Marguerite Abigail Milton
Beloved only daughter of Edmund and Alicia Milton
Departed this life 8th of November 1943
Aged twenty-three years
'Buttercups and daisies,
Oh the pretty flowers;
Coming ere the spring-time,
To tell of sunny hours.'

It had taken them some time to find its position, running their fingers up and down the endless list of names in the official registry kept at the cemetery's gatehouse, then, for Claire, long traipsing up and down the woodland paths, kicking through bark chips and leaves until she found the right path, then the right grave. It was just one of hundreds of other gravestones, and Daisy was just one of thousands of bodies, another civilian casualty to add to the list. She remembered there being something in one of the letters about flowers, and dying. What was it? In her bag, she was carrying all of them. She had thought it might be important to take them to this place where Daisy actually was, buried deep beneath the ground, not like all the other places where she had simply filled the space for a while. Now she turned through the pages, so familiar with them that she found the place almost straightaway. June 1943. *Sooner or later we'll be dead and gone too, and there'll be nothing to remember us by except the flowers feeding off us.* It was something she would have written carelessly, but now it seemed like a premonition. Poor Daisy, thinking she would be remembered at least with purple willow herb and cream-white cow parsley if not with the extravagance of roses. There was nothing but grass around the gravestone, thin and straggly, like all grass at this time of year, and fallen leaves. There was no trace of flowers, no hint that there was someone who cared, and worst of all, it seemed to Claire, not the faintest stir of Richard's name.

She wished that she had brought some bulbs with her – snowdrops or daffodils, maybe – to push into the damp earth, although it was probably not allowed, instead of the cellophane-wrapped bunch of carnations. She didn't even like carnations, but there had been no other choice at the twenty-four-hour newsagent by the bus stop where she had picked them up. The place had been blue-bright with flickering strip-lighting. Yet the flowers looked even more ugly here in the open air than they had when she had pulled them from their plastic bucket. She laid them down in front of the gravestone anyway, knowing that all they would do was rot slowly until someone, maybe, threw the decomposed mess away. It would have been better to leave it to the buttercups and the daisies, just like the rhyme said, pretty, simple words chosen by a father who, as Daisy herself had known, still thought of his daughter as just his baby girl. That rhyme brought other words to Claire's mind now, picked up long ago at school from a teacher who believed in the old ways and insisted on learning by heart despite his pupils' sneers: 'Neglected now, the early daisy lies,' and that was her Daisy too.

It was clear enough that Edmund had never known that she had been married – a wedding's paperwork too slow to catch up with a death certificate and a funeral, a gravestone left to bear a maiden name. She wondered how many times across the wretched years that followed he had said to himself, *If only she had been settled, if only I could be sure she was happy, if only if only if only.* Yet to be in another place than Elm Park Gardens, or there at another time, that would have been all he really wanted for her. Had Elizabeth, too, thought the same, never opening the magazine and allowing the postcard to flutter out on to the floor, or else finding it and not knowing whether to change Daisy's surname on the family tree to that of a stranger? To think, too, that lying in that awful morgue had been, not just Daisy, but Richard as well. Someone must have come for his body, parents or siblings, and known no better than Edmund that here were husband, wife and baby, not strangers. Richard's parents might even have passed Edmund that day, entering as he left, holding the door at the end of a dingy corridor open for him as he walked by, blinded by despair and hardly noticing because of their own grief. Wretched thoughts, and wretched times.

Claire walked on, like everyone else, past all those crosses and gravestones grown side by side with the trees. On every one of them words like peace, sleep, love, rest, loss and longing were engraved. One word would have done, she thought. Forgotten.

Rob was waiting for her at the entrance, sitting on a low, damp wall, behind him a backdrop of heavy, temple-like sepulchres, the kind bought by wealthy people whose relatives would not want to walk far in order to leave their wreaths. She had not wanted him to come all the way in with her, had told him she wanted to be on her own, to say goodbye. She hadn't realised that Daisy wasn't going to be here either, not any more, so there would be no one to say goodbye to. No, Daisy had left this place too. She was nowhere now, nowhere but in the pages of her letters.

He jumped up as he saw her approach. 'Did you find it? What was it like?'

She shivered a little. 'Simple. Neglected.'

'We can look after it ourselves, if you want, now we know where it is.'

She nodded, but said nothing.

'We can bring the baby, when it comes.'

'Yes, we can,' she said, hesitantly. Yet it felt like a dispiriting prospect, wheeling their child over bare bones and coffins split open long ago.

He smiled at her. 'Only if you want to. I thought you'd be crying. I'm glad you're not.'

It had not occurred to her to cry. Maybe it was because now she had finally come to realise that tears were best left to Daisy's father and Elizabeth and Richard, people who had really loved her.

'Are we going home now?' she asked.

'Is that what you want? I was hoping you might want to see the final picture. I think we should.'

'What do you mean? Which picture? We've seen them all.'

'How about the one she was meant to see? She promised Richard she would go.'

'Oh, you mean the Renoir. Let's go and see it today then, if it's what you want. But then no more, for either of us. OK?'

'OK,' he said, and smiled. 'That's fine by me.'

Les Parapluies was different from all the other paintings that had gone before, in style, in subject matter, colour, everything. It showed Paris in the rain, although there was not really any rain at all, or none that you could see. The only hint of it lay in a woman part-seen in the centre of the scene, who had been caught in the act of unfurling or closing her umbrella as the storm rose or abated. Almost everyone in the painting was holding up an umbrella, the curves and ribs of each one picked out in greys and blues. The painting was famous, like *The Hay Wain*, the sort of painting that Claire felt instinctively she must have seen before, even though she probably had not. The room in which it was displayed was packed with people who had come to see the Impressionists, the Monets and the Manets and all the rest of them, before heading to the shop to buy reproduction postcards for 50p each.

From beneath the umbrellas, amongst the body of the crowd, a handful of figures emerged more clearly. There were two women, one of whom was looking right out of the painting, a basket, black with emptiness, in the loose crook of her arm. She was a brunette, with a lightly curled fringe and the rest of her hair swept up behind her head, just a tendril loose behind one of her ears. She wore a grey dress that reached down to the ground and looked unyielding, with a black shirt beneath it. Then, behind her and giving her an appraising look, a man with a neat beard and moustache in a top hat, beige jacket, black leather gloves and a cravat that looked as if it was made of silk. The other woman wore dark blue velvet. There was an elaborate bonnet hat that seemed to be all feathers perched on her golden hair and tied around the chin with a blue ribbon, and she looked softer, somehow, than the first woman in her formal outfit. Finally, there were two little girls. The younger of the two, who must have been around five years old, was in a smart coat with double buttons down the front and lace around the collar and cuffs, with the edge of a light blue dress trimmed with white showing underneath, and her own feathered bonnet completing the picture. In her hands she held a cane hoop and a wooden stick to roll it with. Behind her stood an older child, her sister perhaps, with one hand laid carefully on the other's shoulder. This girl wore a coat trimmed with fur, a dark dress beneath and a white hat with a brim decorated with flowers.

'Come and listen to this, Claire,' said Rob, who was holding an audio guide to his ear. 'It's interesting. You'll like it.'

She looked away from the painting and over to Rob. 'No, you keep it,' she said. 'Just tell me what it says.'

'Look at the picture again. What's wrong with the two women in it?'

'Nothing. There's nothing wrong with the painting at all. They both look normal enough to me.'

'What about their clothes?'

'I don't know. They're not exactly to modern taste, but that's not surprising. They're bound to look different. The painting's over a hundred years old, after all.'

'Anything else?'

She looked again. Still nothing.

'Well, here it is. The audio guide says that the woman on the left is wearing the fashions that came in after 1885, but the woman on the right is wearing the fashions that were popular before 1885. Look, you can see that they aren't the same. The one on the left, the one with the dreamy expression, is in a grey, elegant sort of dress, but the one on the right is wearing something more elaborate. See? The dark blue velvet, and the bonnet with the blue ribbon.'

She didn't need to look closely to see it now. It was obvious. 'The way he's painted it is different too, isn't it? I'm right, aren't I?'

'Absolutely right. They think that what happened was that Renoir started the painting, putting in the woman on the right, then went off to Italy to seek inspiration as artists like to do and didn't finish it till he came back years later. By that time everyone was wearing something completely different and he had had enough of the Impressionist technique. So that's why the two halves of the painting have such a different style. Now that's interesting, you've got to admit it.'

'It is, Rob. It really is.'

Now, knowing this, when she looked back at the painting it was herself and Daisy that she saw, unmistakably, two generations of women brought together impossibly at one moment in time, who had become friends for a while. She saw, too, that the man with the beard had eyes only for the elegant woman, the Richard to her Daisy. As for Claire, she was like the other woman, the one who seemed more alone and was unable to take her own eyes away from the little girl, who reminded her of Ruby, or any child, the child she wanted and now would have. For some reason she began to laugh, like she used to, before she grew sniping and critical and eaten up inside. Rob looked up at her in surprise. It was the end of it all, the last painting, she wanted to explain. She was certain of it. It was time to walk away from Daisy and into the future, with Rob.

'I've seen enough,' was all that she said. 'Shall we go?'

'Alright. But only after we've had a slice of cake.

I want to try out the café. It's meant to be good, isn't it?' Claire found she didn't give a damn that the last time she had been there was with Dominic. Her smile didn't even falter; there was still laughter in her eyes.

They had to pass through the overlit shop to get there, which was overflowing with things of every price and colour, things that every single visitor to the gallery could trust that a mother, godchild or friend was almost certain to like. They sat at a table and Rob chatted, about exhibitions, books and the latest films, and she wondered when he had had time to find out about any of them. She might as well have been with Dominic, or not just Dominic but anyone else. But she wasn't. She was with Rob, and she had forgotten why she had ever hated him. Because of Oliver, that was it. No, not because of him, but because of grief and despair and loneliness. Rob had not changed. *She* had. Now she was beginning to feel herself, the real self, return, carrying with it the knowledge that inside her something new was growing.

'I love you, Rob,' she said, once the cake was eaten and the tea had gone cold. He had only been asking her if she had finished. 'I'm sorry.'

'I love you too,' he said at last, all that she wanted to hear. 'Now I want to take you home.'

'OK. Let me run to the cloakroom first.'

She stood up and walked away, leaving him already

with his head bent over someone else's newspaper. She pushed open the heavy black door marked Lavatories and found an empty cubicle. Every wall of it was tiled from floor to ceiling in clinical white and black, as easy to clean as an abattoir.

It was then that she found she was bleeding.

Panic gripped her and held back her scream. *Not again, dear God, not again.* She tried to control her breathing but couldn't. She checked again. There was no mistake. But Rob was there. He would know what to do. He would still be able to think even though she could not. She staggered out of the bathroom, back to the table. Rob was already on his feet, seeing as she approached the white horror in her face, even beneath the yellow-green lights that swung overhead.

'Blood,' she said to him, gripping his hand tight. 'There's blood.'

'We'll get a taxi to the hospital. It's the quickest way. The exit's over here. Don't be afraid. I'm going to look after you.'

She let herself fall back against him and he held her up as they made their way out on to the street. A black cab responded to Rob's urgent whistle and waving hand in seconds, and then they were on their way, London's crowded streets for once clearing magically ahead of them. Still, she clung to him desperately, and he to her, supported only by fear. In the background she could hear the taxi driver talking on and on about emergency departments, which one was closest, which one was quickest, which roads were shut. She blocked out the sound and concentrated only on telling her baby to stay exactly where it was.

'Look, there it is. There's your baby. Go on, take a look. Don't be scared. It's right there, safe and sound.'

Her eyes were on the screen but the image meant nothing to her. She was unable to focus on either the doctor or Rob. 'Are you sure? Are you really sure?'

The woman pressed the probe more firmly into her stomach. 'You can see it for yourself. Look, there's an arm, and another one. The head. A nice looking spine. Two legs. All present and correct. And listen – that's the sound of the heart beating. Everything looks perfectly fine. I can't see any problems.'

'There's nothing to worry about?'

'No. Nothing at all.'

'And the bleeding?' Rob spoke now, for the first time.

'One of those things that happens from time to time. There's often a little bleeding at this stage, what with all the hormonal changes going on. They can confuse the body. It should stop in a day or two.'

'Thank God. Thank God.' Rob's head collapsed into his arms and Claire knew he was trying not to cry. She put her arm around him, kissed the top of his head, and then he did start to cry, loud sobs that might once have embarrassed her, but for which she was now grateful beyond belief.

'It's OK, Rob. It's all going to be OK,' she said, stroking his hair. It was still damp with the sweat of rushing and panic. She turned to the sonographer. 'We lost a baby before, you see.' Somehow it had suddenly become easier to say, and she wasn't even crying herself because there was no need, not while that picture of the new baby was still on the screen, the baby that she was determined would be born.

'I understand. It's no trouble at all. Do you want to know the due date? It's always good to be able to plan.'

She nodded, then there was a pause as measurements were taken and typed into a computer. 'By my reckoning, the fifteenth of March. You'll have to plant some bulbs. They'll be out just in time for the baby. Now, we'd better see if we can get this emotional father-to-be out of here. I've got plenty of other people to see.'

They sat together in the park opposite the hospital. There must have been a church there once, gone now, because the red brick walls were lined with discarded gravestones, too worn even to read the names from, and in one corner was a solitary statue of an angel, its arms spread open, its features crumbled away. Rob's face was still red and his eyes wet with tears.

'I thought we'd lost it, Claire. I thought we'd lost our baby.'

'But we haven't. Everything's fine, that's what the doctor said.'

'I did everything I could.'

'I know you did. You did everything right.'

She leant out and put her hand in his. She felt his grasp in response.

'It's real, this baby,' he said. 'I've only just let myself believe it. It's coming. I want it. I want it so much.'

'I know, Rob. You don't need to say it.'

'I've been thinking that if it's a girl, we could call her Daisy. What do you think?'

An image of the pile of letters came into Claire's head, lying in the bottom of her bag, still in their soft, faded ribbon, their story bursting to get out. She was going to put them in the back of a drawer when they got home and leave them there with their ghosts – for a while, at least.

'No,' she said. 'Let's not. Let's call her something completely different.'

She leant against him now, and he put his arm around her, and they sat there together, with nothing to look at but half-bare trees and memorials to the forgotten dead. Leaves skittered around their feet in the cold breeze, scratching the hard, dark earth, and in the background the scream of the hospital's ambulances continued its constant wail, but Claire was aware of none of it. She felt only the warmth of Rob's body close to her, and the imagined flutter of her baby beginning to stir.